**“A writer to watch!**

# THE WEAPON

The top-secret Russian SU-39 covert stealth bomber was far beyond anything the world had yet seen. Its increased maneuverability and firepower, combined with the ability to evade detection, made it a super-weapon that could turn the tides of war in favor of whoever was behind its controls.

# THE THREAT

Russian hardliners and their counterparts in the Chinese Red Army would stop at nothing to get the reins of power back in their hands. Before any government had time to react, the two cunning allies had put into motion the pincers of a two-pronged plan that would force the world to the brink of nuclear cataclysm. Their trump card: the SU-39.

# THE MISSION

Commander T.C. Bogner has just seventy-two hours to retrieve the stealth fighter at all costs. In an international race against time that would test his abilities to the maximum, Bogner had to use any and all weapons at his disposal to make sure his foes' high-tech gambit failed. If not, the day would dawn on a new political order and the world would be shrouded in...

## *RED SKIES*

Other *Leisure Books* by R. Karl Largent:

**THE WITCH OF SIXKILL**
**ANCIENTS**
**PAGODA**
**THE PROMETHEUS PROJECT**
**BLACK DEATH**
**RED TIDE**
**RED ICE**

R. KARL LARGENT

# RED SKIES

LEISURE BOOKS  NEW YORK CITY

A LEISURE BOOK®

December 1996

Published by

Dorchester Publishing Co., Inc.
276 Fifth Avenue
New York, NY 10001

If you purchased this book without a cover you should be aware that this book is stolen property. It was reported as "unsold and destroyed" to the publisher and neither the author nor the publisher has received any payment for this "stripped book."

Copyright © 1996 by R. Karl Largent

All rights reserved. No part of this book may be reproduced or transmitted in any form or by any electronic or mechanical means, including photocopying, recording or by any information storage and retrieval system, without the written permission of the Publisher, except where permitted by law.

The name "Leisure Books" and the stylized "L" with design are trademarks of Dorchester Publishing Co., Inc.

Printed in the United States of America.

To W.J.L.—Thank You.

# RED SKIES

# Chapter One

Datum: Sunday—1142L, September 14

Far below Air Major Arege Borisov was the vast expanse of the featureless Gobi Desert. He was passing over into the airspace of the Mongolian People's Republic. Suddenly there was a disturbing awareness that there was no turning back; it was the final break, Nei Mengu, Inner Mongolia, and soon, Shaanxi. Now he could only hope that Colonel General Viktor Isotov's and Chairman Han Ki Po's plan worked.

The last of the escort planes, a MiG-31 Foxhound, had broken off radio contact at 1111 over Erzin, presumably returning to its base at Krasnoyarsk—but only after losing radio contact and reporting that the scheduled refueling rendezvous with the Su-39 over the Yenisey River had not taken place.

For the past thirty minutes, Arege Borisov

had been on his own in the flight command seat of the top-secret aircraft. Komivov was slumped in the pilot's seat beside him, the thin trickle of blood from the small .22-caliber bullet hole just in front of his right ear seeping out from under his helmet and slowly coagulating into a crusted ribbon. The young test pilot had suspected nothing. The bullet had passed through both his helmet and head and lodged in the foam pad on the head restraint.

Borisov took a deep breath. With nothing below him now but a few isolated Mongolian villages in the foothills of the Uliastays, he repeated his systems check and used the UHR to check for radio beams. He was following the carefully detailed flight plan to the letter; since Tultue, he had maintained an altitude of 51,000 feet, and a covert posture under condition IV-Gray.

The twin Tumanski R-35 engines with their combined 34,000 pounds of afterburning thrust were propelling him through the thin air at speeds close to Mach 1. If he maintained that speed and the Yackof computer calculations were correct, it would be another four hours before he rotated to GB-2 and switched to the auxiliary fuel tanks that had been installed in the armament cavities. Fom time to time he wondered about the Menenski engineers who had stripped out the Su-39's armament and replaced them with the two 8,000-pound-capacity titanium fuel tanks. It was those fuel tanks that would enable him to bypass the scheduled in-flight fueling over the Yenisey.

Did they know?

*Nyet.* Of course not, he decided. Isotov would not have left such a matter to speculation. No doubt they were told that it was merely an endurance flight—something that would not have been uncommon at this stage of the Su-39's development.

The audit screen on the VA-instrument computer stared back at him, passively parading systems checks with only an occasional minor deviation in the digital display. None of them troubled him. The craft was performing like a battle-proven veteran, not at all like the unproven design it was. Like its closest American counterpart, the F-117, the Su-39 was camelback in design and thick through the fuselage. It incorporated geometrically flat panels rather than the smooth aerodynamic configurations of previous Sukhoi and Mikoyan designs . . . and it was both faceted and coated with radar-absorbing material to eliminate radiating radar energy back to the transmitting and receiving source.

In earlier flights, Borisov, who had conducted many of the short- and long-range tests of the Su-39's predecessor, had been uncomfortable.

The cockpit, despite being large enough to accommodate both a flight commander and a pilot, afforded him little headroom and under extreme buffeting his flight helmet actually vibrated against the glass walls of the canopy.

"The aircraft is unstable," he had informed Schubatis, the aircraft's designer, in a debriefing session after one of the Su-39's earliest flights. "We cannot always count on optimum conditions."

Schubatis had looked at him, made note of the comment, and within a short period of time the quadredundant fly-by-wire control system had been installed and the canopy enlarged to minimize the problem.

Now, after six hours in the aircraft, the longest flight to date, his legs were beginning to feel cramped and little things like the microthin wire mesh on the casing of the HUD were beginning to annoy him. He shifted in his seat, elevated the seat pan, and tried to get comfortable. Ahead of him lay the imposing eastern slopes of the Himalayas and the broad, sweeping valleys between the Mekong and Yangtze.

He glanced at Komivov, reached over, and pulled down the dead man's visor to conceal the look on his face.

# RED SKIES

Datum: Sunday—1652L, September 14

Colonel Mao Quan stood at the window of Isotov's office with his hands folded behind his back, staring down at the hydroelectric dam on the Bratsk Reservoir. Isotov was still on the telephone.

It had been eight hours since the initial reports of Borisov's departure and word had been expected long before now. When the Colonel General hung up, Quan turned and looked at him. His face mirrored his impatience.

"You have received word?" Quan questioned.

"Patience, Comrade, patience," Isotov replied. "You must remember that the first four hours of the flight were routine. As far as my blundering colleagues in the Air Ministry are concerned, this is merely another test flight—one of considerable duration certainly, but just one more test, one more shakedown before we proceed to the next level. Not until Major Borisov fails to contact our checkpoints at 25-B and 45-B will there be cause for concern." Isotov paused. "Remember, Comrade, it is a vast land, in some ways even more vast than yours."

Quan lit another in his endless chain of cigarettes and walked to the map on the far side of

Isotov's office. Mentally calculating flying time and distance, he stabbed at a point in the staggering immensity of the Tibetan Plateau. "By now, he should be here."

"You are assuming, of course, that all goes according to plan," Isotov said, "a dangerous assumption in view of the fact that the Su-39 is still in its development phase." He followed his assessment with a mocking laugh.

Quan frowned. "I have read your communiqués to Chairman Han Ki Po. You are the one who pronounced the craft ready for testing of its weapon systems."

"And so it is," Isotov said as he stood up. "But it is the responsibility of the government of the People's Republic to conduct the tests. That is why we have already shipped the hardware to Danjia. As soon as Major Borisov is convinced your pilots are capable of flying the Su-39 and are ready to conduct the tests, we will authorize the installation of the weapons systems and release the calibration data."

"And you are certain President Aprihinen knows nothing of these arrangements?" Quan pressed.

Isotov leaned against his oversize desk, preparing to offer Quan a drink, when there was a knock on his door.

*"Da."*

"I have a facsimile for the Colonel General," the voice said.

Quan, who spoke both Russian and English as well as several Chinese dialects, including his native Szechuan, began to smile. "Perhaps," he whispered, "word has come."

Isotov instructed the man to enter, took the fax, unfolded it, and read it. Then he looked at Quan. "See for yourself," he said. He handed Quan the paper.

*Piskaryovs 1500/1109m/taris konfirmt*
*B-25/B-45 no report*
*Contact/negative/verified*
*Intercept and escort: NA Kirhvia*
*Intercept and escort: NA Uzbekzia*
*Slavutich—trqn: 1507*

Isotov smiled, revealing the gold in his teeth. "Now we must wait until our Major Borisov fails to rendezvous with the second refueling station over Elnivoka. When that fails to materialize, we will dutifully express our concern . . . and, of course, we will alert our air-sea rescue authorities."

"Of course," Quan agreed. It was Quan's turn to smile.

Datum: Sunday—0856L, September 14

The Crospar section of Washington consisted mostly of abandoned warehouses, a few run-down tenement buildings, and an occasional neighborhood bar that no longer had a neighborhood to support it.

Sergei Kovnir lived—or, some said, was dying—in Crospar. He was dying in a second-floor flat that had once been the home of someone Kovnir neither knew nor cared about. The only thing that was important was that they, whoever *they* were, were gone and because of that he had a roof over his head.

At sixty-one years of age, Sergei Kovnir had long since given up hope of achieving the American dream. He worked, when he worked, as a dishwasher at a tiny Lithuanian café that, like Crospar, was in the final stages of decay. The owner of the café, the querulous and aging widow of a man he had once met from Byelorussia, gave him work, sometimes something to eat, and even less frequently an occasional bottle of cheap vodka. She had even given him herself once, but Kovnir had botched the opportunity, falling asleep on top of her before he could consummate his dubious opportunity.

On this Sunday morning he was awakened, not by the church bells, as he usually was, but by the sound of voices, voices elsewhere in the dilapidated old structure he called his home. He pushed himself up on his elbow and listened. The voices traveled through old heating ducts and through the myriad holes in the wall and flooring. They were busy voices, voices that spoke a language Sergei Kovnir did not recognize.

Because the old building often served as the meeting place for local street gangs, he stood and picked up a small piece of steel pipe that he kept nearby to defend himself. Then he shuffled to the staircase leading down to the debris-laden first floor and listened. The voices—he could identify three—sounded hurried and spoke in some sort of Asian tongue—Chinese, perhaps Vietnamese, or maybe even Korean. He crouched in the shadows as the early-September Sunday-morning sun streamed through a latticework of broken and missing windows, and tried to determine what the trio was doing.

Finally, when his curiosity had gotten the best of him, Sergei Kovnir descended several steps so that he could actually observe their activities. Two of the men were huddled over a table, while a third stood in front of an old blackboard propped against a pitted wall.

The man at the blackboard was, in fact, an Asian, slight of build, quite tall, and had long, shoulder-length hair tied into a ponytail. He wore blue jeans, a sweatshirt, and sneakers. From his attire, Kovnir would have guessed him to be a student. The man made rapid sketches on the blackboard that were difficult for Sergei to understand.

"We take a box, preferably a small cardboard one. A large cigar box will do, but we make certain it is long enough and deep enough to accommodate four sticks of dynamite, stacked or standing. Then make certain that the blasting cap is tucked securely in between the explosives." He demonstrated. ". . . like so." Then he repeated the drawing and pointed to a second cavity in the box. "It is important that you have enough room to create a second cavity, separated by a thin wall of material, preferably cardboard. This is the area where you place the two C-type batteries." Again he demonstrated. "Put them in sequence with a small wire leading from the electrode to a safety pin that has been broken and inserted horizontally through the wall of the box approximately one-half inch from the batteries."

While Kovnir watched, the other two men replicated the assembly.

"Now—directly above the area where you have the wire leading from the electrode to the pin is a common nail with a hole bored in it. The nail is driven upward through the lid of the box with the spring we removed from a ballpoint pen positioned between the head of the nail and the box lid."

Tang Ro Ji paused, waiting for the two men to complete their assembly.

"Now insert a small straight pin through that hole in the shank of the nail. A thin wire should be tied around the head of the pin so that the nail can be triggered from a reasonable distance."

The two men nodded their understanding.

Tang inspected their work, then continued. "By removing the pin, the head of the nail is forced down by the tiny spring, making contact with the pin, which sends an electrical charge to the blasting cap and . . ."

His students smiled.

Sergei Kovnir scratched his head. He did not understand. But on this particular Sunday morning, it made no difference; he was more hungry than curious—and besides, they were not there to harm him. He rubbed his eyes and made his first decision of the day; he would head down to the little Lithuanian café on Fillmore Street to see if a couple of hours of work for the widow Sochi would lead to something to eat. Little did Sergei Kovnir realize that he was about to play an important role in a terrorist attack of international magnitude.

Datum: Sunday—1838L, September 14

Air Major Arege Borisov picked up the approaching MiG-23s in the Liuzhou corridor. The in-flight computer flashed telemetric data on the screen in a rapid sequence search for target recognition. The data feedback from the RAD-7 on the synthetic aperture profiled the oncoming aircraft, and Borisov quickly determined that the planes were unarmed. Neither aircraft profiled a weapons configuration. He keyed the sort term REVIEW into his onboard and played the reception against the static profile. The words VERIFICATION and CONFIRMED blinked intermittently on his display. Both chronos indicated he was 03:45:21 ahead of schedule. He double-checked the in-flight and reverified contact instructions. Then he turned on the INS and keyed coordinates into the FLIR. Ten seconds before target acquisition the laser would illuminate the target—if there had been armament.

"Gray on gray. IV-Gray. Ident," the voice crackled through static. The transmission was in Russian, fragmented, but sufficiently clear for Borisov to understand.

"176.484," Borisov confirmed. He changed frequencies.

"Say again," came the garbled command.

"176.484," Borisov repeated. Then he added the words "Red red," as he had been instructed. He could almost hear the sigh of relief. He knew that the pilots of the twenty-plus-year-old MiG-23s had to be concerned until contact had been established and verified.

"We do not have you on our scope," one of the MiG pilots advised him.

Borisov laughed. "Descending to forty-five thousand feet. Airspeed seven hundred." Then he added for the MiG pilot's benefit, "That is the whole purpose of this aircraft, Comrade."

"We will escort you in, Air Major. Our ETA at Danjia is 01.41."

Datum: Monday—0614L, September 15

As most of the world had been doing for the last twelve hours, Robert Miller had spent the night monitoring the terrible news coming out of London. At Packer's request, he had come into the office as soon as they heard about the bombing. Now, because he knew Packer would be up—if he had gone to bed at all—he picked up the phone and dialed the bureau chief.

Packer's sixty-two-year-old voice sounded tired. "Packer here," he said.

"Been watching it, Chief?" Miller asked.

"Yeah, I turned CNN on, but I must have dozed off. What's the latest?"

"They've just announced that the death toll has exceeded two hundred," Miller said. "And they've confirmed that the Queen and her entourage are safe. M1 is confirming that they left somewhere in the neighborhood of thirty minutes before the explosion."

Packer was quiet for a moment. "Suppose that was coincidence, or was it planned that way?"

"I've been surfing back and forth on all the major news channels," Miller admitted. "Right now I'm watching CNN. They've got a feed from the BBC. You can get a pretty good view of it. There isn't much left of it—"

"Did anyone get the call yet?"

"Uh-huh," Miller confirmed, "to the BBC outlet in Liverpool. Just like before. The guy said his name was Tang Ro Ji and claimed the attack was the work of the Fifth Academy. The message was obviously taped and played by someone over the phone from a local telephone. Scotland Yard is trying to trace it."

"It's hard to believe," Packer muttered. "Sara and I went to the Royal Opera House on our honeymoon. We sat in the fourth balcony, stage left, holding hands. I remember thinking that for an Oklahoma farm boy I had come a helluva long way—watching an opera at the Royal Opera House in London. Her favorite uncle, a fellow who actually lived in Covent Garden, played first violin in the orchestra. Sara was so damn proud of him—she watched him as much as she did the performance."

For the moment, Miller refused to interrupt the reverie. He waited until the longtime chief of the Washington bureau of the Internal Security Agency fell silent.

"Chief," Miller finally said, "Associated Press has released the names of the confirmed dead thus far. The only Americans reported killed were the ones actually with the opera company. There were three of them, all in the chorus."

Packer sighed. Finally he said, "Okay, Bob, I appreciate your sticking by the phones all night. Let me grab a quick shower, then I'll be in—"

"One more thing, Pack. An interesting item came over the wire a couple of hours ago from Moscow. Apparently the Russians have lost, I'm using their words now, 'a classified aircraft.' According to the dispatch at 0337, 'The pilots and the plane, believed to be an Su-39, went down somewhere over the Russian–Nei Mengu border sometime Sunday.' "

"Any other details?"

"Naw, just the usual eyewash about the search continues, that sort of thing."

"Su-39," Packer repeated. "Isn't that the one that's supposed to be better than our F-117 Stealth?"

"That's the one."

"And weren't there two of them originally?" Packer probed. He had a good memory—but he didn't trust information like this to memory. As usual, he looked to Miller for confirmation.

"The first one went down in the Urals about four months ago. We offered to help them look for it, but they turned us down. That's the one their air force chief, Isotov, got all upset about."

"If Isotov reported this, I smell trouble," Packer said. Then he added, "Call over to the DOD and the State Department. See who's watching the phones and see if they can flesh out the report on that plane. As I recall, Colonel General Isotov has trouble with the truth. Remember four years ago when we were exchanging weapons counts after the arms treaty? He informed Aprihinen their inventory of airworthy MiG-29 Fulcrums was something under five hundred. Then we discovered he was hiding a couple hundred more in his inventory that he claimed had been shipped to Syria and Iraq."

"Will do," Miller said. "See you in an hour or so."

Datum: Monday—0743L, September 15

Sergei Kovnir awoke to the sound of rain. But that was not important. He had a job to do. The widow Sochi needed him. Her regular dishwasher had quit, and if Sergei proved both prompt and reliable, she had hinted that she would give him the job—for as long as she could depend on him.

He dressed, put on his tattered old coat, and threaded his way down the broken staircase to street level before stepping out into the wet Washington morning.

He paid little attention to three young Chinese men huddled in the doorway across the street.

"That's him," Deng Zhen said. "What did I tell you? To me he looks to be about the right size, and I think he looks old enough."

Zhao Shi wasn't so sure. "How the hell do you know?" he asked. "Shit, all these old winos look the same to me."

Tang Ro Ji continued to watch the man as he shuffled down the street toward the corner. He had studied the photographs of Schubatis carefully and he had read the files, not once, but many times. Deng Zhen was right, there was some resemblance . . . but there would have to be more than just a passing resemblance in order to pull off the stunt as Mao Quan had planned it. The man they selected had to look a great deal like Schubatis; height and weight were important, and so was the bushy mustache. But there were other things to consider as well.

There was the matter of the actual alteration of facial features and keeping the individual alive until Schubatis arrived. If this was the man, they would have to act now. Tang Ro Ji knew it was far too risky to wait.

He watched as the old man disappeared around the corner. Then he turned to Deng Zhen. "What do you know about him?"

"It all fits. I saw him hanging out in that Lithuanian restaurant down by the railroad tracks. He goes there almost every day. Most of the time he just sits around and talks to people, but the last two times I watched him, he went back in the kitchen and worked."

"Yeah—but what do you know about him?"

"His name is Sergei Kovnir. I talked to the old woman who runs the restaurant. She's a talkative old bitch; smells like garlic. Once she started talking, I couldn't get her to shut up. She told me he lives alone, that he doesn't have any family, and that about six days out of seven she gives him a bottle of cheap vodka and tells him to go get drunk and stay out of her hair. That was good enough for me, so I followed him. That's when I found out that a lot of nights he sleeps in the same building where we've been putting our little toys together."

Tang Ro Ji listened carefully. "Think we can get him in the study program at Capital?"

"All we have to do is convince him that the Institute for Human Studies at the university is looking for volunteers for the nutrition program. That should be a piece of cake with this old fart."

Zhao Shi, who actually was a student at Capital, was frowning. "If Colonel Quan's information is correct, Dr. Schubatis will be coming to America for the conference in early October. That gives us less than a month."

"We do not have to fool the Americans for long," Tang reminded them, "just long enough to get Schubatis out of the country."

There was a lull in the rain, and Tang Ro Ji, who much preferred the mild Octobers of his native Hainan Island to the chill, damp days in Washington, buttoned his jacket up close around this throat. Then he smiled. If all went according to plan, he would soon be going home.

Datum: Monday—2019L, September 15

United States Naval Captain Tobias Carrington Bogner had not shaved in over a week. He prided himself on the fact. Nor had he worn shoes or anything even slightly resembling a uniform. He spent his mornings walking the lovely seven-mile stretch of Negril beach, his afternoons playing poker with three long-retired navy buddies who had settled on the island paradise, and his nights sipping scotch and water, listening to Cocoa Jones playing the piano in Mary Mary's Tree House. It was a good life, and Toby Bogner felt he had earned it.

He had planned to look up an old acquaintance, Francine Cyre, a dark-haired French girl who ran a small boutique on the strip where the tourists shopped. But as it turned out, Francine was gone, departed, and no one was quite sure where. She had left a forwarding address, but folks indicated that when they had tried to contact her, phone calls were not returned and letters were eventually returned with the letter marked "Unable to Deliver."

Despite that, the first eight days of leave had proved rewarding, and the remaining two weeks promised to be even more so. First there was Jocelyn, who worked at the Caribbean Bureau, and then there was Margot, who worked for the French sugar-processing company six miles down the Montego Bay highway in Machapo. Each had possibilities, and Jocelyn was planning to meet him this very evening—at Cocoa's, of course.

Bogner was still getting dressed—a pair of wash pants, sandals, and a short-sleeved old blue denim shirt—when Queet Bonea showed up at his room at the Harmony House and knocked on the door. Queet was smiling, and he had a bottle of Cardhu malt scotch under his arm.

"Look what I found, mon," he said. "Are you not the one who told me this was the nectar of the gods?"

Toby Bogner took the bottle out of the man's hands. "Something tells me I don't think I want to know where you got this. Right?"

Queet's ebony face released in a broad smile. "You can ask questions if you want to, mon, but I don't have to answer."

Bogner broke the seal, splashed some of the Cardhu into glasses, and handed one to Queet. That's when the Jamaican's smile faded.

"Have you heard the news, mon?"

Bogner laughed. "You know the rules. Same as they've been for every one of the eight years that I've been coming down here. No radios. No television. No newspapers. And above all, no phone calls. If it's an emergency, they call Harper down at Rick's bar—and I get back to them only if I agree it's an emergency."

"Terrorists blew up the Royal Opera House in London," Queet said evenly. "At last count they had recovered over two hundred bodies."

Bogner sobered.

"They think it was an attempt to assassinate the Queen, but they say she left a half hour or so before the explosion."

Bogner stood up, walked across the room, and looked out the window at the last rays of color in the western sky. "Do they know who did it?"

"Some group that calls themselves the Fifth Academy," Queet said.

Bogner turned away from the window. "Queet, old buddy, you're about to see me break an eight-year-old tradition. Where's the nearest damn telephone?"

# Chapter Two

Datum: Sunday—0932L, October 5

"Those bastards," Capelli muttered.

"I can't believe it," Breeden said, shaking his head.

As the camera from the news helicopter scanned the billowing clouds of black, acrid smoke and the wall of flame belching from the rig's production platform, Bogner closed his eyes. It was Oklahoma City, the Royal Opera House, the World Trade Center, and Flight 800 all over again. Now there was a new name in the growing list of terrorist attacks: Tuxpan.

All three video receivers in the Bolling Hangar 7 VIP lounge were showing the same scenes of carnage and devastation. Only the voices of the anchormen, and in the case of CBS, his ex-wife, Joy, were different.

Frank Myers, the ISA agent from New York

City, snuffed out one cigarette and lit another as the camera zoomed in on a combination emergency and firefighting vessel dredging bodies from the water. The aft deck of the ship was littered with the charred remains of victims hurtled overboard by the initial blast. No one was paying any attention to the bodies—there was no need to.

In the background, Bogner could detect the burning hull of one of the rig's supply support ships. The three-story-high superstructure was enveloped in flames, and its cargo—supplies, crates, barrels, replacement personnel, and wooden containers, all crammed into the ship's open aft hold—were rapidly becoming victims of the same fate.

As Bogner watched, the crew of the listing craft began leaping into the oil-coated sea, quickly disappearing beneath the turgid surface.

The scene changed to the CNN newsroom, and the camera zeroed in on a silver-haired, visibly shaken news commentator who began again reciting the grim details Bogner and the three other ISA agents had already heard several times.

"This is Reed Barkley in the CNN newsroom," the man said, trying to clear his throat and give his voice authority. "What you are viewing is Saratoga Rig Seven-Two some seven miles off the coast of Tuxpano and approximately eight miles east of Islas Marias—where, just two hours ago, Mexican President Carlos Cerralvo attended ceremonies opening this latest Saratoga Oil Corporation super rig for production.

"The blast occurred at 7:47, just moments after President Cerralvo boarded the rig's helicopter for the trip back to the mainland at Tepic—"

The camera panned right and another man joined Barkley on camera. The newcomer was short, his tie was loose, and he wore an expression of shock and disbelief. Unlike Barkley, his voice was measured and somber. "We are joined now by Blake Harold, who has been in touch with Saratoga authorities and with Rosa Sales of our CNN affiliate in Guadalajara. Ms. Sales is on the scene of the disaster. . . ."

The short man looked into the camera and began repeating much of what had already been reported.

"The initial blast occurred shortly before eight o'clock this morning, just moments after President Carlos Cerralvo boarded a helicopter to take him back to the mainland. Witnesses aboard the Cerralvo aircraft say that the blast occurred in the area of the blowout preventer on the second level of the seven-hundred-foot-tall rig and directly beneath the area where President Cerralvo had made the dedication only a few minutes earlier.

"At this point officials on site claim that a hundred thirty-seven bodies have been recovered. Most of these were officials and families of officials of the Saratoga Corporation who were on hand for the rig's dedication ceremonies.

"One Saratoga official, according to Ms. Sales, claims that approximately one hundred and twenty workers conducting shakedown tests were below deck at the time of the blast—and so far there is no word on their fate."

The camera panned from Harold back to the silver-haired Barkley. "At eight-fourteen EST, five-fourteen in California, the station manager at our CNN affiliate in Los Angeles received a call from a man who played an audiotape by a man who identified himself as Tang Ro Ji. Tang claimed to be an officer with a faction of the Chinese army, a terrorist group known as the Fifth Academy. Tang stated that the group, who has claimed credit for a number of recent terrorist attacks, including the bombing of the Royal Opera House in London just three weeks ago in which two hundred and thirty-seven died, was responsible for the explosion on Saratoga Rig Seven-Two, and he repeated what many are now calling the Fifth Academy anthem, '*Chin wha` do˜ dun kow—*' "

Bogner translated the words: "China, one

world, one universe." He got up from his chair and walked out of the lounge. When he did, Harvey Breeden, the youngest of the four men assigned to the Schubatis detail, followed him. In the hallway, Breeden checked his watch and stared out at the cold, wet tarmac.

"You know, T.C.," he began, "there was a time I thought if you lived in the States you were safe from this kind of thing."

Bogner knew better. Instead of looking at the young man, he scanned the deck of low-hanging, steel-gray clouds and allowed his thoughts to careen away from the wholesale slaughter he had been witnessing on the Saratoga oil rig, to the image of Joy sitting behind the CBS anchor desk. Finally he looked at the young agent.

"We should have known we weren't safe after that thing at the World Trade Center," Bogner said. "If nothing else, it proved those bastards could go anywhere—do anything."

Breeden agreed.

For Harvey Breeden, this was a special occasion. It was an opportunity to work with T. C. Bogner. Clancy Packer had advised him once that if he wanted to find a role model in the ISA, there was no need to look any farther than Tobias Carrington Bogner. Now he was actually working the Schubatis detail with the man.

Bogner was a twenty-year veteran, a Navy

captain, and a former carrier pilot. Like Breeden, he was assigned to the Washington-based ISA, the Internal Security Agency. He was a Colchin man, inclined to be somewhat withdrawn, and when not withdrawn, a bit taciturn. But on this occasion, he seemed inclined to be neither. Breeden assumed that Bogner had decided the occasion was appropriate for neither. What Breeden didn't know was that the other two men on the detail, Capelli and Bogner's longtime friend Frank Myers, were equally sober in view of their assignment.

"What's the skinny on this guy Schubatis?" Myers asked, coming out of the lounge.

Bogner reached in his coat pocket and handed him the abbreviated dossier Miller had passed out in Packer's office at the Friday meeting. Myers opened it and scanned it.

*Milo Schubatis, DOB 04/06/30, born in Novorossisk, graduated from the Moscow Technical Institute. Wife, Reba. No children. Joined Sukhoi staff in 1960, involved in development of the Sukhoi Su-25 Frogfoot close-support aircraft. Design head on Sukhoi Su-7 Flanker, an air superiority fighter. Generally considered to be the brains behind the concept and prototype design of the Su-39. Official DOD designation: Covert.*

Myers examined the two photographs in the packet. One was nothing more than a straight-on mug shot that Packer had quipped was probably lifted from Schubatis's Party card. The second was slightly more flattering. It had been taken several years earlier at one of the endless round of official Party functions. Schubatis's chest was covered with medals and he was standing next to the present Russian president, Moshe Aprihinen.

Myers handed the packet back to Bogner without comment.

Capelli walked out of the lounge, joined them, and stood studying the rain for several minutes. Then he wondered aloud if anyone had thought to bring umbrellas. No one had, and Breeden went inside to inquire if the VIP officer-in-charge could provide them.

Myers, visibly concerned, glanced at his watch every few minutes. "His plane's twenty minutes late," he said.

Capelli nodded. "Shitty weather; you gotta expect it."

There was a shift in the wind and the rain suddenly invaded the area where the four men had been standing. Bogner moved back under the overhang and wondered if Schubatis had been informed of the explosion on the Saratoga oil rig. Then his thoughts catapulted back to Joy again and he wondered if she was happy. He had to admit that she looked good, sitting there in front of the cameras; cool, collected, together—there wasn't any doubt about it, she was in her element. She loved a big story. His mind played with the thought for a few minutes and then he shrugged. If by some miracle they had still been together, he would have been in the way—not only today, but every day. "You're so damned old-fashioned it's ridiculous," she had once said. He knew that—and he knew that wasn't the reason they weren't still together.

From Joy his thoughts went back to Jamaica, and he chastised himself for living in the past. It served no purpose.

Bogner shifted his weight from one foot to the other, trying to fight off the damp chill. He hadn't noticed that the young airman working behind the transient arrival desk had opened the door.

"Captain Bogner," the young man said, "that Tupolev Tu-204 you were asking about . . ."

Bogner nodded.

"It's on final, sir. The ADO says he'll have the pilot bring her right up to the front door of the terminal here. Ground control says it'll take another ten minutes, though, after he puts her down."

Out of habit, Bogner looked around. The parking lot was empty and there were no other nonuniformed personnel in the waiting area.

Miracle of miracles, so far the press hadn't discovered that Spitz had changed Schubatis's arrival location from Washington National to Bolling.

He sighed, decided to try one of the vending machines for a cup of coffee, and headed back into the VIP lounge to check the death toll at Tuxpano. Somewhere along the way he had made up his mind not to watch the CBS affiliate. Even then, the thought crossed his mind again, as it frequently did: Joy was a helluva name for an ex-wife.

Datum: Sunday—1047L, October 5

When Milo Schubatis stepped from the plane, he looked decidedly different from the photographs in the ISA profile packet. He was even shorter than Bogner had anticipated—perhaps five feet, five inches tall—had a crop of long, wiry, gray-brown hair parted on the left, and an improbable white splayed mustache that failed to soften or conceal his uncompromising mouth. He wore round, wire-rimmed glasses and had enormous pouches under his dull-brown eyes.

After watching him deplane, Bogner decided that if he had been listening to Joy describe him to her viewers, she would have used the word "humorless."

Schubatis's wife, Reba, was taller than her husband, and more personable. She shook Bogner's hand; it was an unusual gesture for Russian women. The third member of Schubatis's party was a woman named Itia Akimerov. She served in the dual capacity of Mrs. Schubatis's secretary and Milo Schubatis's interpreter. She was talkative and charming, and Bogner decided he liked her. There was one other man in the party, but Bogner curtailed the introductions to get the entourage into cars and out of the rain.

Everything had been carefully planned. Capelli had been assigned to drive the first car, a black Lincoln. Bogner would ride shotgun with Schubatis and the Akimerov woman in the rear seat. Reba Schubatis, along with the fourth member of the entourage, a young man with the old Russian look of uncertainty about all things American—and, Bogner figured, probably one of Aprihinen's stoolies—were to ride in the second car. Frank Myers was assigned driving duties, with Breeden, who spoke Russian, attending to the protocol.

The caravan was waved through the Bolling gate, proceeded on to 295, the Anacostia Freeway, and headed north toward Pennsylvania Avenue.

As they pulled into traffic, Bogner made several attempts at casual conversation with the Russian, but by the time it had been filtered through the man's interpreter, all of the spontaneity had gone out of it. The Sukhoi official admitted that, yes—it had been a long trip, yes—he was tired, yes—he was looking forward to the symposium, and finally, no—no special accommodations were necessary because he and Mrs. Schubatis would be staying at the Russian Embassy. Even then, Bogner was unable to detect whether Milo Schubatis was able to understand English. The responses had been carefully spaced and the words even more carefully weighed. There was no way to be certain.

Finally, the Akimerov woman, freed from the need to translate Schubatis's responses, leaned forward and asked Bogner a question of her own.

"I was wondering, Captain Bogner," she said. Her voice was hopeful. "Will we be meeting any American movie stars?"

Bogner laughed. "Is that what Dr. Schubatis wants, to meet some American movie stars?"

The young woman was embarrassed, and shook her head. "Oh, no," she stammered, "I was asking for myself."

Capelli and Bogner were still chuckling when Capelli turned east on Pennsylvania Avenue.

Frank Myers, at the wheel of the second car,

squinted through the rain-streaked windshield and wished he had a cigarette. "What's the weather gonna do?" he grumbled. "With all this rain, I can barely see the blasted road."

"Don't sweat it," Breeden advised him. "It's Sunday. When you've been around here as long as I have, you learn that nothing ever happens on Sunday in Washington."

Datum: Sunday—1103L, October 5

Deng Zhen had been selected by Tang Ro Ji because of his expertise in electronics. Now he crawled along the cargo-area interior of the 1987 Dodge panel truck, carefully tucking the primer cord into a small gap between the steel sidewall and the corrugated metal flooring. The truck was white with the words STACY CLEAN PRO painted in bold, black letters on the side.

Zhen's primer cord was attached to a black box rigged with a tension-release detonator that would explode when they evacuated the target area. It had been rigged in that fashion so that the truck would explode into smaller pieces on impact . . . and it was done that way because Tang Ro Ji liked to say that a puzzle was more difficult to solve when the pieces were very many and very small.

Tang applauded him when he was finished. "Well done, Comrade. There will be very little left of the van, our comrade Mr. Kovnir, or any of the Schubatis entourage when we are done."

There was a loud peal of thunder, and Tang paused to listen to the rain. The rain would add to the confusion. For Tang that was an unexpected benefit.

At the rear of the van, Zhen rotated the sidebar gun mount into position and began checking the post-mounted Checheno-Ingush 750 RFR with twin .50-caliber, thirty-round clips. Beside him was the box of bangalore torpedoes and the homemade grenades. The torpedoes consisted of nothing more than a stick of dynamite in a thin plastic sleeve, headed with a blasting cap and a six-second standard fuse.

The homemade grenades were constructed of a piece of thin, pliable plastic tubing, black powder encasing a nonelectric blasting cap, compacted under pressure with iron and steel scraps and detonated by a six-second fuse. Deng Zhen picked up one of the devices and examined Zhao Shi's handiwork.

Zhao Shi was the appointed triggerman. He was very young, very quick, and very good at what he did.

As Deng Zhen crawled down out of the truck, he heard the phone ring. He stopped while the answering machine announced that the offices of Stacy Clean Pro were closed on Sundays. Then he waited to see if there would be the expected follow-up call. When it rang the second time, Tang Ro Ji answered.

"They passed through the main gate less than ten minutes ago," the feminine voice announced. "We are monitoring their car phones. The second car was inquiring about traffic conditions after they leave Pennsylvania and proceed on Lobard." The caller did not wait for confirmation, nor did Tang offer any.

Tang Ro Ji hung up and turned to his colleagues. "We are ready except for one small matter—that of Mr. Kovnir," he said. "And I will tend to that."

For Tang Ro Ji, the dispatching of Sergei Kovnir was a matter of expediency; there was no emotion involved. As the hour of Schubatis's arrival approached, the terrorists had sedated the old man, dressed him in an inexpensive dark blue business suit complete with shirt and tie, and informed him that they had a very important job for him.

Now, as Kovnir waited, Tang Ro Ji walked into the room and, from a distance of less than three feet, put a .45-caliber bullet into the back of the old man's head. When the bullet erupted from the man's face just below his left eye, it destroyed most of his facial features. That, too, was according to plan.

Then Tang Ro Ji walked around in front of the body, assessed the magnitude of the destruction, and smiled. Identification would not be easy.

When he walked back into the garage area, he instructed Deng Zhen to put the body in the back of the van and motioned for Zhao Shi to open the garage door. *"Chin wha` do˜ dun kow—,"* he said, smiling.

While Deng Zhen and Zhao Shi eased the Dodge van out into the alley, Tang Ro Ji went back into the building and picked up a small canvas valise containing two bottles. The bottles contained cacodyl, a mixture that assured them of spontaneous flammability. Tang Ro Ji knew the mixture, designed to explode on contact, would give off a dense white smoke. He had used it before. That dense white smoke was a deadly arsenic. At the strength Tang had formulated it, one inhalation of the cacodyl would cause death in a matter of seconds. Then, almost as an afterthought, he picked up the three gas masks and took them with him.

Outside in the rain, Tang crawled into the passenger's seat and checked his watch. "We have approximately eleven minutes," he said.

Datum: Sunday—1133L, October 5

Mike Capelli glanced at the veteran ISA agent in the seat beside him. Like Bogner, he was eager to hear the latest on the burning Saratoga oil rig. When Bogner nodded, he turned on the radio.

"We're coming up on checkpoint two at East Fifty-seventh, Pack," Bogner advised. "We'll go north and intersect at Saint Martin's on Lobard."

"How's the traffic look?" Packer inquired.

In the rearview mirror Bogner could see Breeden. The redhead was monitoring the conversation. He smiled and gave Bogner the thumbs-up signal from the second car.

"Harvey says the coast is clear," Bogner confirmed. "So far, so good."

At the corner of Fifty-seventh and Lobard, Capelli eased to a stop for a red light. Bogner, still on the car phone with Parker, was explaining the delay in their anticipated arrival time at the Franklin. "We lost some time on the belt because of the rain."

Across the street, churchgoers from the 10:30 mass at Saint Martin's were starting to stream out of the old edifice. A few darted through the rain oblivious to the traffic. The driver of an approaching station wagon rolled to a stop and opened the door to pick up passengers. Few noticed the white Dodge van that rolled to a stop immediately behind it. Only Bogner saw the rear doors of the van fly open and the man with the .50-caliber automatic drop to his knees into firing position.

Bogner shouted, but it was too late.

Zhao Shi opened fire and the scene became an instant sensory blur. There was a silence-shattering cacophony of gunshots, explosions, and screams.

The station wagon tried to accelerate through the intersection, the driver lost control on the wet pavement, and the rear end of the car came around, plowing into the Lincoln. Capelli was trying to back up as Bogner began shouting instructions.

"Get us the hell out of here! Swing out on Lobard." Then he spun in the seat to see if Schubatis and the Akimerov woman were still safe. As he did, a hail of bullets shattered the Lincoln's windshield and Capelli's head exploded, showering the others with bone shards and fragments of flesh.

Bogner threw open the door and dropped to the pavement. When he did, he realized that the rear door had been blown open and the Akimerov woman was lying in the street beside him. There was an ugly hole in her body where her stomach should have been, but she was still alive. Bogner knew she was pleading for help, but the only thing coming out of her mouth was a torrent of red-purple fluid. He tried futilely to reach out to her. He was giving his body commands—but there was no response.

He could hear gunfire and then an explosion. The second car, driven by Myers, erupted in a ball of flame. He saw Myers lying in the road. He was on fire.

It had evolved into a world of half-images. He saw a man—his brain registered the word *Asian*—holding some kind of long-barreled weapon. He was firing it from his shoulder. There was another explosion and the front of the church disintegrated, erupting into an inferno. There were more screams and Bogner rolled over again and again, trying to pull the pieces together. The rain had become something terrible: a thing of bricks and mortar, stone and steel, glass and marble—and flesh.

He looked for Schubatis. Then he realized one of the terrorists had an AK-47. It belched out more destruction, more explosions. Holes were being gouged in the street. Bogner covered his head.

He heard the cry of a child. The frantic screams of a mother. Then he saw a man, dressed in black. The back of his robe was gone and what was left of it was covered with a wet, ugly crimson color.

Bogner began to shake. It was Vietnam all over again. He was lying in a rice paddy, the wreckage of his downed A-4 smoldering behind him. His vision blurred as his eyes clouded with tears. There was smoke . . . and fire . . . and women and children screaming.

For a moment there was silence, then more gunshots, and ricocheting bullets. He could smell wet asphalt and blood . . . and, when he least expected it, the distinct scent of perfume. He looked back at the second car. It was on fire and the doors had been blown off. He saw Reba Schubatis clawing her way away from the holocaust. He saw people running and screaming. He saw men with weapons. He tried to get up, his legs crumpled, and he fell back to the pavement.

Then, as suddenly as it all began, the shooting ceased. He saw one of the terrorists, wearing a gas mask, loft some kind of bottle into the chaos and begin to run. He saw the body of Schubatis still in the burning car.

Somehow he managed to get to the car and grab hold of the Russian. When he looked at him he realized that the man no longer had a face. Still, he had enough strength left to drag Schubatis out of the car and pull him away.

A cloud of blue-gray smoke hovered over the

carnage, and he saw one of the parishioners clutch at his throat and fall to the pavement. Then he saw another—and a third.

Myers's car exploded, and Bogner realized that the fire had finally gotten to the gas tank. If there had been any hope for Myers or Breeden, it was gone now.

Then, without warning, there was a mocking silence. He could hear people crying—but the gunfire had ceased. All that was left were sounds of the aftermath of terror.

Far away in the distance there was the sound of sirens and people running. Bogner dropped to his knees, looked back at the devastation and carnage, and finally at the body of the motionless Schubatis, and collapsed.

# Chapter Three

Datum: Sunday—1345L, October 5

When Bogner opened his eyes, the room was dark. There was a small night-light next to the door, and in the pale illumination he could see the cloaked silhouette of a man.

The man saw Bogner stir and moved to the side of the bed. "How are you, Toby?" The voice showed concern.

Bogner wetted his lips and tried to organize his thoughts. Out of the chaos and confusion, all he could come up with was the flickering, half-formed images and fragments of a recurring nightmare. He saw Schubatis's face, and then a woman with her body broken. She was crying and holding the body of a child. Part of the child was missing.

Bogner closed his eyes, trying to seal out the nightmare. Only then was he aware of still another voice. It was on the far side of the room, near the heavily draped window. Despite its familiarity, it took an eternity for Bogner to quite make out whose voice it was. Finally it got through to him. It was Joy. He called out to her.

Packer looked at him.

"Joy's here, isn't she?" Bogner's voice was edgy and uncertain.

Packer looked across the room at the floor nurse and shook his head. Bogner closed his eyes again when he realized he had been wrong. Then he forced out the question he knew he had to ask. "Schubatis?"

Packer hesitated. In the semidarkness, Bogner could hear the man's measured breathing. Finally Packer answered, "I'm afraid he didn't make it."

There was another prolonged silence before Bogner stirred and tried to sit up. When he did, the nurse protested. She did it in such a way that Bogner knew she didn't expect him to pay any attention to her.

Packer reached over, turned on the small light on the nightstand next to Bogner's bed, and pulled up a chair. He kept his voice low, almost at a whisper.

"Look, Toby, I'm not going to pull any punches. No matter how bad you think it is, I'm here to tell you that it's a helluva lot worse. Not only is Milo Schubatis dead, those bastards got

Mrs. Schubatis, the interpreter, and Aprihinen's liaison officer as well. Myers, Capelli, and Breeden—none of them made it. Right now you may not think so, but you're the lucky one."

Bogner closed his eyes again. "What about all those people at the church?"

"At this point we don't have anything even close to a final count. So far we've got seventeen confirmed dead and forty-one known casualties—several of those aren't expected to make it."

"Who the hell was it?" Bogner managed.

"At twelve noon, the CNN people in Atlanta received a call from a man identifying himself as a representative of the Fifth Academy. He played a tape by a man who calls himself Tang Ro Ji. Tang claims that the Fifth Academy death squad faction of the PRC was responsible for the attack on Schubatis."

"Tang Ro Ji," Bogner repeated. "That's the same guy who claimed the Fifth Academy was responsible for the Saratoga explosion."

"And the Royal Opera House," Packer added. "But that's not all. Exactly one hour after news of Schubatis's death went out over the wire and was picked up in Moscow, Aprihinen was on the phone to President Colchin. The son of a bitch was already doing a little saber rattling."

"Did Colchin tell him about Tang's phone call?"

Packer nodded. "Affirmative, but Aprihinen isn't buying it. And, under the circumstances, I can't say I blame him. Aprihinen finally feels secure enough to let Schubatis attend the AMBA conference, and less than an hour after the old boy lands on American soil, he gets his face blown off. He has reason to be suspicious."

"I don't suppose it helps any that we're, too, saying it was the Fifth Academy," Bogner added.

Packer was silent for a moment. Then he asked the question he had been sent there to ask. "How are you feeling?"

"A tad wobbly," Bogner admitted. Then he poked around to see how just how wobbly he was. "Why?"

"Lattimere Spitz called here less than thirty minutes ago. If you can make it, he wants us over at the head shed at 1800 hours. I told him we'd try. According to the doctor, you've got an assortment of bumps, bruises, and a couple of first-degree burns—but outside of that you're in one piece."

Bogner had to try twice before he was able to swing his legs over the edge of the bed and sit up. When he did he was still shaking, and the nurse stepped forward to protest.

"We can do without the macho routine, Captain. You stay right where you're at."

Bogner forced a laugh and waved her off.

"Look, sweetheart, I know you've got your instructions, but whoever you got them from, I can damn well assure you I take my cues from someone with a helluva lot more clout than some doctor."

Datum: Sunday—1745L, October 5

Bogner knew the routine: David Colchin, a Texan by birth, favored the Southwest Room of the White House for his meetings. A Charlie Russell painting of a cantankerous bronc tearing up a cow camp in the morning mist was hanging above the gas-fired fireplace to set the tone for the President's meetings. Colchin called the painting symbolic.

Now Bogner, with skin abrasions on his left cheek and right arm, and burns on both hands, waited with Packer for the Chief Executive.

Lattimere Spitz, Colchin's volatile but longtime aide, and the President's conduit to the ISA, had already arrived. He was wearing what Bogner considered Lattimere Spitz standard issue: a single-breasted navy blue suit, white shirt, and regimental red and dark blue Princeton tie. Spitz, a homely man, had a hawk nose, pinched eyes, and thick glasses. On the coffee table in front of him was a manila file folder with the words TOP SECRET emblazoned across it in rubber-stamped bold red letters. As usual, Spitz was sitting in the chair by the fireplace with his fingers tented and his face creased in a scowl—a posture Packer was convinced was the only one the man knew. Packer also conceded that it wasn't Spitz's job to smile.

"Have you seen the pictures of Schubatis, T.C.?" Spitz questioned. "The ones taken at the hospital."

"You mean they've already cataloged the—" Bogner began.

"We don't waste time," Spitz cut in. He handed Bogner the folder. He removed the contents, began to read the medical report, then glanced at the black-and-white morgue photographs. Suddenly he looked up, first at Packer, then at Spitz. "Look, Lattimere," he said, "I know I'm still a little shaky, but something isn't right here."

Spitz cocked his head to one side. "What isn't right?"

"Let me put it like this," Bogner said haltingly. "Unless someone reversed the negative, this isn't Schubatis. It sure as hell isn't the man I picked up at Bolling this morning."

# RED SKIES

Datum: Sunday—1812L, October 5

Dr. Lo Chi Lyn was a small man with a twitch in his eye and the nervous habit of talking to himself. Even though his wife had called it to his attention hundreds of times, Lo Chi Lyn, at the ripe old age of seventy-one, had decided he was too old to do anything about it.

Now he walked around his patient, studying the nature of the man's wounds. As he did, he recited his appraisal of each of the lesions and abrasions to a young woman who sat at the desk in the far corner of the room, carefully making note of his comments.

"You are most fortunate, Tang, most of the wounds are superficial," he said, "particularly the ones in the cephalic region. There are abrasions extending from the left auricular region down, across the parotid-masseteric area, and forward into the oral region. There are also some minor contusions in the parietal locality where the hair has been abraded." He paused for a moment, then added, "And there is a slight tear in the left lateral canthus where the folds of the eye meet. Fortunately, all will heal in good time."

Impatient, Tang Ro Ji glanced at his watch

and wondered if the schedule was still intact. "You will hurry?" he urged. "My only concern is, are any of Comrade Schubatis's injuries serious? Any fool can see that he has a few minor scrapes and scratches. That is to be expected. My concern is that there may be damage to the respiratory system caused by the cyanide."

Lo Chi Lyn studied the foreboding-looking young man with the long black hair and deep, brooding brown-black eyes. He wondered where Colonel Quan found men like Tang. Tang Ro Ji certainly did not look like the young men he had seen in the square in Beijing. "If that is your concern, I can assure you I see no evidence of damage to the larnyx, the trachea, the bronchi, or the lungs. I have examined him closely."

Tang Ro Ji did not look relieved. He continued to glower.

"You are uneasy because you were not instructed to use the cyanide mixture. Correct?"

"Be quiet, old man. It is not your concern. I receive my instructions from Colonel Quan. I was told to intercept the Russian and see that he was safely in our custody. Beyond the matter of his health, he is not your affair."

Lo Chi Lyn stepped back from the examining table and lit another cigarette. For a fleeting moment his features were shrouded in a blue-gray haze. The smoke was the same color as the rare and infrequent strands of hair that still graced his aging scalp. Looking at him, Tang Ro Ji decided, as he had many times before, that he did not like old people.

Despite Tang's obvious hostility, Lo continued to assess the condition of the man who had been brought to him. He used a knife to split the seam of the man's pant leg and examined the discolored eruption in the skin. "There appears to be a compound fracture where the head of the femur connects with the coxal bone, although without further probing I cannot determine whether or not it involves a separation of the head of the femur from the greater trochanter."

The young woman continued recording Lo's observations in Chinese characters, and as the time passed, Ro Ji became more and more agitated. "What is she writing?" he demanded.

"She is simply making note of my assessment of our Russian friend's condition. That is all. The doctors in Danjia will want to know."

Tang Ro Ji snatched the tablet away from the nurse and studied the string of columnar symbols. He generally disliked reading. Ro Ji would never have revealed as much, but as an orphan growing up on the streets of Haikou, he had managed to avoid school. He was self-taught, and his whole orientation toward the land of his birth came from the fevered writings of Quan Jo Shu, the Eminent and Revered, not to mention the money he was paid by His Eminence's grandson, Colonel Quan . . . money he was paid to be a mercenary for the Fifth Academy.

Tang Ro Ji handed the tablet back to the girl. "Hurry up," he ordered.

Lo Chi Lyn pulled a sheet over Schubatis and looked at Tang again. "I have neither the tools nor the strength to repair the Russian's leg," he said. "But I can tell you that he must be kept immobile to avoid any further damage to his leg and hip. When the sedative I have given him starts to wear off, he will be in a great deal of pain. Which, of course, raises other questions. How do you propose to get him to Danjia in this condition?"

"You will sedate him to the point that he feels nothing," Tang insisted, "and it must be strong enough to get him out of the country and into Hong Kong."

"If you are still planning on shipping him back to Hong Kong as the deceased member of an influential family, there is the matter of making certain the proper paperwork is completed and the coffin is appropriately decorated and prepared."

"I do not anticipate any difficulties getting him past the American authorities. They are lax"—Tang Ro Ji smirked—"and we have . . . how shall I phrase it, certain advantages when we arrive in Hong Kong."

Lo Chi Lyn knew that Tang simply meant that some custom officials in Hong Kong would, for the right price, avoid asking, or in the case of Schubatis, avoid looking too far into the matter.

Lo, although he did not show it, was equally concerned about the time. He glanced at the clock and stepped away from the table. "I am finished," he said. Then he urged Tang Ro Ji to make his preparations.

Datum: Sunday—1830L, October 5

While Lattimere Spitz waited for the phone call, he laid the three photographs side by side. He agreed with Packer: The first appeared to have been lifted or copied from Schubatis's Party card. The second was the one taken at the official Party function. The third, taken by the hospital, showed the difference. "It shouldn't take long for Palmer to check it out," he said.

Before either Packer or Bogner could reply, the phone rang and Spitz snapped it up. "What did you find out?" he asked. As he did, he switched on the speakerphone.

Thomas Palmer was new to the department. Packer had dispatched him to the hospital morgue as soon as Bogner had raised the question.

"The hair is definitely parted on the right side," he began.

Spitz looked at the first photo and nodded to Bogner. "You were right about the hair, Toby." Then he turned back to the telephone. "What about the rest of it?"

"They measured him. The Schubatis we've got down here is a good three inches taller. And this is the clincher: The coroner says there is evidence of some pretty sloppy skin grafting around the hairline and the back of the scalp. He said it looks like it was a hurry-up job and that it was done fairly recently. The skin grafts aren't holding."

"What about the facial features?" Spitz pressed.

"Like Bogner said, there isn't much to go on."

"Did you check personal effects?"

"The passport photo is of the guy we've got down here," Palmer said. "They were careful about some things, careless about others."

Packer leaned forward with his hands on the desk. "The question, then, is which one is which? Did Aprihinen send us a bogus Schubatis because he was afraid to let the real one attend the conference?"

Palmer hesitated. "Miller gave me copies of everything in the dossier before I came down here, and about the only thing I can say with any degree of certainty is that it's two different people. The one thing that doesn't add up is the comment one of the surgeons made when I started asking questions. He said that he was surprised at the level of rigor mortis considering the time of death."

"Meaning?" Spitz said.

"Actually, nothing conclusive. From what the doctor tells me, it varies from individual to individual. But the Schubatis we've got down here was already showing surprising signs of muscle stiffening. To me that supports the switch theory."

Spitz made several more inquiries about passports, personal effects, and papers, ending by instructing Palmer to grab everything he could. Then he hung up and made a second call. Within minutes, a White House staffer had arrived with a stack of folders. Spitz took them from the man and closed the door.

"Better get comfortable, gentlemen; it's going to be a long night," he said with a sigh.

Datum: Monday—0540L, October 6

Gurin Posmanovich was a recent graduate of American Institute, and the only son of parents who had fled from Kiev when they were mere youths. A student of social structure, and particularly communism, he thumbed idly through the final pages of a laborious dissertation on collectives during the Stalin years, and wished he had something better to read.

For young Posmanovich it had been a long night, thanks to the frequent exchange of calls between Washington and Moscow. The calls had concerned both the Saratoga explosion off the coast of Tuxpano and the equally disturbing news that Milo Schubatis had been killed by Chinese terrorists who claimed to be a dissident faction of the Red Army.

Adding to his dismay was the fact that it had been nearly three o'clock in the morning before the Ambassador had finally fallen asleep on the daybed in his office on the second floor. The Ambassador could be a difficult man in times of stress.

Even then, Gurin had been left with explicit instructions. "Wake me up if any calls come through."

Gurin had anticipated a call from the man at the night desk at the State Department, or possibly even a call from the ISA, since a man by the name of Miller had already initiated two earlier calls. But he was caught off guard when the red light began to flash.

"A-42," the voice on the other end snapped.

Gurin riffled through the pages of the receiver

code. Finally he managed a none-too-authoritative "GP-95."

"Prometheus," the caller informed him. "We are using scramble four. Press four and wait twenty seconds."

Gurin's throat tightened when he referenced the code and realized that Prometheus was the code name for the President. "Oh, my God," he blurted. The book dropped to the floor.

"Ambassador Wilson, please," the voice demanded.

"I'll have to wake him, sir," Gurin said, pressing the route-through button to the Ambassador's office.

Wilson's response was groggy, but it cleared the moment Gurin recited the code name Prometheus.

"GP-95, recitation for voice-pattern check," the monitor instructed.

Wilson recited his ident number and repeated his name.

"Pattern valid," the monitor verified. "Go ahead, Prometheus."

"I know it's barely the crack of dawn over there, Frank," Colchin began.

"That's quite all right, Mr. President. I just dozed off here in my office. What's the latest?"

"The Schubatis affair has gotten a bit sticky since we spoke a few hours ago. Our ISA people believe they've uncovered something."

Wilson waited for the President to continue.

"Hospital officials are reasonably certain that the body they recovered from the terrorist attack at Saint Martin's earlier today is not Milo Schubatis. Both the CIA and ISA have rather extensive dossiers on the man, and if our information is accurate, the body at the hospital is not Schubatis."

"I'm not sure I understand, Mr. President."

With Colchin's Texas drawl, the story took even longer to unfold. "We believe the scenario goes something like this. Somehow a group that calls themselves the Fifth Academy, a faction of the Red Army, learned about us trying to slip Schubatis into the country prior to the conference. And, as far-fetched as it sounds, they had this attack so well planned today that they were actually able to substitute a Schubatis look-alike at the site of the attack."

Wilson was mentally trying to put the pieces together. It would be difficult to convince the already suspicious Aprihinen that the Americans weren't up to something. It sounded too contrived even to him. Still, he asked, "What's our plan of action, Mr. President?"

"Tap your local sources for what information you can find, then get to Aprihinen. Tell Moshe what we think happened. See what you can do to quiet him down. He wasn't buying much of what I was telling him in my earlier call."

"Do I hold anything back?" Wilson asked.

"Level with him. Tell him we've got our hands full. I don't need to be looking over my shoulder every twenty minutes worrying whether or not Moshe is getting ready to jump ship on us. Tell him I'll update him as soon as we've got something to go on."

Wilson wondered if there was anything he had overlooked. He did inquire whether the Secretary of State knew of the matter, and Colchin informed him that the Secretary was standing next to him.

When Colchin appeared to have nothing further to say, Wilson mumbled something about the weather.

"Raining like hell," Colchin informed him. Then he cautioned the Ambassador to "stay loose." After that, the line went dead.

Frank Wilson waited a moment, then pressed the button on his telephone a second time. Gurin answered.

"Gurin," the Ambassador said, "remember that little bistro you drove me to last week, the one next to the Ostankino on Botanicheskaya Street?"

Gurin was nodding, even though he knew the Ambassador couldn't see him. "I believe so, sir," he said.

Wilson didn't waste words. "Good. Get the

car out. We're going down there just as soon as I make another call."

When he was certain that Gurin had left for the garage, Wilson used the electronic scanner to make certain that no one was monitoring his call. Secure, he dialed the 416 number. When a voice answered, Wilson conveyed his message in three words: "Vilnius, thirty minutes."

There was the usual cryptic response. *"Da."*

Datum: Sunday—2045L, October 5

The death of Zhao Shi in the attack on the Schubatis caravan had not, of course, been anticipated, and Deng Zhen was saddened. Twice he had tried to talk to Tang about it, but the man refused to discuss it. Zhao Shi had been his friend—and now he would be alone when Tang Ro Ji returned to Hainan.

Earlier he had told one of his fellow students at Capital that they had been evicted from his apartment and needed the enclosed truck to move his belongings. The ruse had worked. But now there would be the matter of explaining Zhao Shi's involvement in the terrorist attack—a fact that would perhaps make his own situation difficult to explain.

For the time being, though, Deng Zhen had

to put his concerns aside and do as Tang Ro Ji instructed. He inched the borrowed truck into the narrow alley behind the building housing Lo Chi Lyn's office and turned off the ignition. It was still raining, and in the darkness he was not certain if he was close enough to the loading dock to ease the cylinder onto the freight platform.

When the door opened, the light outlined the slender figure of Lo's nurse. She was holding a flashlight and indicating how close he was to the dock.

Deng Zhen crawled out of the cab, went around to the rear of the truck, opened the doors, and began working the empty six-foot-six-inch aluminum cylinder onto the loading platform. Without all of the internal life-support mechanisms, it would have been an easy task, but with the heavy steel air tanks installed, the cylinder had become quite cumbersome.

The young woman said nothing as he struggled with the bulky container, nor did she offer to assist him. She had helped to the extent that she opened the freight-elevator door and blocked it. The only illumination was a single sixty-watt lightbulb.

Deng Zhen managed to maneuver the cylinder into position and waited while the door closed. As with Tang, a major element of his concern was that the task of getting Schubatis into the cylinder and to the airport was taking a great deal longer than anticipated. Even though the flight did not leave until the early hours of the morning, the cylinder had to be in the customs compound by midnight. That was when Comrade Mi Po went off duty.

The elevator door opened and Tang Ro Ji was waiting. "Over here," he ordered. He indicated a location next to the gurney containing the unconscious Schubatis.

While Deng Zhen watched, Lo and Tang Ro Ji secured the Russian's body on the support board, temporarily disconnected the silicone rubber tubes from the needles administering the sedative, and placed Schubatis's body in the cylinder. Then Lo put the oxygen mask on the Russian and adjusted the straps. He was still connected to the auxiliary system.

"You are certain of the time interval?" Lo asked Tang.

Tang Ro Ji glanced at the clock, mentally calculating the sequence. "We will seal the cylinder at 2200 hours. The flight leaves tomorrow morning at 0530. Actual flying time, including the stopover at LAX, is about eighteen hours. Long before the thirty hours we have provided for have passed, Comrade Schubatis will be safely in Hong Kong. The flight is scheduled to arrive in Hong Kong at 2300 hours our time."

"What you are attempting is risky," Lo Chi Lyn assessed. "His condition is unstable."

Tang Ro Ji ignored the old man's concerns and began adjusting the tanks inside the aluminum cylinder. The thin copper shields that normally line a transportation pall had been removed to allow the installation of the life-support systems. As he arranged each of them, he extended the wires to the small monitor concealed at the head of the cylinder. Since Lo's nurse would be accompanying the body, she had been carefully instructed how to adjust each component of the monitoring system. One adjusted the morphine dosage, the second controlled the three compressed-air tanks, and the third administered the sedative. All three controls had been cleverly concealed behind a panel inscribed with the supposedly deceased's official crest and documents.

"Americans," Tang Ro Ji sneered. "They even require paperwork of the dead." Then he laughed.

Lo, still cautious, went over the configuration of the control panel with the young woman once again. Then he repeated the procedure a second time. The woman smiled and repeated the sequence exactly as he had detailed it.

When everything had finally been arranged to Tang Ro Ji's satisfaction, he stepped back and motioned for Lo to reconnect the tubes to the needles. Lo took out his stethoscope, checked Schubatis's heart and pulse, and as a final precaution, put an additional strip of tape over the areas where the needles had been inserted in the Russian's arm.

"He is completely immobile?" Deng Zhen asked.

"He could not scratch his nose if he wanted to," Tang said with a laugh.

"Any movement at all could be fatal," Lo said.

Tang Ro Ji again checked the time. "Now we wait. We will close the cylinder at precisely 2200 and activate the life-support systems."

Finally the young woman spoke. "What will happen if the Russian dies?" she asked.

Tang Ro Ji sat down at a nearby table and lit a cigarette. "He won't," he said. For the first time, Lo noticed a lack of conviction in the young militant's voice.

# Chapter Four

Datum: Monday—0648L, October 6

The American Ambassador, Frank Wilson, was a tall man with thick gray hair and eyes that resembled steel marbles. He had a precise military walk and referred to himself as a born-again Christian. As he stepped from his dark blue Volvo sedan, he instructed young Posmanovich to remain with the car.

Inside the Vilnius, he looked for Andrakov, the headwaiter, and waited until one of the servers summoned the Lithuanian. When Andrakov emerged from the back room, still tucking in his shirt, he saw Wilson, arched his eyebrows, and inclined his head toward the stairway.

Wilson uttered one word: "Korsun."

"Second floor, second door on the right," Andrakov confirmed.

"Tell my driver to go around behind the building," Wilson ordered. "The fewer people that know I'm here, the better."

The second-floor hallway was not well lighted. Wilson tried to ignore the large rat scurrying through the duct where the fascia plate was missing. It was appropriate, he thought to himself.

He knocked twice before he entered.

Korsun, who reminded Wilson of 1940s movie star Sidney Greenstreet, because of his bulk and sinister laugh, was seated at a small table in the middle of the room. There was a wispy layer of cigarette smoke hovering like a cirrus cloud over his head. Korsun had procured a bottle of vodka, an off brand that he had no doubt purchased from a small black-market distiller in a little second-floor shop not far from the Hotel Russia on Ulitsa Rzina. Wilson didn't drink, but his Russian guests did, and he used the shop himself to obtain vodka.

Always a taciturn man, Korsun greeted him with his fat, rheumy eyes, then looked at his watch. "What took you so long?" he growled.

"What the hell is going on?" Wilson snapped.

Korsun ignored the question and motioned for the American Ambassador to have a seat. When he did speak, Korsun's voice was little more than a wheezy whisper. Wilson had heard that the fat man had once been diagnosed as having cancer of the larnyx. If that was the case, Korsun, with his constant parade of cigarettes, made no concession to his affliction.

"What kind of game is Kusinien playing?"

Korsun shrugged. "As you well know, Secretary Kusinien is President Aprihinen's personal confidant and strategist. And I would think you know equally well that Georgi Kusinien does not consult me on matters of state."

"All right, let me put it another way. What the hell is going on with Schubatis?" Wilson demanded.

Korsun pushed himself away from the table, stood up, and waddled to the window. He pulled back the drape and stared out at the still-sparse early-morning traffic. "How long have we been doing business, Comrade?"

"Three years," Wilson answered. "What the hell does that have to do with it?"

"And how do you regard me?"

"You're a mercenary bastard."

Korsun authored one of his infrequent laughs. "Then what makes you think that if I knew something about Milo Schubatis, I would not make that information available to you?"

Wilson leaned forward with his hands on the table. He disliked looking at the back of his obese informant. Not being able to see the man's face put Wilson at a disadvantage. Mikolai Korsun, for all his value as a conduit to

Kusinien, and thus Aprihinen, was the kind of man that, if Wilson had the choice, he would have preferred not to do business with at all.

"Are you aware," Korsun asked in his unpleasant voice, "that twenty-one days ago, an Aviation Major Arege Borisov piloting the prototype of the top-secret Su-39-Covert disappeared on a high-altitude test flight?"

Wilson nodded. "I saw nothing of it in your papers or on your telecasts. I learned of it through my own government. Why? Was it a defection? Where?"

Korsun laughed again and turned to look at him. "You saw nothing of it on television because the state still controls fifty-one percent of the only network that covers all of the former union. News is still monitored. As to where? Where indeed? Where else but the very nation that a few short years ago we were referring to as the capitalist warmongers."

Wilson shook his head. "If your man, Major Borisov, had flown into American territory, it would have been on the front page of every damn newspaper in the country, and you know it. Besides, how do you know Borisov didn't deep-six that Sukhoi, involuntarily or otherwise? There's a helluva lot of water out there."

Korsun walked back to the table with his arms folded behind him. The gesture only accentuated his bulk. He was still smiling. "Major

Borisov did not deep-six it, as you suggest, Comrade Ambassador. On the contrary, when he disappeared, he was acting on orders from a very high-ranking Russian official."

"How high?"

"The highest."

"Aprihinen?"

Korsun did not answer. He went back to the window, where he was silhouetted by a thin orange streak on the horizon. The splash of color betrayed daybreak through the dark, low-hanging clouds. "I have always said that I prefer dawn to sunset," he said, changing the subject. "Dawn is a promise. Sunset is a verdict."

"Dammit. Was it Aprihinen?"

"Have we progressed from philosophy to business?" Korsun asked.

"Has my government ever been anything but generous?"

Korsun continued to look out the window. The American Ambassador had told him what he wanted to hear. He began slowly.

"What I am about to tell you is known to very few. Following the death of our beloved President Zhelannov four years ago, and the subsequent election of Moshe Aprihinen to the Presidency of the Confederation, Air General Cosmo Ansovich instructed Milo Schubatis to continue work on what could be termed a strategic equivalent to your much-ballyhooed F-

117. When General Ansovich saw how successful your design was in the Gulf War, Ansovich instructed Schubatis to redouble his efforts. As a result, just eighteen short months ago, the first test flights were conducted."

Wilson lit one of his infrequent cigarettes. Smoking was inconsistent with his "born again" philosophy.

"Go ahead," he said. Frank Wilson had heard about the Sukhoi Covert project, but certifiable information had been even more difficult to come by than usual. Now he was getting it from a surprising source: Mikolai Korsun, the man *Izvestia* had once called "Mikolai the Merchant."

"Subsequent tests," the fat man continued, "revealed that the aircraft was capable of performance perameters that far exceeded what our sources believe your Stealth to be capable of."

"For example?"

"Will it whet your appetite if I tell you that it has a tactical range of twenty-five hundred kilometers, and can be armed with a variety of nuclear missiles?"

"A bomber?" Wilson pressed.

"An attack bomber with fighterlike performance, capable of carrying a dozen or more bombs similar to your MK.84."

Wilson sagged back in his chair.

"Exactly three weeks ago, Air Major Borisov and a Sukhoi test pilot by the name of Arid Komivov took off from a top-secret test facility in Volgograd, and neither of them was heard from again. Initially, everyone assumed that they experienced mechanical difficulties and that the aircraft was lost. Then we received a delayed report from Irkutsk that a high-performance aircraft of unknown origin was spotted by a MiG-29 pilot crossing the Tashkent range over the border into Mongolia."

"Then you damn well know he didn't cross over into American territory."

"We always knew that, Comrade," Korsun wheezed. "When we realized what happened, we also knew that Air Major Borisov was not acting alone."

Wilson looked puzzled. "Meaning?"

"You are aware of the growing ideological chasm between Colonel General Isotov and President Aprihinen?"

Wilson nodded. He had heard rumors. Korsun's admission was the first time he had heard anyone speak openly about the rift.

"Isotov accuses both President Aprihinen and Secretary Kusinien of an ideological sellout. He is an outspoken advocate of impeaching Aprihinen and reinstituting Party control."

"So he has this guy Air Major Borisov hijack the Su-39," Wilson speculated, "because it gives

Isotov the upper hand if it comes to a showdown with Aprihinen."

Korsun resumed his seat. "Exactly, but this is Russian theater, my friend—and, as you well know, we are a people that thrive on melodramatic plot twists. Originally I believed that Borisov landed, as he was instructed, at a small base in Guangdong province where he was told he would be given sanctuary by the Kong Ho regime. As far as cogent political philosophies go, some of Kong Ho's detractors share views more in line with Isotov than Aprihinen."

"Is that what happened?"

"The plot took another twist. Air Major Borisov flew to Danjia on the island of Hainan."

"Hainan," Wilson repeated, "the Fifth Academy."

"Exactly. See how the plot thickens?"

"What you're saying is that Isotov has himself some powerful allies if it comes to a showdown with Aprihinen and the Fifth Academy takes over in China."

"Remember, I said this was Russian theater. There is more. Kong Ho is fighting his own ghosts of administrations past. The nooks and crannies of Beijing are full of people who think China's finest hour came under the leadership of Zhou Enlai. They're the real muscle behind the Fifth Academy. They're the ones who are aligned with Isotov—and now they're the ones with the Su-39, not the Kong Ho regime."

Wilson let out a sigh. "Then we're caught in a cross fire—damned if we do, damned if we don't."

"You are indeed," Korsun acknowledged. "I believe this is what you Americans call a lose-lose situation."

Suddenly, Frank Wilson had a new problem. Now what did he say to Aprihinen? He was in the unfortunate position of knowing more than he was supposed to know. Kusinien would want to know where he got his information.

He stood up, put out his cigarette, and started for the door.

"Have you forgotten something?" Korsun asked.

Wilson nodded. He reached into his coat pocket, extracted an envelope, and laid it on the table.

Korsun smiled.

Datum: Sunday—2205L, October 5

Tang watched as Lo Chi Lyn's nurse removed Schubatis from the bottles of intravenous solution and connected him to the solutions contained in the supply chambers concealed in the double wall of the aluminum funeral cylinder.

When the woman had completed the task, he watched the monitor for signs of change in Schubatis's vitals. As much as Tang disliked it, he was still dependent on the doctor's assessment. "What do you think, old man?" he asked.

"Between here and Hainan is a long journey with many perils," Lo Chi Lyn said.

Tang ignored the comment, moved to the head of the cylinder, removed the small medallion with the crest, and examined the digital monitor and three control valves. The monitor gave him readings on the air, the painkiller, and the sedative. Then he leaned over and laid his head on the cylinder, with his ear next to the surface of the metal. He could hear nothing—and if there were no sounds, the Americans would not be suspicious.

Tang stepped back, glanced at his watch, nodded to Deng Zhen and the woman. "It is time," he said.

The unconscious Schubatis was now sealed in the cylinder that would be his home for the next twenty-four to thirty hours. Deng Zhen wheeled the cylinder into the freight elevator, and Tang waited until the lift disappeared below floor level before looking at Lo Chi Lyn again.

"You have arranged the necessary papers for the woman?" the doctor inquired. "Passports, tickets, interior travel papers, and Party card?"

Tang nodded. "I have taken care of everything except one small matter."

As Lo Chi Lyn watched, Tang pulled back his coat, reached into his concealed belt holster, and produced a dull-black 92D Beretta. It was the same gun he had used on the unfortunate Kovnir. He released the safety and pulled the trigger. There was a single report—a cracking sound—but there was no one except Tang Ro Ji and the old man to hear it.

For a fleeting moment Tang wondered about that. Did the sound of the Beretta slam its way into the victim's brain before the message of death? It was a conundrum. He liked philosophical riddles.

It was finished.

Doctor Lo Chi Lyn, admirer of Kong Ho, was sprawled on the floor with a tidy bullet hole in his chest, arms and legs akimbo, and, as Tang assessed it, with not all that much blood to manifest the process of dying.

Tang tucked the Beretta back in the holster, went to the still-open drug locker, took several cartons, made certain he spilled some of the capsules on the floor, and flushed the remainder down the toilet. He littered a second carton in the hall on the way to the freight elevator. Then he rode the elevator down to the loading dock. When Lo Chi Lyn was found, police would assume his death was drug related.

Americans, he believed, were easily duped.

Deng Zhen and the woman were waiting. The cold October rain had turned to a heavy downpour. "Everything is ready?" Tang asked.

Both Deng Zhen and the woman nodded.

"I almost forgot." Tang smiled, looking at the woman. "Doctor Lo Chi Lyn said to tell you that he wishes you a most pleasant journey home."

Datum: Sunday—2320L, October 5

In large measure, Bogner was amazed at what could be accomplished on short notice, especially on a Sunday night. Spitz had paraded them in, one by one, making certain the ISA trio of Packer, Miller, and Bogner had all of the information available.

Seth Lambert of the DOD had been first, bringing them up to speed on the performance capabilities of the Su-39 Covert. In less than an hour he had profiled the aircraft, its range, its armament capabilities, and the DOD's admittedly extrapolated test data. And he had concluded with what for Bogner seemed to be the real reason Schubatis had been abducted.

"Make no bones about it, this guy Schubatis has built one hell of an airplane. Whoever has it has the edge. The most disturbing part of which is, we don't have anything that compares, not even on the drawing board."

The second briefing came from the State Department's Mel Courier. It took him less than twenty minutes to detail the political situation in the Russian Commonwealth.

"Aprihinen is no sweetheart. He's got a hard-on for the Americans, but he's politically savvy enough to know that without our backing and the cooperation of the World Bank, his economy is in a shambles. On the other hand, this guy Colonel General Isotov makes our boy Aprihinen look like a teddy bear. He's a hard-liner, a Party loyalist, and he's the man who pushed Schubatis and Sukhoi to develop the Su-39."

"In other words," Colchin added, "Isotov is the worst kind of a son of a bitch; an ambitious son of a bitch."

"At the same time," Courier continued, "we've got what amounts to damn near a mirror image of the Russian situation in Beijing. The right-wing Kong Ho regime is in power, but there's an old man by the name of General Han Ki Po who leads a dissident faction of hard-liners known as the Fifth Academy. Kong Ho's people haven't had much success ferreting them out because they're buried deep in the bowels of the Red Army. Now comes the scary part: From time to time we get reports of a possible coalition between Han and our Russian friend, Isotov."

Finally, it was the CIA's turn. Oscar Jaffe had sent his first lieutenant, a man Bogner respected, Del Harper. Harper had already sifted through the political debris of the Saratoga explosion off the coast of Tuxpano earlier that morning.

"I spent most of the afternoon sorting through this with Jaffe, Dahmer, and Felix Masterson of our synoptic group. What I'm about to give you is what we call the most likely scenario."

Both Colchin and Spitz got up to pour themselves another cup of coffee. Bogner thought the President looked exhausted. But the fact was, Bogner wasn't feeling too well himself.

"We're beginning to see a pattern in all this, and if we're right, we've been set up. Just moments after the blast at the Royal Opera House, we received a call from a guy who identified himself as a representative of the Fifth Academy. He played a tape by a man called Tang Ro Ji. In it, Tang claimed the blast could be laid at the feet of the turmoil in the PRC. Kong Ho denies it. Key to this is the fact that the Queen had already departed. We don't think this guy Tang or whoever he's working for wants a bunch of pissed-off Brits if Tang kills their queen.

"Same thing," Harper continued, "with the

Saratoga situation. Tang is on the phone taking credit for it twenty minutes after it happened. But once again, it happens after the key figure, namely Cerralvo, has departed.

"True, we've got two major disasters on our hands, but let's face it, not nearly as big as if they had killed the Queen or Cerralvo."

"As a result of all this," Spitz said, looking around the table, "as of noon today, we are redoubling our security measures on Prometheus."

Colchin smiled whenever he heard himself referred to in that fashion. Raised on a Texas ranch, and a lawyer by education, he admitted to a gap in his education about Greek mythology. Early on, he'd felt compelled to ask Spitz to explain the significance of his code name. When he heard Spitz's explanation, he'd laughed.

"You know the rest," Harper continued. "We thought we were taking more-than-adequate security measures with Schubatis's arrival today—but it wasn't enough."

"Put a bow around it," Packer said.

"Twenty minutes after the massacre at Saint Martin's today, we got the obligatory call from—you guessed it—Tang. He said it was the Fifth Academy wing of the Red Army. At the same time, we're in touch with Kong Ho's people and we're getting the standard disavowal.

Bottom line, we're buying what Kong Ho's people tell us. Why? Because what happened at Saint Martin's today is an altogether different M.O. than what happened earlier.

"At this point, we believe the most likely of three possible scenarios is that Han Ki Po and his Fifth Academy dissidents have the real Schubatis."

"And . . ." Spitz pressed.

"Well, he sure as hell isn't going to do them any good here in the States, so we figure along about now they're either hustling him out of the country or are about to do so."

Bogner sagged back in his chair. "Taking him out of the country—where?"

"Best guess, Danjia on Hainan Island. Our sources claim that's where Han Ki Po's faction hang their hat. It's the stronghold of the Red Army's Seventh Garrison . . . the group known as the Fifth Academy."

"Or . . . we could be chasing our tail," Colchin cut in.

Miller looked at Spitz. "Can we get any of this verified?"

Colchin stood up. "I'm waiting on a call from Ambassador Wilson. He has instructions to tap his sources and try to get Aprihinen to cool down long enough for us to sort through the pieces."

"So what's our next move?" Packer asked.

"We've got the airports covered," Harper said. "Every major airport with direct or connecting flights to Hong Kong, Singapore, Beijing, Shanghai, and Macao has one of our agents acting as a customs agent. If they try to smuggle Schubatis through, we're damn sure going to know about it."

Colchin looked at his watch. "It's almost one o'clock. Let's get some sleep. Leave a number where Spitz can locate you. If you haven't been contacted before then, be back here at 0800 hours."

Datum: Sunday—2313L, October 5

Deng Zhen had driven to the most congested part of the Washington National short-term parking lot and selected a place between two similar-size vehicles for cover. Like Tang, he had already changed into a conservative, dark, two-piece suit, with a white shirt and tie. He put on a raincoat, then headed for the International Terminal and the Northwest ticket area to verify flight times and check the weather.

The young woman, meanwhile, began to disrobe, shedding the long, now wrinkled, off-white cotton uniform she had been wearing in Lo Chi Lyn's office. Tang watched her, and when she had stripped to her undergarments, he reached out and touched her breast. The young woman recoiled.

"Well, Mrs. Yan," Ro Ji said, reminding her of her new name, "you've been a widow now for a couple of hours. I figure by now you must be getting pretty horny." He took a quick look at his watch. "I've had a good day. Now's your chance to reward a true hero of the people. If you do, I can put in a good word for you with Colonel Quan."

The young woman turned her back and continued to change. She was small and delicate, and Tang was tempted to press the issue. She had just slipped into a long black mourning dress when Deng Zhen opened the rear door of the van. The rain had stopped, but the wind was raw.

"They are predicting improved weather by daybreak," Deng Zhen announced. "There is no flight delay, but it is quite cold in Minneapolis; snow flurries."

The woman turned to Tang. "You approve?" she asked in Mandarin.

"Listen," he admonished, "we're not taking any chances. Go over your conspectus in English one more time. I don't want any slipups."

"My name is Yan Shi Ho," she said, tears forming. "My husband's name is Yan Yao Ping. He died of Borneo fever. We are returning to my husband's homeland in Xuzhou in Jiangsu province. Here are his papers. . . ."

"Good," Tang said. "Other than that you are not to speak in English. If they start asking you questions, give them some shit in Mandarin. Let them do the work."

Tang leafed through the packet of papers she handed him. It contained a passport that showed that the woman's husband had entered the country only six months earlier, a death certificate signed by Lo Chi Lyn indicating that death was due to a rare and highly contagious virus resulting from a bout with Borneo fever, the necessary signed-off customs papers with seal affixed, and a letter from the State Department instructing airport officials to assist Madam Yan wherever and whenever possible.

Tang was pleased with himself. He turned to Deng Zhen. "Back us up to the loading dock at customs. Let's get this shit over with."

Datum: Monday—0017L, October 6

Whenever he was in Washington, Bogner shared a two-bedroom apartment with Reese Smith of the Associated Press. The arrangement worked out well for both men. Smith was normally wherever news was breaking and Bogner averaged about a week a month in the capital. The two men seldom saw each other.

He tucked the rented Olds Aurora into the cramped parking space on the first level, noted with some satisfaction that Reese's BMW was nowhere in sight, and took the elevator to the third floor. What surprised him was the slash of light coming from under his door.

Bogner took out his key, opened the door, and stepped back. She was the last person he expected to see. The former Joy Bogner was curled up in an easy chair with a sheaf of papers in her lap. On the floor beside the chair was his bottle of Scoresby. The shaved ice had already melted. She had been napping, and there was no denying that old dewy-eyed-fawn look she had when she woke up. After all these years, she still had it.

"Surprised?" she asked.

Bogner nodded.

Tobias Carrington and Joy Ellen Bogner still had a thing for each other. Both of them knew it, both of them denied it.

Even now, when she was playing the role of frowning spouse, scolding him for the late hour, a small, almost secret smile played with the corners of her mouth.

He brushed her cheek with a kiss, picked up her glass, replenished the ice, and topped it off with the Scoresby. Then he sagged into a chair opposite her. "You always were full of surprises," he said. "What's the occasion?"

Joy shrugged. "Is it enough to say I was worried about you when I heard you were involved with what happened at Saint Martin's today?"

In Bogner's eyes she was just as beguiling as she had been in Pensacola back when he was in flight school. She lifted her glass in a toast.

"Let's drink to winter," she said. "It isn't far off."

"Okay," he said, "considering the hour, one of two things brings you here. One, you've heard from Kim at school—and she has a problem. Or, two, some of the brass at the network found out you use to be married to the only guy that survived the Saint Martin's massacre."

Joy frowned. "Wrong on both counts. Kim is doing fine. She made the dean's list. And no one in the Washington bureau at CBS knows about us."

"Then, reason three, you missed me."

"Tobias," she said with a slight nod, "there isn't a day that goes by that I don't miss you. And don't let your male ego run away with you. You were good in bed, but I loved you for other reasons as well."

Joy Bogner, professionally known as Joy Carpenter when she was on assignment for CBS, had, after a brief stint with a couple of PBS stations in Southern California, caught on with the

CBS affiliate in Los Angeles. The rest was history. Now she was the grand dame of prime time, the queen of penetrating interviews, the darling of the celeb circuit, with Nielsen ratings that made her, according to *Time* magazine, the "High Dollar Harriet of Network Schmooze."

She still wore her sable-colored hair shoulder length, still had a voice that was both an invitation and a threat, and, despite the years, was still as exciting and beautiful as T.C. had always remembered her.

There was a protracted silence before she asked how he was.

Bogner nodded. "Other than a few cuts and scrapes, I think I'll make it. I'm a tough old bird."

"I have to ask, you know. You don't stay in touch."

"I didn't know there was any reason too. Seems to me I recall the word 'final' being printed across the divorce decree." Bogner couldn't help himself. Despite the passage of time, a tinge of bitterness still had a way of creeping into his feelings about the woman who had been unwilling to share him with the Navy.

Joy studied him over her glass. "Mike was with you today, wasn't he?" She was referring to Mike Capelli. Capelli had been in their wedding. He was the one who had introduced Bogner to Clancy Packer back in the days when the

ISA chief had been recruiting for the Internal Security Agency. That was just one more dimension of the unevenness of their lives: She knew the people in his. He knew nothing about hers—except what he read and what he occasionally saw on television.

Bogner nodded. He had tried not to think about Capelli, or what he would say to his wife, Barbara, at the funeral.

When Joy thought she saw a tear in his eye, she got up, walked across the room, sat down on the arm of his chair, and put her arm around him.

"That's why I'm here," she said. "I'm here because I know you're too damn macho to cry—and because I know deep down under that 'me tough guy Navy pilot—I can handle it' facade, you're hurting like hell."

Bogner sagged down in the chair and closed his eyes. The tears came. Joy was right. It did hurt like hell.

Datum: Monday—0122L, October 6

At fifty-five years of age and working two jobs to make ends meet, Henry Davidson had put in a long day. The man who was supposed to relieve him at midnight, Mi Po, had called in sick, and the supervisor had asked Davidson to work through until the morning shift. "If you do, I'll get Bricker to come in early," the man promised.

Davidson had agreed, but the penalty for cooperating had been having to update the week's logs, work he wasn't used to, and double-checking two shipments of machine tools that had shown up without the proper paperwork. The phone calls had been lengthy and the courier with the paperwork wouldn't arrive until just before flight time. If the courier didn't understand Washington traffic, it would be late, and Henry Davidson knew that he would have done a lot of work in vain.

Now, however, he was faced with the disagreeable task of checking the aluminum cylinder containing the body of some minor Chinese diplomat. He walked into the waiting room, took his usual seat behind the customs desk, and called out the woman's name: "Madam Yan."

A young Chinese woman stood up and approached him slowly. She was small, slender, and, he judged, more than slightly confused by the bureaucratic proceedings. The dress she wore was black and ill-fitting. She took a seat in front of him. She was accompanied by a young man.

"Madam Yan," Davidson began.

She nodded, but the young man clarified, "Madam Yan Shi Ho."

Davidson shuffled through the papers. Unlike the shipment of machine tools, everything appeared to be in order. All that was left was the questioning.

"My name is Yan Shi Ho," she said. Then she began to cry. "My husband's name is Yan Yao Ping. He died of Borneo fever. We are returning to my husband's homeland in Xuzhou in Jiangsu province. Those are his papers."

"Borneo fever?" Davidson repeated. "When did he contract it?"

Lo Chi Lyn's nurse followed instructions. She smiled and gave a demure shrug.

"May I speak on behalf of Madam Yan, Officer?" Deng Zhen offered.

"Who are you?" Davidson asked.

Deng Zhen presented his card. "We are the transfer agency appointed by the Chinese Embassy. I'm afraid Madam Yan does not speak English very well. And, as you can well imagine, she is very distraught."

"What about this Borneo fever thing?" Davidson pressed.

"We have been told that he contracted the disease working as a minor official in an assignment in Malaysia prior to being transferred to Washington. He died four days ago."

Davidson pushed back his chair and stood

up. He motioned for Deng to follow him. The two men walked through the customs office and out to the shipping dock. It was raining again and the wind had increased. Davidson shivered as he walked around the cylinder. "Borneo fever, huh," he repeated. "Never heard of it."

Deng shrugged. "We picked the body up at the funeral home earlier today."

Davidson stopped, glanced at the papers again, and studied the aluminum container. "Better open it," he said. "If he wasn't going to China, it wouldn't be necessary. Your government over there gets on their high horse when we don't follow procedures. I guess they think we're gonna ship them some bombs or something."

Deng Zhen did not smile. "I'll open it, but I don't advise it. Madam Yan is Chopan. The Chopans' religion doesn't allow for embalming. Besides being contagious, I'm afraid he might be a little ripe."

Davidson stepped back. "No shit? No embalming?"

Deng Zhen nodded. "Just thought I'd warn you. Still want me to open it?"

Davidson shook his head. He laid the papers on top of the cylinder, initialed them, took the seal out of his pocket, and embossed the papers. Then he handed them to Deng Zhen. "Borneo fever, huh?" he asked again. "Never heard of it. Contagious?"

"Highly contagious, I'm told."

"Hope we don't get that shit over here."

The two men walked back to his office, and Davidson instructed Deng to take Madam Yan to the Northwest terminal.

"Tell her everything is okay," he said. When he did, he bowed slightly to the young woman. "And you might tell her that we are sorry we had to put her through all of this. . . . Red tape, you know."

"Red tape," Deng repeated. "I know all about it." He managed a smile. It was one of his infrequent attempts at humor.

Datum: Monday—0537L, October 6

Harry Driver was in the process of making his first important decision of the day: whether or not to shave. He was leaning in the direction of avoiding the ordeal. He had shaved the previous evening before he left Nellis, and the current crop of stubble was barely visible.

He decided against shaving, walked into the sitting room of his suite, and poured himself another cup of coffee. It was his third, and it occurred to him that if he did not have to meet the swabbie at 0800 hours in the hotel coffee shop, the coffee would have been bourbon. Bourbon, in Harry Driver's opinion, was a helluva lot better way to start the day than coffee.

Harry Driver was known to the world as an Air Force man, a colonel, a full bird, a bird that had managed to somehow screw up each and every chance he had to move up to brigadier. There was the infamous escapade in Hickham's officers' club in 1988, the ill-timed flyover at March Air Force Base during his longtime friend General William Shilling's retirement party in 1993, and the all-too-recent "tell-it-like-it-is" incident concerning a young lieutenant's flying capability at March. That young lieutenant had turned out to be the grandson of the Chairman of the Senate Armed Services Committee. Strike three.

Despite the hour, he dropped down on the edge of the bed, picked up the receiver, and punched out a nearly forgotten number.

The foggy voice on the other end was decidedly feminine and openly disgruntled. It was exactly what Driver had anticipated at a quarter to six in the morning.

"Susan?" he grunted.

There was a pause before the expected response. "Harry?" Another pause, this time longer because he knew she was fumbling around for a cigarette. Finally she said, "I just looked at the goddamn clock. Do you know what time it is?"

" 'Course I do," he blustered. "I've had my ass cramped up in a borrowed F-16 for the last couple of hours flying in from New Mexico."

Susan Driver, forty-seven years old and onetime bed and board partner of the man she called H.D., was used to her former husband's odd-hour, middle-of-the-night telephone calls. He called whenever he thought of it—and he thought of it often, something he'd failed to do when they were married.

"You're in Washington, I take it?" she said. The voice was a little clearer.

Driver grunted again. His ex-wife recognized the guttural sound as his version of an affirmative response.

"For how long?" If she wanted information, she knew she would have to work it out of him. She had once likened it to prying the hook out of the mouth of a slippery bass.

"Who knows. I'll tell you at dinner tonight. I'm meeting some guy later this morning. As soon as I get rid of him, I'll give you a call. You still workin' at the same place?"

"Suppose I told you I had a date tonight?"

"You know what I'd say," he shot back.

"You'd say, 'Bullshit'?"

"You got a great memory."

Datum: Monday—0645L, October 6

When Bogner rolled over, he felt Joy's hair brush against his cheek. He paused to savor the sensation before he answered the phone.

"Hello," he mumbled. Few people besides Reese Smith's boss down at AP knew the telephone number. Even fewer knew that Bogner hung his hat there when he was in Washington. Packer was always the exception.

"Didn't want to roust you out too early in the morning," Packer said. He sounded like a man who had been up for hours already. "I knew you went to bed late, and I don't figure you had a chance to get much sleep. How do you feel?"

"Sore," Bogner admitted. He glanced over at the clock and then at Joy's clothes on the floor. The CD player was still playing the sounds of an obscure Chopin piano concerto. She moved her foot and caressed it down the length of his leg. Bogner felt that old tingling sensation race up his spine and spread into his shoulders. There were other sensations, but he tried to ignore them. "What's up?" he finally managed. He was still laboring under the illusion that he could get Packer off the phone and accept Joy's invitation.

Packer was brief. "Eight o'clock in the coffee shop of the Claypool. Driving time from the Corydon shouldn't be any more than twenty minutes."

"Set it back an hour." It came out sounding more like an order than a request. He hadn't intended that.

"Can't. This is Lattermire Spitz's show. While you've been sleeping they've flown in some hot jock from Nellis. You, Miller, Spitz, and I are meeting this guy at 0800 sharp."

Bogner felt Joy slide out of bed, heard her walk across the room into the master bath and close the door behind her. Her movements had been quick, a shade edgy even, colored with anger. It occurred to him that in some ways people never change.

"I'll be there," he said.

Bogner knew what to expect when he hung up the receiver. He got out of bed and walked to the closed door. "That was—" he started to say.

"I know who the hell that was," she snapped over the sound of the shower. "When Clancy Packer barks, Toby Bogner jumps. Same old shit; Navy first, Joy second. I don't like the batting order."

"Dinner tonight?" He knew his voice and the invitation sounded empty—a peace offering that was destined to be rejected before it was acknowledged.

"Like hell. Where you're concerned, Tobias Carrington Bogner, I'm planning on having one helluva headache."

Datum: Monday—0803L, October 6

For Bogner, there was a smell associated with hotel coffee shops. During the morning rush hour, sweet rolls, citrus juices, bacon, perfume, shaving lotion, soap, overstarched linen, and coffee all competed to dazzle the senses. Bogner would have preferred any number of other scents, especially that of Joy after her shower.

He searched the montage of people in the room before he found Packer and Miller tucked away at a table at the far end. Then he realized that Spitz was standing behind him. Standing beside Colchin's assistant was an Air Force colonel, short in stature with a decidedly unmilitary bulge straining his blues. He had a small cigar cupped in his hand.

"Toby," Spitz said, "I want you to meet Colonel Harry Driver."

Driver grunted and forced an uneven smile. "You must be Bogner."

The two men shook hands. Driver took a drag

on his cigar and Bogner took measure of the man he had been briefed about as being instrumental in the early testing of the F-117 at the Tonopah Test Range. Prominent in the array of service ribbons were ones that indicated Driver had seen action in Vietnam and Desert Storm.

Spitz, oblivious to the brief power encounter, led the two men toward Packer's table.

Coffee shop heads turned; Colchin's right-hand man with the hawk nose and lack of hair was easily recognizable. It was said that of all of Colchin's aides, Spitz enjoyed the least anonymity.

As they approached, Packer and Miller stood up and headed for the back of the room. The five men walked through a door, down a long hall to a door marked EXIT, left the building, and crawled into a Winnebago RV with Minnesota license plates.

By the time the big RV had inched its way into Washington's morning rush-hour traffic, Spitz had pulled down a viewing screen and turned on an overhead projector. "All right, gentlemen," he began, "let's get down to business."

# Chapter Five

Datum: Monday—1659L, October 6

"This is Inspector Konstantin Nijinsky," the woman said. She made a pronouncement out of it, as though he were a visiting dignitary instead of a homicide officer.

Nijinsky nodded to the two men and inclined his head in the direction of the door. "You are the ones who found the body?"

Both men nodded. The taller of the two appeared to be on the verge of volunteering more, but thought better of it and remained silent. Nijinsky recognized that the ways of the Party died hard.

He opened the door, looked around the room at the array of books, overturned furniture, papers, and clothing before he glanced at the body. The victim's facial features had been obliterated, beaten into an unrecognizable mask. Even after all of the times he had seen it he still had difficulty with something like this. Nijinsky swallowed hard and closed the door again.

"I have a few questions," he said. "May I sit down?"

The woman gestured toward a table, and cleared away some papers.

Nijinsky took out his notebook, opened it, and fished around in his pocket for the chrome-plated ballpoint pen he had purchased at the market. It had the word *Chrysler* written on the barrel. "What time did you discover the body?" he asked.

The two men glanced at each other again. Nijinsky could tell that they were nervous. Finally, the taller of the two said, "Shortly after three o'clock or so . . ." He appeared to be uncertain about the time. Nijinsky wondered if the man would still be so uncertain if the time of death had already been established.

"May I ask what were you doing here?"

"We—we had business," the tall one faltered.

"What kind of business?"

"Every Monday we go to the market."

"And what do you do at the market?"

Nijinsky waited while the taller of the two lit a cigarette, puffed hurriedly, and avoided looking at him. He had already taken note of the two men's clothing. Both were dressed in a way that betrayed their profession. Their clothing was soiled—stained with the kind of grease and grime he would have expected to find on men who toiled with their hands in one of Moscow's many back-alley, black-market automotive shops.

"We . . . obtain parts," the shorter one finally answered. Then he waited to see if Nijinsky reacted. When he didn't, the man continued. "Mikolai had contacts. We paid him a percentage . . ."

"Mikolai?" Nijinsky questioned.

"Mikolai Korsun."

Nijinsky nodded and began to write. He recorded their names, where they could be contacted, and numerous other facts before he dismissed them. The two men appeared to be relieved. When they were gone, Nijinsky turned to the woman.

"How long have you known this man Korsun?" he asked.

When she seemed not to understand him, he rephrased the question. "How long has he been a renter?"

She was an old woman, heavy through the trunk, wearing a faded print dress, thick stockings, and a sweater. The sweater was worn and frayed. She stood with her arms folded to ward off the chill in the unheated hallway. "Two years," she said emphatically. "He was a good tenant. He paid his rent on time. Not many do that."

As he had with the two men, Nijinsky took her name and telephone number, made a few notes, then excused her. He watched her disappear down the dimly lit stairway, and when she crossed over to the second-floor landing, he went back into the room.

With a cold Moscow rain pelting the windows, he picked up an overturned lamp, set it on a table, and turned it on. Then he began systematically sifting through the debris. He found two books that would have been large enough, but both were intact. They had not been hollowed out. The closet, although obviously made to look as if it had been ransacked, revealed that it was at best a halfhearted effort—perhaps even an afterthought.

Under the bed, he located several notebooks that contained jottings, little more than musings. On the surface, at least, they revealed nothing. Next to them was an inexpensive Kiriosk computer. Using a handkerchief, he opened the housing and noted that the boards had been removed. Even though they had been clumsy, they had been thorough.

Finally Nijinsky turned his attention to the body. Mikolai Korsun had been a man of considerable robustness. Now he merely looked fat. For the most part, he was bald with tufts of gray wiry hair around the ears. His face had been obliterated, another ex–KGB practice. Either old ways died hard . . . or someone had gone to a great deal of trouble to make it look as though they had.

Korsun's throat had been laid open from ear to ear and the body had been draped over the edge of the bed, facedown.

Peasants.

Poachers.

The blood was drained from a deer in the same fashion. Did they think that a homicide officer was a fool? Mikolai Korsun had been dead long before the scene had been staged.

When he was convinced that he had not overlooked anything of importance, Konstantin Nijinsky sat down on the edge of the bed, picked up the telephone, and dialed the number.

"*Da,*" a voice responded.

"Is he there?"

There was a pause before he heard the phone being placed on what he knew was the leather-bound notebook the secretary kept beside the phone. While he waited, he turned to watch the rain trace patterns in the grime-coated window. It was cold enough, he realized, for the rain to soon freeze. He hoped he would be home before that occurred.

Finally there was a voice on the other end. It

was flat, raspy, and impersonal. *"Da,"* the voice said.

Nijinsky weighed his words. He knew the conversation was being taped. "It is not here," he said.

After a moment of hesitation, the voice said, "Then we must assume that our comrade Korsun disposed of it. And we must also assume that he would have disposed of it only after obtaining the maximum return on his investment. Would you not agree?"

Nijinksy agreed.

"We must likewise assume that the Americans know," the voice continued, "that Air Major Borisov and the Su-39 are missing."

Nijinsky was nodding, even though he knew the gesture was going unrecorded.

"Isotov is a fool," the voice proceeded. Then it trailed off into a protracted silence.

Nijinksy waited before he said, "This will be handled as a routine homicide. I will say that the motive was probably robbery." He looked around the room, wondering if the motive was believable. Mikolai Korsun's belongings were sparse. A thief who robbed Mikolai Korsun would receive little in return for his efforts.

"You will say nothing of the obvious KGB tactics?"

"Nothing," Nijinsky confirmed.

"Excellent."

Next Nijinsky called his superior and informed him he would require assistance.

Datum: Monday—0931L, October 6

Tang Ro Ji stepped out of the terminal barbershop and paused just long enough in front of a mirror to straighten his tie. Now he looked every bit the part of a member of the Chinese trade delegation that had been prominent on Washington television for the past seven days. He had even purchased a number of gifts, brazenly carrying them through customs to complete the picture. The transformation was complete. He was now a businessman/tourist.

By taking a later flight than the one carrying both Madam Yan and Schubatis, and arranging an itinerary that routed him through Los Angeles on American Airlines instead of Northwest, he had done everything he could to ensure that none of the customs officials he had encountered earlier that morning would recognize him.

At a newsstand, he purchased a copy of the *Washington Post* and scanned the front page. The Saint Martin's massacre, as it was being called, had been given precedence over the bombing of the oil rig in Tuxpano. The death toll at the oil rig now stood at 287, with nearly as many still missing. At Saint Martin's, the toll stood at twenty-seven. He read the article carefully, but there was no mention made of Schubatis. Either the Americans had not yet discovered the switch, or, as he suspected, the discovery had been made and now they were trying to figure out what to do about it.

Tang Ro Ji folded the paper, put it under his arm, and made his way from the newsstand to a bank of telephones near the concourse where his flight waited. It was his first attempt to make contact with his superiors since the attack on Schubatis's motorcade. He was aware that there was a three-hour time difference between Washington and Los Angeles, but Quan had insisted.

He was also aware, of course, that Quan would not be there. The phone, located in a warehouse in Brentwood, rang three times before the familiar signal indicated he was to proceed. Tang Ro Ji carefully recited the message as he had been instructed. "Accomplished, 0745-0940." The first number confirmed that Madam Yan and Schubatis were safely aboard the Northwest flight to Minneapolis, while the second number confirmed the time of his call. As an extra precaution, Tang had altered his voice. He waited to see if anyone came on the line. When no one did, he hung up. All Tang Ro

Ji had to do now was get something to eat and wait for his flight.

Datum: Monday—0947L, October 6

While two children played outside of the parked Winnebago and a woman busied herself fixing breakfast at a nearby picnic table to give the illusion of tourists taking a respite from their travels, Lattimere Spitz continued his briefing.

"At 0500 hours this morning, Ambassador Wilson confirmed what has been a suspicion for some time now. Aprihinen has been a little testy lately, and now we know why. Some three weeks ago, a Russian pilot by the name of Arege Borisov took off from one of the Russian test facilities in Volgograd. Supposedly, he was flying a top-secret Russian aircraft, Su-39, NATO designation Covert, on the second in a series of long-range test flights. Four hours into the flight it became apparent that Borisov had deviated from his flight plan."

Driver leaned forward, fished out a cigarette, lit it, and slouched back in his chair. There had been rumors of such an aircraft. Now it was confirmed. He looked at Bogner. "And the clouds parted."

Spitz continued. "For some time now, we've been aware of the political infighting between Aprihinen and a hot dog by the name of Colonel General Viktor Isotov. Isotov is a no-holds-barred hard-liner, and as far as he's concerned, Moshe Aprihinen is selling the old Russia down the river."

"So where's our boy Borisov?" Packer asked.

"Last spotted crossing the Tashkent range and headed into Mongolia."

"Let me guess," Bogner interrupted. "The boys in Beijing are now the proud possessors of an Su-39. Correct?"

"Not exactly," Spitz countered, "It's a little more complicated than that. The Kong Ho regime has their own problems. Aprihinen is fighting a rearguard action with Isotov. Kong Ho has someone called Han Ki Po and his so-called Fifth Academy to deal with. CI is guessing Borisov probably delivered the Covert to Han's troops."

"Somewhere in China, huh?" Driver mused. "Shit, that's like lookin' for a virgin at a whores' convention. That goddamn plane could be anywhere."

Spitz held up his hand. "No, Colonel, we don't think so. In fact, after an all-night session with Sabrini of the CIA and Goetchel of the Far Eastern Affairs Bureau, we think we have a pretty good idea where Borisov ended up."

Driver leaned forward with his hands on the table. "So? Where?"

"South of Guangxi and Guangdong province there is a small island called Hainan. Gateway to Hainan is the northern port city of Haikou. West of Haikou is the Songtao reservoir, one of Zhou Enlai's more significant achievements. The old boy built a water catchment that stretches out over five hundred and fifty square miles. Zhou had one thing in mind, but a guy by the name of Han Ki Po had another."

Packer repeated the name: "Han Ki Po." Then he looked at Miller. "Have we got a book on him?"

Robert Miller never ceased to amaze Bogner. The man was a walking encyclopedia when it came to the ISA files. This time, however, Packer's chief administrative assistant was hesitant. He shook his head. "Outside of the fact that we have him listed as a former general in Zhou's military command, we don't have much. I can tell you one thing: He's an old man. Our sources tell us he's actually holed up in some compound in the south of Hainan."

Spitz began to recite the man's dossier. "Han Ki Po is the reputed head of an organization known as the Fifth Academy. He hails from Yazhen, a fishing center on Hainan. When he fell out of favor with Zhou, he went home. We believe Zhou thought that was the end of things, but Han Ki Po has since emerged as a power figure. If the Kong Ho regime has a laundry list of internal concerns, we figure there's a damn good chance Han heads that list."

"So where do we fit in?" Driver pushed.

"Let me give you a list of ifs," Spitz began. "Let's start with the fact that we have two contacts in Haikou. One of them, a woman by the name of Shu Li, is the concierge at the Haikou Tower. She was educated at Columbia, speaks English and several different regional dialects, and is on our payroll. Oscar Jaffe will vouch for her. She isn't mainstream, but she's a good in. The other is a fellow by the name of Father Hua, a Roman Catholic priest. He runs a mission in the low hill country not far from the Songtao reservoir. The bad news is, Hua isn't in our pocket. He won't compromise. If we're wrong, he tells us. On the other hand, if Han Ki Po is leaning the wrong way, he tells us."

"You said 'if,' " Bogner reminded him.

"If Borisov and the Su-39 are in the hands of the Chinese, we think there's a damn good chance Han Ki Po has them. That's the first if. The second if is contingent on the first. If Han does have the Covert, we think it's likely it's at the Fifth Academy installation on Hainan known as Danjia. Why? Because our sometime friend, Father Hua, as recently at two weeks ago confirmed that Han's pilots were scooting in and out of the base at Danjia in some state-of-the-art Russian Fencer upgrades. Not only that, they were armed with AA-6 Acrid missiles. If that's the case, it stands to reason that's where they would attempt to hide the Covert."

Bogner took a deep breath. "Isn't the Fencer supposed to be Mikoyan's antiradar creation?"

"If and when they get one off the ground. That's why we think Han is so interested in the Su-39. Schubatis's design gives him what he's been looking for . . . and it, unfortunately, already exists."

"In that case, the ifs make sense," Driver decided. "So how do we put all this to the test?"

"As we speak, we're establishing contact with both Shu Li and Father Hua," Spitz went on. "Jaffe has had his people working on it since we received Wilson's confirmation."

"When will we know?" Packer asked.

"We've already established contact with the woman. From here on out it's anyone's guess."

"Best-guess scenario?" Bogner pushed.

"We're convinced that whole scene at Saint Martin's yesterday was designed for one purpose only: to abduct Schubatis. Those poor slobs coming out of that church just happened to get in the way."

"What the hell do they need Schubatis for," Driver wondered, "if they've already got the Su-39?"

"Look at it this way, Colonel. If they've got Schubatis and the aircraft, Aprihinen's cupboard is bare. That makes him very, very vulnerable. And that's what Isotov wants."

"Suppose Schubatis doesn't cooperate?"

"Han still has the Su-39 and Aprihinen has egg on his face. It's a good bet that if the Russian people know that plane exists, they sure as hell don't have any idea of its capabilities. If Aprihinen thinks he's got troubles now, wait until his constituents find out he's authorized all that money for the development of the Covert."

"But he didn't," Packer reminded them.

"They don't know that."

Datum: Tuesday—0013L, October 7

The Qingyuan Binguan did not compare with the upscale Haikou Tower, but the rates were much lower and Shu Li supposed that was why Zhun Be stayed there. It was generally believed that despite his posturing, Zhun Be had not been all that successful selling to the procurement and supply officers at Danjia.

As the taxi came to a stop at the Haifu Road address, Shu Li realized that the temperature had dropped several degrees in the last hour. She stepped from the rickety old Simca taxi, handed the driver the fare, and, as was her practice, entered through the service entrance. She took the elevator to the third floor. In their phone conversation, Zhun had confirmed that he was in his usual room.

She knocked, and when he opened the door there was the predictable scent of his Western cologne. Shu Li remembered that Zhun had admitted buying it on the black market from a vendor who could be found on Thursdays walking along Datong Road near the Jinrong Dasha.

Zhun Be was no taller than Shu Li, but he wore Italian shoes with lifts so that he would appear taller than he actually was. It was equally obvious to Shu Li that he had showered, shaved, and donned his finest attire for their meeting. Zhun Be had long entertained the fantasy that someday Shu Li would be his lover.

The room, like most rooms at the Qingyuan Binguan, was a clash of cultures: Western furniture intermingled with traditional Chinese, and a window with the panoramic view of a now-abandoned farming commune. In the daylight, it provided a view of rambling, makeshift housing and rutted, unpaved streets—a view that the Kong Ho government had attempted to conceal with a twelve-foot-high fence. At night the area became a haven for those who populated the seamy side of Haikou, called Ghengdi.

Zhun, smiling, ushered her into the room, offered her a drink and a seat, in that order, and complimented her.

Shu Li was a striking woman. An attractive five feet, six inches in height, she was tall by her native country's standards. She was educated in America, and her dress and demeanor were decidedly Western. For her meeting with Zhun Be, she was wearing a dark linen suit and high heels that offset the small advantage he had gained with his lifts. As usual, her communication skills were impeccable regardless of whether she was speaking in English or any of the local Yazhen dialects.

Zhun glanced at his watch. "I suppose I should assume that because of the hour, this is not a social call," he said. He smiled anyway.

"You have checked the room?" she asked.

"I have checked," he acknowledged. There was a trace of disappointment in his voice.

"There is a rumor that the fishermen on the Songtao reservoir are annoyed by the sound of arriving and departing aircraft at the Danjia base," she said. Then she paused while Zhun's smile erupted into something akin to a full-throated laugh.

"And you are . . . shall I use the word *curious*, about all of these noisy aircraft. Correct?"

"I am curious about one particular aircraft," she admitted.

"You are even less subtle than I am," he teased.

"We are two of a kind," Shu Li assured him.

He leaned back in his chair, reached into his suit-coat pocket for a pack of cigarettes, and offered her one. They were a Canadian brand, filtered. He lit one, exhaled, and took a sip of his drink. There was no need to hurry. In all probability, when she had the information she was seeking, she would be gone. He was not eager for her to leave.

Shu Li took out a small piece of paper and a pencil. She sketched a long cylinder with its nose tilted down. Then she drew two rectangular boxes, one on either side of what was becoming an illustration of an aircraft. The boxes were parallel with the cylinder. After she added the wings, she worked right-angle configurations into the sketch. Finally she made a loop at the rear of the cylinder that was intended to represent the vertical stabilizers.

Shu Li leaned back and studied her effort. Satisfied, she drew a five-pointed star on the stabilizer and pushed the drawing across the table to Zhun.

"Does this look familiar?" she asked.

"I have seen it," he acknowledged.

"It has arrived just recently?"

Zhun nodded. "It is unlike the others. It is painted a curious color: a dull, flat, almost ominous gray. I have an associate. We have discussed it. He has seen it up close. The plane itself generates much conversation among personnel at Danjia."

It was Shu Li's turn to smile. She had what she had come for. "Now I'll have that cigarette," she said, "and maybe even a drink."

Zhun Be was pleased.

Datum: Monday—1359L, October 6

Henry Davidson stumbled across the floor of his third-floor apartment and opened the door. He had slipped into a pair of trousers and put on his robe. The floor of the apartment was cold, and his toes curled in protest.

The two men who confronted him, one more heavyset than the other, were wearing dark raincoats. One wore a hat; the other's hair was wet, betraying the kind of weather that had beset Washington for the past several days.

"Mr. Davidson?" the heavyset one inquired.

Davidson blinked.

"My name is Agent Drucker and this is Agent Seboneller," the man continued. He opened a worn leather wallet and displayed a badge. "Federal Bureau of Investigation. May we come in? We'd like to talk to you."

Davidson nodded, stepped aside, and allowed the two men to enter. "What's this all about?" he muttered.

Drucker opened his briefcase, extracted a manila folder, and opened it. Then he handed the customs agent a series of eight-by-ten photographs. "Can you identify any of these people?" Drucker asked.

Davidson sorted through the stack until he came to the photograph of a young man in what appeared to be a visa photo. The picture had been taken at an awkward angle and he couldn't be certain . . . but there was something about the man.

Then he recognized the image of Deng Zhen—or, as Davidson knew him, the agent appointed by the Chinese Embassy to handle the matter of Madam Yan. He handed the photograph back to the agent. "Him I think I recognize. He came through early this morning. They were shipping the body of some Chinese official back to Hong Kong . . . had some kind of disease or something. All the paperwork checked out."

"What airline?"

"Northwest, through Minneapolis." Davidson glanced at his watch. "Hell, by now that flight is probably long gone."

"Gone where?"

Davidson thought for a minute. "Singapore, through Hong Kong."

Drucker looked at his partner, then around the room. "May we use your phone, Mr. Davidson?"

Davidson nodded. "Sure, it's over there." Then, as an afterthought, he asked, "Am I in some kind of trouble?"

Drucker had already started dialing. He did not answer.

Datum: Monday—1741L, October 6

Lattimere Spitz slumped into the chair across from the ISA trio and motioned for Driver to take a seat. "I have to apologize, gentlemen," he began, "but under the circumstances we think it's necessary."

Miller, who had twice left the motel to make a telephone call and run an errand, had unplugged the small electronic eavesdroping device that had been monitoring the motel switchboard. For Bogner, that was a sign that Spitz was either ready to move on or call a halt to the operation.

"Unfortunately, the folks we are after have been just one jump ahead of us most of the day," Spitz continued. "Still, I think we've got enough to hang our hat on.

"First, we believe we know what happened to Dr. Schubatis. Jaffe's office, in conjunction with the FBI, has put together a pretty convincing scenario. It would appear that our Russian friend left Washington this morning—in a casket, on a Northwest flight bound for Hong Kong with a stopover in Minneapolis. If our friends had continued on that flight, we probably would have been able to call the flight down before it got out of our territorial jurisdiction. But when the flight landed in Minneapolis, a Madam Yan who was accompanying the casket claimed to be ill. She got off the flight, had the casket removed, and it was picked up by a local funeral home. We've since ascertained that there is no such funeral home in either Minneapolis or Saint Paul."

Driver looked at Bogner. "The cagey bastards probably have him on another flight by now."

"Exactly," Spitz continued. "The FAA log shows that a small private cargo carrier left the Minneapolis Airport less than two hours after the casket was removed from customs. The carrier filed a flight plan for Winnipeg. It wouldn't take a rocket scientist to figure out the rest."

Packer put down his pipe. "There was a flight out of Winnipeg for Hong Kong?"

"Canada Air, flight seventy-four," Spitz confirmed. "We've checked with their officials, obtained a copy of the passenger manifest, and as you might guess, the grieving widow is on board . . . and so is our friend Schubatis, still tucked away in his temporary casket."

"How do we know Schubatis is still alive?" Miller asked.

"They sure as hell wouldn't be going to all of this trouble if he wasn't," Spitz said.

"Can't we force it down?" Driver pressed.

"No authority," Spitz countered. "Besides, at this point, if we jerk the wrong chain, we could create the kind of international incident that would leave the President with his ass hanging out."

"So what happens now?" Packer asked.

Spitz cleared his throat. "The President has been in contact with Aprihinen. Aprihinen knows what we know . . . and, as you may have already guessed, he isn't buying it—at least not all of it. Under the circumstances, however, he doesn't have a lot of options. Aprihinen's relations with the Kong Ho regime aren't a helluva lot better than ours. If he sends some of his muscle in there, the situation could worsen."

"I don't like where this is heading," Driver grunted.

"We've told Aprihinen we're going in after Schubatis," Spitz said.

Driver laughed. "What the hell are we supposed to do, march in there and tell Kong Ho to hand him over?"

"Earlier today we were able to confirm that the Su-39 is under wraps at the Danjia installation on the island of Hainan. Our contact can confirm two sightings. Best bet is that Kong Ho doesn't even know about it. So two plus two equals that's where they're taking Schubatis. Han Ki Po wants him. And lately, what Han Ki Po wants, Han Ki Po gets. The State Department says we have a helluva lot more to fear from Han than from Kong Ho."

"You still haven't told Harry and me where we fit in," Bogner reminded him.

"You're going in after Schubatis."

"Why two of us?"

"You get Schubatis, Toby, and, if at all possible, Harry flies the Su-39 out of there."

"Fly it out to where?" Driver laughed.

Spitz's expression didn't change. "Taiwan."

"Suppose Harry can't get it out of there? Then what?"

"Burn it," Spitz said. "We sure as hell don't want it left behind."

Bogner looked around the room. His initial reaction was that despite his admiration for the man, Colchin had lost his mind. His second thought was that it would take some kind of miracle to pull it off. "Harry and I are going to stick out like a couple of sore thumbs. How the hell are we supposed to move around over there? They're going to see a couple of Americans and either Kong Ho or Han Ki Po will have their people trailing us night and day."

Spitz smiled, reached down, picked up his briefcase, and dumped the contents on the table. "Show our friends what you've come up with," he said to Miller.

"Ever hear of the Jade cartel out of Toronto?" Miller asked.

"Arms dealers?" Bogner clarified.

"Exactly," Spitz confirmed. "We've traced them through every hot spot in the Middle East. They've boasted that there isn't anything they can't get their hands on. And they've got a reputation for delivering. Our sources have learned that Han Ki Po has expressed interest in widening his sphere of contacts. You'll be welcomed with open arms."

"What have we got that he wants?" Driver asked.

Spitz laid a thick computer printout on the table. "There's your inventory. It includes everything from a pair of Mirage IIIs to a couple of Bulagian MiG-23 BNs. And if that doesn't whet his interest, tell him you can produce just about anything he wants out of the U.S. bases in South Korea. To make it look realistic, you can offer him a deal on a couple of ancient Su-7 Fitters. Tell them they've been in your inventory quite a while, but that they still provide a stable weapon platform for low-level strikes and that your supplier is eager—no, *motivated* to find them a new home."

"What about armament?" Bogner said.

"Get familiar with your inventory, Toby. Knowing what Han Ki Po has already amassed, more than anything else we think he needs a few planes to launch his missiles."

"That Su-39 is a helluva start," Driver said.

"How about our cover?" Bogner asked.

Miller spread them out on the table. "Passports, credentials, even a letter of introduction. The rest of it is fill: pictures of the family, background profiles, prior sales. From here on out you're a couple of Canadian gun peddlers."

"Priorities?" Bogner asked.

"Schubatis is first priority. The Su-39 is second. If you can't fly it out of there, Harry, make damn sure no one else does."

"Suppose the real Jade contingent shows up while we're courting this guy Han."

"They won't," Spitz assured them. "The RCMP took both brothers into custody this afternoon. And as we speak, the offices in London and Cairo are being boarded up."

"When do we start?"

"The meter's running," Spitz said.

"I didn't like the way you phrased that."

"And I didn't like it when Aprihinen gave us seventy-two hours before he starts moving his own pawns."

# Chapter Six

Datum: Wednesday—1758L, October 8

The *chuzu qiche* ride from Haikou Airport into downtown Haikou had taken no more than twenty minutes after Bogner and Driver finally located a taxi. Even their seventh-floor rooms at the Haikou Tower had been a pleasant surprise. They had most of the amenities: a telephone, closed-circuit television, a well-supplied minibar, mostly European stock, and the real bonus, an air conditioner. Bogner had been in China numerous times before; air-conditioning was a luxury.

Their flight had originated in Montreal and landed in Hong Kong. Now, a full three hours after, with the flight from Hong Kong to Haikou behind them, there was nothing to do but wait for Shu Li Wan, Spitz's contact. The Haikou's concierge had yet to get in touch with them.

While they waited, Driver fixed himself a scotch and soda, lit a cigar, and periodically scanned Spitz's bogus arms inventory. Bogner, meanwhile, already comfortable with the arms dealer identity, was content to stare down from the room's exterior balcony at Haikou's rush-hour traffic. If he hadn't known better, he could have believed the commerce of the southern island city hinged solely on the lowly bicycle. They outnumbered the cars twenty, perhaps thirty, to one.

From where he stood, the colors around Haikou were more yellow than green now that the city had moved into the dry season. And, as their young taxi driver had informed them, the days were now supposedly cooler. That part Bogner found hard to believe. The temperature hovered in the mid-eighties and the air was close and damp.

He loosened his tie, unbuttoned his shirt collar, and stared out at the crowded freighter traffic in the harbor. He counted eleven ships, all but one flying the PRC or North Korean flag. The exception was a Dutch freighter, sitting low in the water. Outbound, it could have been headed for Macao or Hong Kong—or, for that matter, up into the East China Sea.

In the sky over the lowland hills to the west of the city, there was an ominous cloud deck, occasional displays of distant lightning, and the even more remote rumble of infrequent thunder. It was, Bogner decided, a long way away.

As he watched the traffic, he seemed to be the only one paying any attention to it. It was as if the people of Haikou, scurrying through their late-evening routines, were oblivious to the world around them.

Bogner walked back into the room and glanced at his watch. Even though they had been expecting her, the concierge's knock on the door surprised him.

Bogner thought it was curious that the woman was calling to them through the door. "Mister Boggs, Monsieur Cormea?" She was even speaking louder than necessary. "My name is Shu Li Wan. I am the concierge for the Haikou. I have instructions to deliver a message to you."

Bogner opened the door and stepped back. Spitz's contact was not at all what he had expected. She was tall, with soft, straight, ebony hair that hung down to her shoulders. She had a wide sensuous mouth, high, finely sculptured cheekbones, amused hazel eyes, and a demeanor that was decidedly more American than Asian. She wore a white linen business suit, tailored to accentuate a slim waist and her decidedly feminine proportions. The way she smiled, there was little doubt that Shu Li Wan was pleased she had caught the American, Bogner, off balance.

When Bogner closed the door after her, she lowered her voice. "You'll have to excuse the theatrics, gentlemen. I'm afraid your arrival in Haikou has caused quite a stir."

Driver frowned and motioned for the young woman to have a seat. He arched his eyebrows. "A stir?" he repeated. "What kind of stir?"

Shu Li laughed. "That louder-than-necessary greeting was for the benefit of the little man who is tailing you. Poor thing; he looks rather uncomfortable standing down there at the elevator, pretending to read the newspaper."

Driver looked at Bogner. "So much for Spitz's cover."

Shu Li assessed the two men. "Let's see, you would be Colonel Driver," she guessed, "and you would be Captain Bogner." It had been easy to single Bogner out because of his height and athletic build.

"Excellent," Bogner complimented her. "You've done your homework."

"Not at all. Your Mr. Packer was quite thorough. He faxed dossiers—including photographs."

Then, while Driver and Bogner watched, Shu Li Wan opened her briefcase and produced two files. As an afterthought, she handed each of them a newspaper. "The *China Daily,*" she said.

"It's sold at the newsstand in the lobby. It's the only English-language newspaper in China. Westerners make a habit of carrying it with them everywhere they go. You'll be even more conspicuous than you already are if you aren't carrying it."

Bogner ignored the file folder. "You said we had picked up a tail?"

Shu Li nodded. "Welcome to China. My country may be making noises like solid citizens in the world community, but I'm afraid Westerners are still curiosities in Haikou. Colonel Quan likes to know what's going on."

"Then we haven't blown our cover?" Bogner said.

"Quite the contrary. The moment you cleared customs, the word spread. I'd say the odds are good that even the customs officer who worked you through is on Quan's payroll. The mere fact that a couple of representatives of Toronto Jade got off the plane in Haikou is enough to raise more than a few eyebrows. It's a small town, and the comings and goings at Danjia generate most of the street talk around here."

"I'm curious, Miss Shu, just how much do you know?" Bogner asked.

The young woman gave Bogner her most engaging smile. "No more than I have to. . . . That's the way my contacts in America like it. But I can tell you this much: Haikou's been a busy place since the Russians showed up."

"Russians?" Driver repeated.

Shu Li leaned back in the chair and crossed her legs. "It's my guess that they're interested in the same thing you are, Mr. Boggs."

"You mean the Su-39," Driver said. "Out of curiosity, do you think Colonel Quan is having them trailed as well?"

"Most assuredly."

"Okay, we're being tailed. We can live with that. When do we get started?" Bogner asked.

"There's no time like the present. But first I think we'd be smart to throw an element of confusion into the equation," she said. "And we do that by splitting up. A friend of mine has agreed to be Mr. Boggs's escort for the evening. You will like her, Colonel, she's an instructor at the university . . . and she speaks English."

"So what do we talk about?"

"I told Ti Minn that the two of you are here to do business with the Han Ki Po people at Danjia. Consequently, she will not be surprised if you ask questions about the Danjia installation. If you ask your questions in the right fashion, Colonel, you will learn a great deal. Traditional Chinese seldom volunteer information. Ti Minn used to be an instructor at Danjia before she received her appointment to the university."

"Just exactly how do we pull this off?" Driver asked.

"You and I will walk down to the elevator together. We will discuss quite vocally how your colleague is exhausted following your flight from Montreal. And since we are the ones who are leaving, the man who is supposed to be tailing you will do the obvious: He will follow us."

Driver waited.

"In the lobby, I will introduce you to Ti Minn and I will excuse myself to go to my office. It will be a simple matter for me to exit through the hotel offices and meet Captain Bogner in the service area at the rear of the building." She turned to Bogner. "Wait until the Colonel and I have taken the elevator, then proceed down the hallway to the right until you come to the service elevators. It will be marked with a *qi.* The symbol is a lowercase *T* with a tail on it. If anyone stops you, say *'Wo bu shufu.'* That means you don't feel well. Then say *'Nali you yao,'* which, loosely translated, is asking where you can buy medicine. Whatever happens, I'll be waiting for you near the service door. Got it?"

Bogner nodded.

When Shu Li and Driver left the room, Shu Li's conversation was overly animated. Bogner could hear her talking all the way down the hall and until the elevator door closed. Moments later, he heard another elevator door open and close, and when Bogner peered into the hall, the little man that had been standing near the bank of elevators was gone.

Bogner, heeding Shu Li's advice, slipped the copy of the *China Daily* under his arm, opened the door, and headed for the freight elevator.

Datum: Wednesday—1912L, October 8

Shu Li Wan was a rarity in Haikou. She owned her own car. And even though it was a Renault Dauphine of early-fifties vintage, only perhaps one of every two hundred and fifty citizens of the seaside city had a car at their disposal.

They parked in the alley behind a row of identical, nondescript, two-story frame structures that Bogner figured had been built by the Kong Ho regime in an effort to alleviate the city's infamous housing shortage.

Shu Li was about to open the door, but paused when Bogner put his hand on her arm. "Two rights, two lefts, and two more rights—you know someone is following us, correct?"

The woman nodded. "What really surprises me is he didn't pull into the alley. Either he intends to wait until we leave, or he's taking a chance on finding us. It's a labyrinth back in here."

Bogner looked back, stepped out of the Renault, and waited for Shu Li. "Here," she said as she worked her way past him, "you may need this." She reached in her handbag and handed him a steel-gray .45-caliber Beretta.

"Use this often?" he asked with a smile.

"Not unless I have to. Most people back off when they see what I'm packing."

With that she started up the steps to the second floor. Bogner stepped back, pinned himself up against the masonry partition, and waited. From the alley he was completely hidden by shadows.

Shu Li knocked, and when the door opened she went in. Within minutes, a black Subaru sedan began inching its way into the alley beside the Dauphine and stopped. The door opened and the dome light flashed on and then off, just long enough for Bogner to see that there were two men in the car.

One of the men crawled out, circled Shu Li's car, glanced in, and looked up at the light on the second-floor landing. Then he motioned for the driver to pull ahead and wait.

For Bogner it seemed like an eternity until the man sized up the situation, circled the landing, and started up the open stairway to the second floor. This was where patience came in. He waited. Then he leaped. He caught the intruder in the middle of the back with his forearm, heard the air gush out of him, and then heard him cry out when Bogner's weight pinned him against the steps.

Bogner jammed the barrel of Shu Li's Beretta into the hollow area just below the base of the skull, making certain the man heard the metallic click of the automatic being cocked.

"Understand English?" Bogner growled.

The man tried to nod, and in the process scraped his face against the rough-hewn steps. At the same time, Bogner was frisking him for a gun. When he didn't find one, he jerked the man to his feet, spun him around, pinned him against the wall of the building, and lodged the barrel of the Beretta against the man's temple.

"Listen very carefully, because I'm going to say this one time and one time only, cowboy. You're fucking with something bigger than you are. You and your partner would be real smart to find yourself another diversion." He spun the man around, slammed him down against the steps again, reached in his pocket, and stuffed one of the cards Spitz had given him into the man's shirt pocket. "Got the message?"

The man nodded and started to get to his feet. That was when Bogner realized, if only for one split, ultimately painful second, that he had forgotten all about the man's accomplice. He heard the thud even before he felt it. The blow caught him across the side of his head and the whole world went from black to blacker. Bogner felt himself rock backward, start to crumble, and the wind rush out of him. He fell forward, but it seemed to take forever until he went down. When he did, he plummeted three steps down to the alley level, rolled over, and viewed an abbreviated panorama of pure pyrotechnics.

In the distance there were footsteps, the sound of screeching tires—and then silence.

There was something cool and damp on his forehead, and something equally cool and hard on the back of his head.

"I'm sorry," he heard Shu Li say, "ice is at a premium in Haikou. It's the best we can do."

Bogner pushed the woman's hand away and sat up. When he did, he felt a wave of nausea and shooting stars began erupting from places that hadn't previously hurt. "No sorrier than I am," he managed. "I'm a little out of practice for this kind of stuff. I might have expected this in New York—but not Haikou."

"That's us," Shu Li said, "all the accoutrements of a big American city, I'm unhappy to say."

"Welcome to Haikou," Zhun Be said. Under the circumstances, he was being a shade too glib to suit Bogner.

In the light of an unshielded incandescent

bulb hanging from the ceiling in the middle of the room, Bogner got a look at his host for the first time. Zhun Be was short, fragile looking, wearing a white silk shirt and a carefully tailored pin-striped business suit; he smelled like a fugitive from the cologne bar in an upscale men's department store. It occurred to Bogner that he looked too young to drink, and far too young to be involved with anything Shu Li might have up her sleeve.

Shu Li Wan glided through the introductions. "This is Monsieur Marcel Cormea," she said, "the gentleman from Toronto."

Zhun Be smiled and bowed slightly. It was not so much what Shu Li had said as what she had implied. Zhun had obviously heard the street talk, and he had long heard of the organization known as Toronto Jade.

Despite his discomfort, Bogner managed a semicivil grunt and handed Zhun Be one of his bogus business cards.

"And, Monsieur Cormea, this is the gentleman I was telling you about, Zhun Be. Zhun Be is also a supplier to our friends at Danjia."

Zhun Be preened. He was pleased with the way Shu Li had introduced him. It made him sound important.

"I apologize for the welcoming committees," Zhou Be said. "It comes with the low-rent district."

"Did you get a good look at them?" Shu Li asked.

"They were driving a black Subaru sedan."

Zhun Be nodded. "An encounter with our Russian friends," he confirmed. "They have been here before. Like you, Monsieur Cormea, they wish to do business with Han Ki Po."

"What kind of business?"

Zhun Be's response was cautious. Bogner deduced he was aware that he had to be careful how he answered the question. If he intended to sell information to the Canadian, offering too much without negotiating would make him appear less than professional. "I believe it has something to do with an airplane," he said.

Datum: Wednesday—2100L, October 8: Danjia Installation, Hainan

It was Milo Schubatis's second session of the day with Colonel Quan and the fourth time he had met with Quan since he had informed his abductors that he felt strong enough to make the journey from the infirmary to Quan's office.

Now he was sitting across the teak desk from Quan and sensing the evil in the man who it was said would someday replace Chairman Han Ki Po. Quan stood no more than five and a half feet tall and weighed less than 120 pounds. He had hollow temples and pockmarked cheeks, and wore thick glasses to shield his dull-gray eyes. He smoked an endless chain of cigarettes, always with an ebony and ivory cigarette holder, and he had a deceptively deep, raspy voice, frequently punctuated by a racking cough. At each of their previous meetings, Quan had worn the drab, olive-green "people's uniform" Schubatis associated with the late Chairman Mao.

The wall behind Quan was decorated with starkly framed portraits of Mao Zedong and Zhou Enlai. Only the image of Hua Guofeng, the Party Chairman following Mao Zedong's death, seemed inconsistent. Compared to the others, Hua was a lightweight.

Quan offered Schubatis a cigarette and invited him to take his usual seat across from him. "You are feeling better, Comrade?" he inquired.

"Somewhat," Schubatis admitted, "but I will feel even better when I am told why I am here."

During their three previous meetings, Quan had said nothing of the Su-39. Instead, their conversations had revolved around philosophy, the state of China's economy, and the comparative political views of Russia's Moshe Aprihinen and Chairman Kong Ho of the People's Republic. Quan not only saw but recited significant similarities. Schubatis did not share his views.

When the Russian was seated, Quan lit a cigarette, exhaled, and studied the smoke as it drifted about the room. Then he leaned back. "You know why you are here, do you not, Comrade Schubatis?"

"I have not been told, but I think it is quite apparent, Colonel. You have the Su-39—and now you think you need me."

Quan waited. The smile was forced and empty, almost a mocking gesture.

Schubatis tried to give his voice authority. "Even your, how shall I say it, considerable accommodations cannot muffle the distinctive sounds of the engines on an airplane that I, in large part, built with my own hands, Colonel."

"You have indeed fathered a marvelous instrument of war, Comrade. We applaud you."

For the first time, Schubatis felt as though he had the strength to rebuke the officer. "Colonel, I am being held here against my will. Why?"

Quan tented his fingers and looked up, avoiding the Russian's eyes. "Many years ago, when I visited one of the Sukhoi factories, I read something that you had written. As I recall, you said that your designs, your concepts, your innovations were like children . . . that they required ongoing nourishment. Do you recall?"

"I do."

"Then perhaps you will understand when I tell you that our *adopted* children need nourishment as well. You see, Dr. Schubatis, our children are ideologies, and unlike those of Kong Ho and your President Aprihinen, they cannot sustain themselves with mere power. Today, despite our considerable numbers, it will take more than the sheer will of the people. It also requires technology."

"I hear words coming out of both sides of your mouth, Colonel."

Quan stood up and walked around his desk to the far side of the office before turning back to confront the Russian. "Through the centuries, Comrade, my country has chosen to turn its back on the power alliances of NATO and the Warsaw Pact. But the world grows more complicated and alliances shift. Dangers and threats are evident now that were, at one time, of little concern to us. As we learn of such weapons as the American YF-22 and YF-23, and now your Su-39, our once-great distance from opposing ideologies is no longer reassuring to us. The American Stealth, the Russian Covert, and Western Europe's Eurofighter and Rafale place others far ahead of us."

Quan discarded the remains of one cigarette and lit another.

"This, then, is our quandary. We are vulnerable now. To gain parity, we must design, develop, build, and employ state-of-the-art weapons such as our adversaries possess. That takes time . . . and resources—resources we do not now possess. So what is our alternative? Perhaps less honorable than developing the technology, but far more expedient, is the method we have chosen, to use existing technology—and that Comrade Schubatis, is where you come in. Now we have the Su-39, and as insurance, we have the man who conceived of this marvel of military technology." When Quan paused, he again manufactured his ingratiating smile.

"But," Schubatis declared, "you do not now have, nor will you have, the cooperation of the man who designed the Covert. Clearly we have differing ideologies."

For a moment, Quan was silent. Then he said, "I would advise you to reconsider, Comrade."

Schubatis's answer was emphatic. "I am here against my will, Colonel. I have no intention of helping you overthrow your government. Kong Ho is the rightful head of government in the People's Republic."

"That is your final answer?"

"It is."

Quan's pinched face was unable to conceal his anger. He returned to his desk and picked up the telephone. He shouted the word "guards," sat down, and waited. When the doors opened, two guards appeared, followed by a young officer. Quan began reciting orders.

"It would appear that our esteemed colleague, Dr. Schubatis, has decided not to cooperate, Lieutenant Yew. Perhaps a change of scenery will alter his somewhat distorted perspective. Put him in the east cell block and demonstrate for our comrade why it is that cooperation would be a more prudent course of action in his case."

Datum: Wednesday—2241L, October 8

Zhun Be checked his watch and waited until he saw Shu Li's Renault pull out of the alley and into the sparse, late-night Haikou traffic before following. The Jinyo Café, where he had instructed the Russians to wait for his report, was less than two blocks away.

When he arrived, he saw the black Subaru parked across the street from the club's entrance. The Russians, he decided, were either careless or blatantly stupid. The car could easily have been spotted by Shu Li or the Jade representative, Cormea, when they left. He made a mental note to advise them against such arrogant behavior—this was not Moscow or Kiev or even Novgorod, and their GRU status meant nothing on the island of Hainan.

Inside, he ordered a beer and spotted the two men sitting in a booth at the rear of the café. He elbowed his way across the crowded dance floor and smiled. "You did not trust me, Comrades?"

Kusava, the one with the swollen face and cuts, grunted. "There will be another time."

Andrei Provnosky, whom Zhun Be regarded as the elder in both seniority and rank, and who was the one with whom he had done most of his negotiating, motioned for Zhun to sit down. "He is American, right?"

"On the contrary," Zhun said, "Monsieur Cormea was exactly as my colleague Shu Li Wan represented him." Then he laid the card Bogner had given him on the table and read it for them. " 'Marcel Cormea, Representative.' " Then he pointed to the words "Jade, Ltd."

Kusava grunted and spat a mouthful of blood into his napkin.

"And this Cormea, why is he in Haikou?" Provnosky asked.

Zhun Be laughed. "Because he has business here."

Kusava frowned. "What kind of business?"

The fact that the Russian had not heard of Jade did not surprise Zhun. From the outset it had been apparent that both of the men had been ill-prepared for their mission on Hainan—

namely, monitoring the activities of the Han Ki Po forces on Danjia.

"Their business is that of selling weapons," Zhun Be informed them, "and they have presented me with a representative inventory to show to my associates at Danjia."

"For what purpose?" Kusava demanded.

"It seems that my associates at Jade have recently come into possession of a number of aircraft. . . ."

"French aircraft?" Provnosky prodded.

Zhun was still savoring the sound of "my associates" and linking himself with the Canadian arms cartel. "Tomorrow," he said, "I will visit with some of my contacts at Danjia and make discreet inquiries."

"At the same time you will be seeking information for us?" Provnosky asked. "Correct?"

Zhun ignored the Russian a second time, and Provnosky bent forward until his large frame was leaning halfway across the table. His eyes were hard.

"Do not play us for fools, little man. Play your mercenary games. Comrade Kusava and I are interested not in what you attempt to sell Han Ki Po and Colonel Quan. We are interested in what they actually buy."

Zhun leaned back in his chair to avoid the Russian's glare. He lit another cigarette and finished his beer. Then he looked at Provnosky.

"Do you not find it curious that there is suddenly a great deal of outside interest in Danjia?"

Neither Kusava nor Provnosky knew how to answer.

Zhun decided to elaborate. "You are here. Earlier today, Shu Li Wan was making inquiries for the Americans about the Russian aircraft that suddenly arrived at Danjia. And now the Canadians appear on the scene. I find that curious. Perhaps I should expand my business . . . either that or take bids for my services."

Provnosky reached into his pocket and passed an envelope across the table. "An oversight," he apologized.

Zhun Be knew the risks in overplaying his hand. The Russians were already on the hook. At the moment, the Canadians were little more than a possibility. If he could open the door for Cormea, he was certain that Cormea would express his gratitude with a "finder's fee," as he chose to think of it. On the other hand, the Russians were a steady source of income. He did not wish to jeopardize his position. He supplied them with information—and they forwarded that information back to their superiors in Moscow. It was the way the system worked.

Zhun Be cared little for politics, and it made no difference to him who was in charge. It mattered only how much he was paid for what he could learn. His philosophy was simply to make certain he was on the side in power. On Hainan Island, that was Han Ki Po. On the mainland it was Kong Ho. Zhun Be justifiably considered himself a chameleon.

Datum: Wednesday—2345L, October 8

Harry Driver got up from the table, walked to the window, and let out a sigh. "So what do you make of it, T.C.?"

Bogner studied the sketch and looked at Shu Li. "How about it? How accurate is Harry's sketch?"

Shu Li shook her head. "Ti Minn worked there for many years. She knows the installation well. The only things she would not be aware of are the changes Colonel Quan has instituted in the last three or four years."

"No one changes the location of buildings, hangars, or runways," Driver said.

Shu Li agreed. "I have been to Danjia twice, but the general layout is as I remember it."

Bogner's pencil drifted over the layout that Driver had sketched during his dinner with the woman. "Okay, to the west you've got the Gulf of Tonkin. That means that whole channel down the inlet into the supply docks is probably mined. To the north you've got the reservoir, all

1,440 square kilometers of it. And, according to Shu Li, they've got patrol boats on the southern end of the reservoir all the time . . . and the rest of the reservoir some of the time."

"I've seen them," Shu Li confirmed, "small gunboats. They even turn back the fishermen when they get too close to the barrier."

"To the east of the base is the highlands and the railhead. According to Ti Minn, it's heavily patrolled," Driver said. "So . . . if we can't arrange to walk through the main gate, we've got our work cut out for us."

Bogner dropped the pencil and pushed the sketch across the table toward Shu Li Wan. "Who does have access?"

Shu Li shook her head. "Danjia is famous for its tight security. No identification—no admittance. And Quan has a reputation for coming down hard on his security people. How is it we used to say it back at Columbia? 'One screwup and you're out.' That pretty much sums up Quan's philosophy."

"What you're telling us is that if Quan isn't interested in our so-called inventory, the chances of getting on that base are damn slim. Right?"

Shu Li nodded. "If that inventory list you handed Zhun earlier tonight doesn't capture Quan's interest, you're going to have to crawl under the fence somewhere. And as you can see, those security fences are a long way from where you want to be."

Driver walked back to the table and stabbed his pencil at the sketch. "Ti Minn tells me that this five-mile stretch between the fence and the perimeter road is heavily mined all the way around the installation."

Bogner studied the sketch again and circled an area northeast of the installation. "Access here puts us closest to the landing strip and hangars. If Ti Minn is right about the location of the big hangars, it stands to reason this is where they've got the Su-39 stashed."

"But where," Driver interrupted, "are they keeping Schubatis? That damn plane is only part of the equation."

"How do we know Schubatis is even there?" Shu Li asked.

"We don't," Bogner admitted, "but it's the only logical answer."

Shu Li closed her eyes and Driver began pacing again. "Does the name Father Hua mean anything to you?" she asked.

Bogner nodded. "I'm told we haven't been able to establish contact with him for several months. We're not even sure he's alive. When our government was trying to establish whether or not the Su-39 had been flown to Danjia, we tried to contact both of you. We never were able to get through to Hua."

"I can take you to him," Shu Li said.

# Chapter Seven

Datum: Thursday—0531L, October 9

From the cockpit of his Su-27 Flanker, Air Major Arege Borisov could observe the young Fifth Academy pilot as he put his Su-21 Flagon F through a series of maneuvers designed to show Borisov how well he had mastered the now-twenty-year-old aircraft. The young officer, Li Jiwei, was the third of Quan's three candidates for Su-39 training.

Now, into the second hour of the flight, Borisov was not impressed. Like the others, on three separate occasions the young pilot had failed to handle the less-sophisticated Flagon in response times that Borisov felt were little more than baseline performance levels needed to command the Covert.

As Borisov peered over the glass dome containing the Su-27's combined FLIR and laser rangefinder, he followed the young officer's flight path, momentarily losing him as his own head tilted to one side under G force and the aircraft dipped below the blank spot in his vision created by his HUD.

Borisov recorded the young pilot's response time in the PiRev log. In completing the tactic, the young officer had allowed his plane to slip below the computer-mandated equivalent of Mach 0.8, and Borisov was even more convinced the man was not qualified.

"You will bring her around, Lieutenant," Borisov commanded, keeping his voice even, and at the same time wondering if the multilingual voice decoder developed by the Chinese would be reliable under combat circumstances. "And let's try it again."

The lift-inducing vortex streaming back from the LERX and the close-proximity turbulence created by the craft's R-13 engine buffeted Borisov's Flanker, and he was forced to hold on, continually correcting until the young pilot had again assumed the training position forward of Borisov's observation plane.

"Again, Lieutenant," Borisov rasped. "Compute your target's position. For tactical purposes, assume the range is ninety nautical miles. Correct to 037 degrees, activate pulse-Doppler, and identify."

The young officer began reciting coordinates

as Borisov entered the data. After four plot points he knew the coordinates were wrong. "Advise verification," Borisov said evenly.

During the 1,200-kilometer radius check accomplished before dawn, Borisov had identified the bogey, an Iranian tanker positioned in the mouth of the Gulf of Tonkin between Thanh Hoa on the east coast of Vietnam and Dongfang on Hainan Island. Now it was the responsibility of the young officer to identify that particular tanker from the more than thirty ships Borisov had counted earlier.

Slowly, to give the lingual decoder enough time to convert and relay fast his commands in Chinese, Borisov recited the coordinates given to him by the young officer. When he saw the target configuration, he shook his head.

"In theory, your plane is carrying eight AAMs, Lieutenant. Those AA-8 Aphids give you enough firepower to blow that whole flotilla out of the water. If you were in the Su-39, your decision window would be reduced by forty percent and there would have been no prior visual confirmation. No flyovers in the Covert. Now—which one is your target?"

The young pilot hesitated.

Borisov was angered. "Check your T-Ident computer!" he shouted.

It was obvious now that the young pilot was rattled; there was no response.

"Divert," Borisov ordered. He growled a string of commands into his flight voice recorder, reciting and reassessing each instance where the young officer had failed. He had made his decision; he would walk in and hand the flight's digital mission monitor to Quan and let him see for himself.

Only then did Arege Borisov reflect back on the scene at the Komsomolsk plant where the Flagon had been originally assembled. Even then, the planes had been delayed because of persistent flaws in the increasingly complex avionics. The mere fact that Quan had been able to obtain nothing more recent than a handful of outdated trainers and two Su-27s from the Imperial Iranian Air Force was testimony to just how closely other governments were willing to work with the PRC hard-liners like Han Ki Po and Colonel Quan. Until Isotov's decision to ferry the Su-39 to Danjia, Quan's air force could hardly have been considered a threat to Kong Ho's balance of power.

The young officer slipped the Flagon into position aft and below Borisov's craft and waited for orders.

"You will be glad to know," Arege Borisov said, "that we are returning to Danjia. That is all for today."

Even though he knew he hadn't, Borisov could have sworn he heard a sigh of relief.

Datum: Thursday—0713L, October 9

There had been a sign reading 35 KM along the side of the road where Shu Li had turned south off the Danjia highway winding around the Songtao reservoir. From that point on, the surface of the narrow, one-lane road had deteriorated rapidly.

The tiny Renault protested, and on one occasion overheated, but Shu Li pressed on until they came to a small rise overlooking an overgrown cemetery on one side of the road and a narrow path leading down to a small stream on the other.

Bogner commented on the fact that a few of the grave sites were marked with whitewashed crosses.

"Christians," Shu Li said matter-of-factly. "Father Hua is permitted to bury them here—it's the only place on the island. Christians are an embarrassment to the Han Ki Po regime."

Shu Li Wan backed the Renault into a crop of tall bunchgrass, turned the car around, and inched the ancient Dauphine into the underbrush. She opened the hood, left the windows rolled down, loosened the distributor cap, wedged a small piece of paper under it until it was hidden, then bent over and began scooping dust and sand on the car.

Bogner watched her, and she anticipated his question.

"The Russians call them 'hooligans.' You Americans call them 'thieves' and 'street gangs.' In China, we call them 'guo.' It's just another way of saying 'trouble.' " She pointed down the narrow road. "The only thing between us and the Danjia installation is about twenty-five kilometers of worthless land. And just about the only people who use this road beside Father Hua and his charges are the 'guo' that can't find jobs at Danjia. If they see my car sitting along the side of the road with the hood up and dust all over it, they'll figure it's been abandoned because it quit running. I loosened the distributor cap just in case one of them knows how to hot-wire it."

Bogner looked around. "Where the hell do we go from here?"

Shu Li, dressed in what Bogner would have loosely described as a Chinese version of a safari suit, pointed at a narrow footpath leading down a hill. "It's about a half a mile or so—in that direction." Then she added, "I should have warned you, the chanko flies are terrible this time of year."

"Ever been in Greenland in the summertime?" Bogner laughed.

Shu Li shook her head.
"Believe me, they're worse."

Datum: Thursday—0839L, October 9

Colonel Quan led the aging entourage of Party officials down the ramp into the oily air of hangar 11 and waited for the last of the seven to arrive. The young officer pushing Han Ki Po's wheelchair moved the eighty-seven-year-old Party Chairman of the Fifth Academy around to a vantage point in front of the group. Even though he was seeing the Su-39 for the first time, the old man's expression did not change.

Quan nodded to the waiting Borisov and his interpreter.

"Please proceed, Major Borisov."

"Chairman Han," Borisov began, "what you are looking at is the latest in my country's technology. The Su-39 has been constructed primarily of aluminum, with the liberal use of titanium components in certain critical areas. The exterior is coated with radar-absorption material consisting of magnetic iron, ferrite particles, and polymer binders."

Borisov waited for the translator to clarify some of the terminology before moving closer to the plane's engines.

"The aircraft is powered by two twelve-thousand-pound Tumanski R-35 engines. These engines are nonafterburning variants of earlier models. We have partially concealed the inlet ducts with foils coated with the same radar-absorbing material I mentioned earlier."

Han Ki Po gestured with palsied hands, and in a barely audible voice said, *"You shenma tebiede haochi?"*

Barisov's interpreter repeated the old man's question. "Chairman Han asks about your plane's specialty."

"Primarily tactical, although it can carry nuclear weapons of a strategic nature. It can fly faster, farther, and deliver a bigger weapons payload than anything the Americans, British, or French currently have in their arsenal."

For the first time Han Ki Po smiled. He had no teeth and his skin was nearly transparent.

Quan gestured for Borisov to continue.

"The cockpit is equipped with most of what we now consider to be conventional equipment in an aircraft of this type. There is a heads-up display and a FLIR—forward-looking infrared cathode ray tube. Across the control panel there are four five-inch multifunction display CRTs. Both the FLIR and the HUD are, of course, transparent. This allows both transient and fixed-position imagery to be seen without creating a trackable surface."

Borisov again paused for the interpreter and caught Quan's eye. "Enough," the Colonel announced. "Chairman Han is weary from his long journey from the compound at Huangliu. We must give him time to rest."

As the entourage of Party officials began filing out, Quan delayed. He looked at Borisov and then dismissed the interpreter. Borisov knew why.

"Lieutenant Li is not qualified," Borisov said flatly. "I have the flight instruction recorder. It is available. You may listen to it anytime you wish. If a pilot cannot master the Su-21, he has no business being assigned to an aircraft with the complexities and capabilities of the Su-39."

"Then they have all failed," Quan said. There was disappointment in his raspy voice.

"It will take more time," Borisov said. "They must receive further training in aircraft with less sophisticated demands."

"Time is a luxury, Major Borisov, we do not have. You must find a way."

Datum: Thursday—0946L, October 9

Father Hua Xiling was not at all what Bogner had expected. At eighty-two years of age, his once-supple body had been twisted into a caricature, crippled by arthritis and ravaged by time. He spoke English fluently, but his sight was failing and he relied upon a tall and slender, somewhat balding man who seemed so much like the aging priest that he had become an extension of the old man. The man was known as Le Win Fo. Unlike Hua, he offered no welcome even though Shu Li had revealed Bogner's real identity from the outset. There was no mention of the Jade cover.

"I have no sons," Hua explained. "But I have something even better than a son—I have Le Win Fo. He has been with me since the final days of the war. His mother was my sister. The Japanese killed her." Hua spoke plainly, without trying to soften the reality. "He was but a youth then; he brought her home with him. She is buried on the hill."

Bogner estimated Le Win Fo to be in his late fifties, maybe even his early sixties. With his deep-set eyes and high forehead, his face appeared to have been chiseled out of sorrel stone.

Hua lit his pipe and looked at Bogner. He ignored Shu Li. "Why are you here, Captain?"

Bogner began a methodical account of the last five days: the explosion of the Saratoga oil rig, the Saint Martin's masacre, the abduction of Schubatis, even down to the Americans' conviction that it was the Fifth Academy and not a dissident faction of the Red Army that had perpetrated the terrorist attacks. "From what we've been able to learn so far, the trail leads to the Danjia installation and some of Han Ki Po's more ardent supporters . . . specifically, a man by the name of Colonel Quan."

Through it all, Hua was silent. He stared out at the children in the courtyard. There was nothing to indicate whether or not he had even been listening to Bogner. It was Le Win Fo who spoke up and asked the questions in impeccable English. "I find it curious, Captain, that you did not mention the strange aircraft that has flown on several occasions from the Danjia installation. Is there a reason?"

Bogner looked at Shu Li and smiled. "Bingo." Then he looked back at Le Win Fo. "Describe it."

Le thought for a moment. "It is curious in shape, constructed with geometric angles unlike anything I have ever seen before. Perhaps even more curious is the color: dull black like the eyes of a shark."

Bogner decided to explain further. "Our intelligence sources tell us that Air Colonel General Viktor Isotov has formed an alliance with Han Ki Po. Supposedly this alliance was formed because Isotov, a very powerful figure in Russia, is Aprihinen's adversary—and Han Ki Po has likewise voiced his opposition to the leaders in

Beijing. Both men want the Party back in control in their respective countries."

"I am even more curious, Captain," Le Win Fo said, "to know why you think a humble and aging priest and his impoverished nephew can help when we are barely able to feed our children. As you can see, we are dependent upon the mercy of the Danjia leadership. Would you ask us to risk that?"

Hua laid down his pipe and folded his hands in front of him. There was a weariness in his voice that for Bogner defied description.

"Did you see the children playing in the courtyard?" Hua asked. "How many of them were there? Did they number twenty? Or thirty? Or even more? You see, Captain Bogner, I do not see well and I have lost count. I can no longer call each of them by name. Still, this is their home and I am their father. I dare not jeopardize that, even for the American money that has often sustained us."

Le Win Fo stood up and motioned for Bogner to follow him. The two men walked out into the midmorning sun, across the hardpan surface to a small rise that afforded a view of the distant hills. "I sense an urgency on your part, Captain. But you must understand, men the age of my uncle and me are conspirators in the planning phase only. There is little we can actually do to help you accomplish whatever it is you hope to accomplish."

Bogner studied him. "I need to get into Danjia."

"For what purpose?" Le asked.

"To get Schubatis out of there."

"But you have already admitted that you do not know for certain where he is. On Danjia alone there are numerous places he could be."

"That's why we contacted your uncle. We thought he could find out where Schubatis is being detained."

"Locating him will be the easy part, Captain Bogner. Getting Dr. Schubatis out of Danjia will be difficult . . . much more difficult."

Le Win Fo turned, went back down the hill, and again crossed the playground area toward a small cluster of derelict buildings. The largest, a Quonset hut with a partially collapsed corrugated tin roof and sadly in need of repair, appeared to be abandoned. It was surrounded by a thick growth of kimho and shag saplings. It looked to Bogner as though it hadn't been used in years. Le cleared away the broom brush and opened the heavy doors. When he did, Bogner couldn't believe his eyes. Inside was a small helicopter.

"Do you recognize it?" Le asked.

Bogner nodded. "A McDonnell-Douglas Defender—with the Hughes thirty-millimeter chain gun removed. What are you doing with it?"

Hua's nephew laughed. "We call her Ki Ling after Father Hua's maternal grandmother. She is the one who influenced Father to join the priesthood. Some of our friends in Washington arranged for it to be sent in—in pieces, of course—from South Korea after the war."

Bogner looked at the layers of dust, dirt, and bird droppings covering the tiny craft. The landing gear consisted of four crudely fashioned steel struts and two eight-foot-long neoprene and canvas pontoons. It had been painted a muddy black color and stripped of all insignias. "It flies?" he finally asked. He was half afraid Le Win Fo would tell him yes—and half afraid he would tell him no.

Le began reciting Ki Ling's pedigree. "It has a 420-horsepower Allison turboshaft, can cruise at 125 to 130 miles per hour, and has a range of 350 miles or so—enough to carry three or four Danjia refugees to political asylum in the Anxis, a small group of islands out in the Gulf."

Bogner walked around the tiny helicopter, estimating its overall length. "Twenty-five feet?" he guessed.

Le Win Fo nodded. "The main rotor is slightly over twenty-six feet."

"Who flies it?"

Le smiled. "There is an old Chinese saying,

Captain Bogner. 'A man of many talents is long-lived.' I enjoy what I do here; therefore, I try not to be one-dimensional."

"How long would it take you to get her up?"

"A matter of minutes, Captain."

"Surely you're not suggesting this as a way to get on the base? That rotor makes a helluva lot of noise."

"Why not, Captain? It has worked before. It is simply a matter of timing. When Quan's helicopters go out on night patrol over the reservoir, one more helicopter draws very little attention."

"Sounds risky."

"Have you not heard that life is a risk, Captain?" Le asked with a smile.

With that, he closed the large rusted door to the makeshift hangar and led Bogner to a small whitewashed structure no larger than ten by fourteen. Two of the children from the orphanage followed him. Le went in while Bogner waited, and emerged moments later wearing a black cassock, sandals, and carrying a Bible.

"For a long time there was a great deal of friction between the Vatican and the leaders of the PRC, Captain Bogner. But about fifteen years ago that all started to change. The Chinese Catholic Patriotic Association was formed. We do not boast of the numbers of Buddhists or Daoists on Hainan, but despite our meager numbers, we have become a force to be reckoned with."

The children had obviously seen Le Win Fo dressed in the garb of the priest before. They danced around him and referred to him as Father Le.

"What I'm saying, Captain Bogner, is I believe I can find out where your Dr. Schubatis is being detained. Now, what else is it you need?"

"While you're in there, look around. See if you can figure out how to get a strange-looking aircraft out of there," Bogner said, laughing.

Datum: Thursday—1142L, October 9

Colonel Quan, back in his office following the visit by Han Ki Po's cortege, sat across the desk from the now-uniformed Tang Ro Ji. "You have done well," he advised him.

Tang acknowledged his colonel's brief commendation and lifted his cup of tea in salutation. "It was not without its price. I lost two men."

Quan did not inquire as to their identity.

"And how is the Russian?" Tang asked.

Quan sighed. "He is well, but so far he has refused to cooperate."

Tang settled back in his chair. Quan had requested the audience; now he had to wait until the Colonel proceeded. While he waited, he lit a cigarette and studied the portraits of the Communist leaders behind Quan's desk.

Finally, Quan began. He exhibited a certain amount of hesitancy—with long pauses between each sentence. To Tang Ro Ji it was an indication that his leader had not yet worked through all of the details.

"I believe," he said, "we are now ready to proceed with the next phase of my plan, my young comrade. We have the demonstration of Air General Isotov's support, and now we have the plane. Already our engineers are becoming familiar with its construction. I see no need for further delay."

"The training of our pilots is proceeding?" Tang Ro Ji inquired.

"It is," Quan lied, "and now we must turn our attention to Han Ki Po. Less than an hour ago, his plane left Danjia so that he could return to the compound in Huangliu."

"And the Chairman's health?" Tang Ro Ji asked.

"It continues to deteriorate. But it does not deteriorate rapidly enough. I am concerned that he will continue his conciliatory overtures to the Kong Ho regime."

"Then he must be stopped," Tang said, "before it is too late."

"And that is exactly why I have sent for you, my young comrade. It is time."

Tang Ro Ji knew what Quan was referring to: the plans to assassinate the Fifth Academy elder. "When?" he asked.

"Unfortunately, your reputation precedes you. At least two members of the Chairman's group inquired about you today. One, Hong Dung Lei, was even so bold as to openly discuss your involvement in the Tuxpano incident in Mexico."

Tang Ro Ji stood up. "Do you have any instructions?"

Quan shook his head. "The signs are right. It must appear that the Chairman died of natural causes. You must find a way to enter and leave Huangliu without being recognized."

"That will not be easy," Tang Ro Ji noted.

"And that is why I have given you the task, Comrade."

Following his meeting with Quan, Tang Ro Ji returned to his quarters in Quonset H to prepare for his assignment. Quan's insistence that Han Ki Po's death appear natural would make his task more difficult.

Han Ki Po's compound was located on the outskirts of Huangliu, high on a cliff overlooking Chuwan Bay. The Chairman, Tang knew, often insisted on being taken for garden walks before he retired to his quarters for the day. It was well publicized that Han meditated and prayed the final hour before he went to bed. Tang Ro Ji suspected that this would be the ideal time. It was said that the Chairman looked forward to the solitude of that hour—and insisted that the only one to accompany him be the young aide who assisted him with his wheelchair. Under those circumstances, there would be more than enough opportunity to do what had to be done.

The only question now was how he would get into and out of the Chairman's compound without being recognized.

Because he had cut his hair before leaving Washington, his appearance was already altered. All that remained was to select clothing that would enable him to blend in with the other tourists in the port city. He discarded his uniform, dressed, donned glasses, and looked in the mirror. Tang Ro Ji smiled, confident that only his closest friends would recognize him.

When he crossed the courtyard to the Danjia motor pool he looked like one of the workers from the village. No one paid attention to him. It was as if he did not exist. Tang Ro Ji considered that a good omen.

Datum: Thursday—1339L, October 9

It was one of the inconsistencies of the Han Ki Po regime on Hainan that permitted Le Win Fo access to the Danjia installation. Because he wore the garb of a priest, it was assumed that he was a priest. The fact that in earlier years he had come to Danjia accompanied by Father Hua only gave credence to that assumption.

As always, when he was making his weekly visit to the installation, Le Win Fo took the crowded people's bus from the crossroad outside of Zebo to the village of Chupin near the mouth of the Hunpo River less than a mile from the main gate. Most of the guards knew him, and it was customary for him to pass through without producing his credentials.

As was also his custom, he left a basket of vegetables at the gate for the guards and walked up the Yingze Road to visit the patients at the hospital. From there he took the base tram to the detention block, a series of long, narrow cinder-block buildings that housed everything from soldiers being reprimanded to peasants caught stealing inside the compound. That portion of his visit always began with a brief and cordial exchange with Lieutenant Yew of Danjia security.

Yew, unlike many of the more passionate young Red Army officers Le Win Fo had encountered over the years, was given to both philosophical and theological discussion, and appeared to enjoy Le Win Fo's visits.

"Good day, Comrade," Le said as he entered Yew's cluttered, cell-like office. It was exceedingly hot in the small cubicle, and Yew's small oscillating fan was not up to the challenge. It barely rustled the papers on his desk.

Yew stood to greet him, his smile sincere. He motioned for Le Win Fo to have a seat. "The heat does not deter you, Father?"

"I know a hotter place," Le quipped, and both men laughed.

"Perhaps you should have worked harder on this one," Yew said, sliding a file folder across his cluttered desk in Win Fo's direction. "We caught him stealing supplies out of our commissary."

"Perhaps he was hungry," Le Win Fo offered.

Yew laughed. "If he had not been stealing ammunition, I might have considered that a reasonable defense."

Le smiled. "You alluded to the fact that he was one of ours. Do you mean from Zebo?"

Yew nodded. "According to his papers, he comes from your village. And, since he speaks very good English for a peasant, I can only assume he received his tutoring from your school."

"He could have learned English in one of the People's Schools," Le Win Fo said, laughing. "Surely you do not think that our teaching methods are superior to those of the Party, do you?"

The Lieutenant saw the humor in Le's reply. "Someday"—he shook his head—"you will see that our way is the only way. Then, and only then, will you understand true enlightenment."

"But until then, I must continue along my uninformed path, doing what I know to do, and praying for that day of ultimate enlightenment."

Yew continued to smile. "Ahh—at last, a sign of hope. I will again make my offer . . . this small book, the writings of Chairman Mao. It is only fair that you should read it. After all, I have read your Bible."

Le Win Fo stood up. He shook the young officer's hand. "I must be cautious. I enjoy our conversations too much. I must not allow these pleasurable exchanges with you to deter me from my real reason for being here." Then, at the door, he turned back to Yew. "By the way, are there any other incorrigibles I should know about?"

Yew laughed again. "You may wish to tell the Occidental that he would be wise to comply with the wishes of Colonel Quan."

"Occidental?" Win Fo repeated.

"Russian," Yew confirmed.

"Unfortunately, I do not speak Russian," Le Win Fo said.

"Use English. I understand he speaks passable English," Yew said. "Then again, you may not wish to spend any time on this one. I cannot vouch for whether or not he is a sinner. I can only vouch for the fact that he is disagreeable."

"And where will I find him?"

Yew glanced at his papers. "The east cell block, building three, number eight."

Le Win Fo was more than passing familiar with the east cell block. While still a young man, during a weekly visit with Father Hua, he had discovered a distant cousin incarcerated in the compound. Younger than Le, the youth had been severely beaten for, as he was informed, "conduct detrimental to the Party of the people." Le Win Fo was never able to learn what the charge meant, because when he returned the next day to visit the young man, he was told that his cousin had died.

Since that time there had been others, and Le Win Fo now knew why the east cell block was referred to as Quan's Gehenna. There was a crude cemetery in the courtyard just outside the cell block, and if a prisoner was one of the few fortunate enough to have a cell with a window, he looked out over the neglected burial ground.

At the heavy wooden exterior door that opened onto the stone corridor to the cells, he encountered a young PRC soldier standing guard. The youth's face was pockmarked and covered with a thin sheen of sweat. He lounged against a section of the stone wall couched in shadows, seeking refuge from the heat. He asked Le Win Fo for a cigarette and passed him through.

At number eight, Le found what he was looking for. The occupant was a homely little man, both surprisingly short and surprisingly thin. It occurred to Le that the man Yew referred to as the "Occidental" was approximately the same size as the man who had imprisoned him.

The cell door was constructed of crude steel framing with heavy steel wire mesh more than a quarter of an inch thick. The eight-by-eight cell contained a straw cot that lay on the stone floor. In the far corner of the tiny enclosure was a small hole in the floor that served as a toilet. The cell reeked of urine and excrement. Le Win Fo checked the cell on each side of number eight and across the narrow corridor; none was occupied.

He stood at the door several minutes before Schubatis looked up and stared back at him without speaking.

"I am Father Le Win Fo," he said. "Are you the one they call Schubatis?"

The man hesitated, his eyes searching Le Win Fo's face.

"I have visited the confined for many years," Le said in English. "Do you speak English?"

Schubatis nodded. "I am Russian," he admitted. "I am being detained against my will. . . ."

Le Win Fo leaned against the wire mesh. "Of course you are. I have never met anyone in here who did not say the same thing."

"I am not an anarchist," Schubatis protested.

"Then why are you here?" Win Fo asked.

The Russian clutched the wire mesh. He was wearing only a pair of coarse-fabric green shorts and he was barefoot. There was a dirty cast on his leg and a bandage on his right arm. He was pale and his hands were soft—not the hands of a worker. "They—they abducted me," Schubatis blurted.

Le Win Fo could hear the desperation in the man's voice. "Abducted?" he repeated. Even though he knew Schubatis was telling him the truth, he recognized that the Russian would quickly distrust him if he did not show some degree of skepticism. The role he was playing was both time-consuming and risky, but it was a scenario that had to be played out if he was going to be able to gain the Russian's trust. "Abducted from where?"

Schubatis's voice was little more than a whisper. "I am Dr. Milo Schubatis. I was in America to attend a symposium as a guest of the United States government when I was abducted—"

"America?" Le Win Fo said. He made certain Schubatis could detect the air of mistrust in his question.

"What I am telling you is true," Schubatis insisted. "My government will be outraged when they learn of this."

Le Win Fo moved closer to the wire mesh. "They already are," he lied. "That is why I am here."

"They know where I am?"

Le nodded.

"You will speak to Colonel Quan? You will explain the magnitude of his actions?"

Le Win Fo smiled. "I'm afraid it's not going to be that easy. Colonel Quan knows full well the ramifications of his actions. If you're going to get out of here, you're going to have to cooperate."

Schubatis hesitated. "How . . ."

Le Win Fo shook his head. "I ask only that you trust me. We have ways of getting you out of here, but they are risky and it's going to take your cooperation." Le Win Fo's eyes darted up and down the stone corridor again. He could see the guard. The man was still slumped against the wall near the door. As Le Win Fo started to back away, he heard the desperation in the Russian's voice.

"But when . . . ?"

"Soon—very soon. Talk to no one. Just be ready."

Le Win Fo opened his Bible and pretended to read as he walked slowly back toward the guard. As he did, the young soldier straightened to confront him. There was no grace in the volunteer's movements. Instead he held out his hand. "Cigarette," he demanded. Le Win Fo breathed a sigh of relief and then realized it was very likely the only word of English the soldier knew.

Datum: Thursday—1631L, October 9

When Serafim Kusava and Andrei Provnosky entered the small Aponton Wor curio shop on Beinji Di, the old man behind the counter glanced up only briefly before returning to his conversation with a customer.

The two men passed through the beaded curtain at the rear of the store, climbed the flight of stairs, and opened the door. Zhun Be was already there, and he was smiling. He motioned toward a rice-paper envelope on the table.

Kusava picked up the envelope, extracted a

sheaf of papers, and frowned. "It is written in Chinese," he said, throwing the documents back on the table.

"And so it is." Zhun Be laughed. He picked up the papers and shoveled them back into the oversize envelope. "I hope I have made my point, gentlemen. But just in case the subtlety escapes you, you are Russian. I am Chinese. This is not Beijing or Shanghai. Unlike those cities, no more than perhaps a handful of the people on this island speak English, and even fewer speak Russian. Do not count on the refugees from Malaysia or Indonesia either—they will be of no help to you."

"What is your point, Comrade?" Provnosky demanded.

"My point," Zhun Be emphasized, "is that I will tolerate no more threats concerning my cooperation. There, in that envelope, is the information you seek—but it is of no use to you unless you can read and understand Chinese. And, quite frankly, I am the only one who can interpret it for you."

Provnosky opened the envelope a second time and spread the documents on the table. "We pay you for information, Comrade, information that we can use. My threats were made out of frustration. Do not attach too much significance to them. Now that you have the information, we must cooperate."

Zhun Be sat down at the table. "This," he said, pointing to the papers, "will confirm your suspicions."

Kusava, sweating and irritable, face still slightly swollen, was impatient. "And what do these supposedly valuable documents tell us?"

"First," Zhun Be began, "they confirm that the Su-39 aircraft is hangared at Danjia. Since its arrival, it has been flown on three separate occasions. All were test flights conducted by a Russian called Air Major Arege Borisov. I am told he is instructing three of Colonel Quan's finest pilots to master the aircraft."

"Have you seen this aircraft?" Kusava demanded.

Zhun Be shook his head. "I am told it is maintained under the tightest security."

"My comrade has a point," Provnosky interrupted. "We have papers, but we do not have proof. These papers tell us nothing."

"But they do," Zhun insisted. "These logs contain the comments of Major Borisov relating to retrofit of both North Vietnamese and Korean armament systems comparable to those used by the Americans and French."

"Explain," Provnosky said.

"I am told these would be vastly superior to the twenty-five-nautical-mile-range radar-guided AA-9s the aircraft carried on its earlier flights."

Neither of the Russians appeared to be knowledgeable about such matters, and Zhun Be felt relieved. It would alleviate questions. "These documents," he continued, "also confirm that with the Danjia modifications, overall ordinance-carrying capability will be increased to eight thousand kilograms."

"And you are certain it is Borisov that is supervising these modifications?" Provnosky asked.

"I am told he is in touch daily with certain officials in Russia."

"Do you know their names?" Kusava asked.

Zhun Be shook his head and leaned back in his chair.

"What about the Canadians?" Provnosky pressed.

"I have been instructed to inform them that a representative of Colonel Quan will meet with them here in Haikou as soon as arrangements can be made."

Kusava leaned forward. His thick hand closed over Zhun's. "What is Quan's interest?"

"It is only preliminary," Zhun replied. "He reviewed the Canadians' inventory. It is quite extensive."

"We must know of any agreements," Provnosky stressed. "My government does not trust Han Ki Po."

"It is Colonel Quan they should fear," Zhun Be reminded them. "He is a dangerous man."

Datum: Thursday—0545L, October 9

Robert Miller had just confirmed the code for the last transmission to Ambassador Wilson in Moscow when he picked up the phone and dialed Packer.

The ISA bureau chief picked up after the second ring. Despite the hour, he sounded alert. "That you, Robert?"

"Roger, Pack. Berry Lucas of the State Department is here. He approved the content and the code. Wilson has read it and confirmed it."

"Let's hear it."

" 'Code R-O-D-A-L. TR-time 05/05/77: COVERT confirmed—Danjia. White Shark—High Flying—on site. Second confirmation—code 55s—TR-time 06/09/77: RM-BL—CAP.' "

"Anything else?"

"Afraid so, Pack. Driver says the place is crawling with Russians."

"Aprihinen said he would give us seventy-two hours. What the hell is going on?"

"Apparently he doesn't think we can get the job done," Miller said.

"Give me a couple of hours," Packer said with a sigh. Then he added, "Sounds like Bogner and Driver have their hands full."

# Chapter Eight

Datum: Thursday—2020L, October 9

Shu Li had selected the Qingyuan Binguan, one of Haikou's lesser hotels, as the site for their meeting because she knew the hotel's manager, and he could assure them of privacy.

She drove Bogner back to the Haikou, and while he changed clothes, again persuaded her friend, Ti Minn, to create a diversion for the man Quan had assigned to trail the two representatives of Jade. To no one's surprise, the ruse worked again. While the little man again pretended to read a newspaper in the alcove by the elevator, Ti Minn, using the hotel telephone and speaking loudly enough for him to hear, agreed to meet Driver in the hotel's bar. Quan's man bought the deception, and the three, Driver, Bogner, and Shu Li, left the Haikou by the service elevator.

On Haifu Road, in her Renault, Shu Li instructed the two men how to make contact with Le Win Fo.

"Le comes to Haikou twice a month to buy supplies for the orphans at Zebo. He always stays at the Qingyuan Binguan. The manager of the hotel is an old friend and very much opposed to the direction of the Han Ki Po government. He will see that you have complete privacy. In all probability, Quan has someone keeping an eye on Le Win Fo, so don't be surprised if you don't make contact right away. He won't make contact until he's certain the coast is clear."

"What about you?" Bogner asked.

"Have you been watching out the rearview mirror?" Shu Li said. "There's a black Subaru following us. Our Russian friends don't trust anyone. That plus, after you roughed up one of them last night, he may have a personal grudge. I'll try to divert them. If they don't see you get out, they'll follow me."

"How do we get back to the hotel?" Driver said.

"Take a taxi. My friend, Yua Lin, will call one for you. It's too dangerous for me to come back. They may have already figured out that you're getting more attention from the Haikou's concierge than normal."

Shu Li pulled into the darkened street market

across from the Qingyuan, walked up to one of the newsstands, and purchased a pack of cigarettes. While she did, Bogner and Driver got out of the car and stood in the shadows of one of the vendor's booths. Then they watched while the Subaru stopped two hundred feet away and waited. Shu Li got back in the car and drove away. The Subaru followed.

"You can bet your sweet ass they'll be back as soon as they figure out there's no one in the car with her," Driver said.

The two men crossed the street, entered the lobby of the Qingyuan, and went into the bar. Following instructions, they sat at the bar, ordered drinks, and waited. Thirty minutes later, a man dressed in a three-piece suit walked up to the bar, ordered a beer, and slid a *shi yuan* note to the bartender. It was the signal.

Bogner asked the man what time it was. *"Jidian zhong?"*

*"San shiyi,"* the man replied, and walked away.

"Third floor, room eleven," Bogner whispered.

"Where the hell did you learn Chinese?" Driver asked.

"Shu Li coached me," Bogner smiled, "all the way back from Zebo."

They waited ten minutes, then Bogner went first with Driver following, making certain they hadn't picked up another of Quan's goons in the process.

Bogner made the introductions brief, and Le Win Fo spread a series of charts and documents on the bed.

"We have a great deal to accomplish, and from what Captain Bogner has told me, Colonel Driver, very little time to do it. So first of all, Colonel, let me tell you what little I do know about the Russian aircraft that has recently arrived at Danjia."

Driver sat on the edge of the bed and looked at the drawings.

"First of all, let me explain the installation. There are three hangars in all, two small and one large. The large hangar contains four military aircraft. Two of the aircraft are Sukhoi Su-27 Flankers, and the third is a MiG-23U trainer. Quite recently, a fourth aircraft was flown in. It is an unusual aircraft in appearance, and since its arrival, the base commander, Colonel Quan, has doubled security. . . ."

Driver looked at Bogner. "That's gotta be our baby."

"Did you get a look at it?" Bogner asked.

Le shook his head. "Only when it flies over Zebo."

"Any other aircraft?" Driver pushed.

"Several, but they are not housed in the main hangar," Le said. "Many of them are quite old, and I am told some of them are not serviceable. They are parked on the tarmac between the infirmary and the commissary."

"Where's the hangar in relation to the airstrip?" Driver said.

Le Win Fo pointed to the map. "The hangars are located here, on the northern side of the installation. The main runway is here—to the right. The flight path is north out over the Sangtao reservoir. The reservoir covers five hundred-plus square miles, and Quan patrols the southern part of the reservoir with four gunboats. Helicopters cover the rest. They are small, but they are armed with machine guns. At Zebo we have heard reports from local fishermen who have tried fishing these waters that both the boats and the patrol helicopters will not hesitate to open fire—and seemingly without provocation."

"Have you noticed any activity with that Russian plane?" Driver asked.

Le Win Fo frowned. "I must exercise caution that I do not ask too many questions. Questions arouse suspicion. But I am told that the Russian pilot who flew the aircraft to Danjia is conducting a series of training sessions for Quan's pilots. The flights are conducted in the very early hours of the morning."

Driver continued to study the map. "What's the protocol on those flights?"

"I am told that the first flight of the day uses the two Flanker aircraft. The Russian instructor puts the students through a series of maneuvers to test their proficiency. Then the Russian pilot gives them a shakedown in the new plane."

"That confirms Spitz's suspicion that the Su-39 Borisov hijacked has an elevated two-seat cockpit to accommodate either an observer or a copilot," Driver said.

"We'll know for sure when we get our hands on Schubatis," Bogner confirmed.

"Then getting Dr. Schubatis out of the cell block is your first priority," Le speculated.

Bogner nodded. "First Schubatis, then the -39."

"What *about* Schubatis?" Driver asked. "What kind of shape is he in? Are we going to have to carry him out?"

"He is very weak," Le Win Fo confirmed, "but he was able to move around the cell when I spoke to him today, even though his leg is still in a cast."

"How and when do we get him?" Bogner asked.

Le Win Fo straightened and looked at his watch. "It is a quarter past nine. In exactly fifteen minutes, Father Hua will call the manager of the Qingyuan and inform him that I am required back at Zebo. That will explain why I do not stay for the evening as is my custom. You will wait fifteen minutes so as not to arouse suspicion, then follow me. I have arranged for a car. It is a dark blue Simca, parked across the street in the marketplace." He looked at Driver. "Captain Bogner knows the way. I have also arranged to have the car brought back to the city—that way there will be no way to trace it to your use."

While Driver phoned Shu Li, Bogner crossed Haifu Road to the people's market and headed for a cluster of cars parked near the playground. A group of young people were listening to a Chinese rock band on a small portable cassette player and discussing politics. From their mixed bag of mostly Western attire and stacks of books, Bogner guessed they were from the nearby university.

He located the Simca, opened the door, and saw the movement in the shadows from the streetlights all at the same time. There was no time to react. Kusava swung and the first blow caught him on the side of the head. Bogner slumped forward and the Russian's knee caught him flush in the face. There was an instantaneous taste of blood in his mouth as he reeled backward against the Simca. Even while he was going down, he could see Kusava's short, squat figure cock his arm for the encore. Bogner, spitting blood, hit the ground, rolled over, and managed to pivot most of his body under the Simca before he scissored his legs. He caught the Russian by surprise, cut his legs out from under him, and sent him sprawling.

By the time Bogner got to his feet, the Russian was already up but off balance, staggering, gasping for air. In the half-yellow light of the streetlamps, Bogner could see the small, snub-nosed revolver. Kusava was gripping it with both hands, and dropping to his knee to steady his aim. He squeezed off two rounds, both tearing into the door of the Simca, before Bogner lunged and buried his shoulder in the Russian's soft midsection. The impact sent both men rolling toward the fountain.

Kusava was surprisingly quick. He managed to get off one more shot before Bogner rolled away, scrambled to his feet, and threw his best cross-body check on the Russian. Kusava grunted, staggered momentarily, and fell backward into the fountain. Bogner went after him, but this time the Russian was quicker. He heard the metallic click of the pin on an empty clip, and saw the Russian swing wildly with the barrel of the revolver. The intent was noted, but it was too late to get out of the way. Unlike the first one, this was no glancing blow; Kusava nailed him right on the side of the head.

Bogner doubled up in pain. The lights flickered, the world started spinning, and the darkness got darker. Bogner staggered, dropped to his knees, and felt the ground move. There was no air to breathe, and he felt himself pitching forward, out of control, into the rust-colored water of the fountain.

All of a sudden, the pain-filled world of Tobias Carrington Bogner made no sense to him. There was a discordant symphony of surreal sounds, a disturbing display of pyrotechnics, and a whole lot of confusion. He could see the young people running and the Russian bending over him. He could feel the blunt barrel of the revolver pressed against his forehead as Kusava pulled the trigger again and again. Each time there was a hollow click. The Russian's face slowly twisted into a mask of rage as he realized the clip was empty.

The only sound to get through to Bogner was a dull thud, a thick, muffled sound—like a hammer hitting meat. The Russian's eyes rolled back in his head and his body swayed momentarily before he crumpled forward on top of Bogner, pushing him down beneath the surface of the water. It was all deadweight, and Bogner, still dazed, struggled to get his head above water. Finally he broke through to the surface, sputtered, and saw Driver standing in the water beside him. For several seconds there was an uneven, almost childlike thrashing in the water, and Bogner finally realized that the struggling sounds were those of a man taking his last breaths. Driver was pressing his foot down on the dazed Russian's neck.

Finally, Kusava's struggle ended. All that was left were the sounds of Driver's labored breathing, the water cascading down from the top of the fountain, and the discordant sounds of a Chinese rock band.

Bogner sat up and tried to clear his head.

"Two times is one time too many," Driver said. "Leave the bastard there. Let the local gendarmes try to figure it out."

Datum: Thursday—2017L, October 9

The gardens of Su Dongpo, named after the great Song Dynasty poet, had charmed Han Ki Po since the earliest days of his childhood. And it was ordained, Han believed, that following his days at the four academies in the north, he would return to his beloved homeland to do his writing, explicate his philosophy, and establish his long-cherished dream of a Fifth Academy.

Long at odds with the views of many of his country's leaders since the People's Revolution, Han Ki Po had in recent years become an outspoken critic of the economic policies of Chairman Mao, and now the more moderate views of the aging Kong Ho.

At eighty-two, he was still beguiled by the intoxicating scent of gardenias and chiwan blossoms in his rose garden. Sitting by the flickering gaslight next to the small statue of Ding Wei, his beloved mid-eleventh-century poet, Han Ki Po idly thumbed through the tattered copy of Sun Tzu's *The Art of War* and allowed his thoughts to float on the fragrance-filled breezes.

The compound where Han had chosen to spend his declining years in Huangliu was situated high on a ridge overlooking a quiet inlet on Chuwan Bay. There, surrounded by a twelve-foot-high security fence, the Chairman of the Fifth Academy was protected by a thirty-five-man garrison under the command of Han Ki Po's eldest son, Han Xihui. The elder Han was under constant scrutiny because of his advanced years and failing health, and it was only in the late hours of the evening that he was permitted the pleasurable solitude of his garden.

Weary from his round of meetings earlier in the day and his return flight from Danjia, Han had permitted his trusted confidant Dung Lei Hong to retire early. He could maneuver his wheelchair himself for a while. Alone for the first time in days, he reflected on his thoughts.

* * *

Tang Ro Ji had arranged to arrive in the village of Huangliu in a small private plane. He landed at a private landing strip near Wunia, a fishing village north of Huangliu. From there a Wunia fisherman, under cover of darkness, took him to the Plei inlet at the base of the forty-foot cliffs reaching down from Han Ki Po's Fifth Academy compound.

Tang Ro Ji constantly checked the time; timing was critical. Quan had informed him that the Chairman usually retired at 2200 hours. It was now 2037. If the ever-present Dung Lei Hong was with Han, his task would be more difficult . . . and he would need the extra time. If he was in luck, and Han was being checked on hourly by one of the garrison guards, the task would be considerably easier.

Tang wasted little time thinking about the third possibility: the fact that the aging Chairman might be too weary after his long day to visit his beloved gardens before retiring.

The cliffs overlooking the inlet were steep, and Tang Ro Ji double-checked his equipment before he began his climb. Carefully trained by Quan's own guard garrison for just such a mission, he used the outcroppings and tangled vegetation to secure his holds and methodically work his way to the top. From the photographs Quan had shown him, he knew that there was a small ridge, just big enough to survey the gardens from, shielded by a dense growth of evergreens and shale bushes. From there, Tang Ro Ji knew he would be able to see the Su Dongpo fountain and the rosebushes near the place where the Chairman prayed. Since the fountain was lighted only by gas lanterns, Han would probably be close by.

He shimmied over the rim onto the ledge, and paused when he heard voices. Then he inched his way into the shale bushes and peered into the garden. He was in luck. Dung Lei Hong was nowhere in sight and he could see only one guard, a young soldier in full uniform. The guard stood a respectful distance from Han, and as far as Tang Ro Ji could see, the man was unarmed.

"Do you wish to retire, Comrade Chairman?" the soldier inquired. He was standing with his back to Tang.

Han Ki Po dismissed him with a feeble wave of the hand.

"Do you want me to return for you in an hour, Comrade Chairman?" the young man persisted.

Han gestured the guard away a second time, ignored the salute, and continued to look out at the water.

Tang Ro Ji held his breath and waited until he saw the guard disappear up the path leading to the house. There was the metallic sound of a gate opening and closing . . . and finally, stillness. Only the gentle sounds of the surf and the plaintive sound of a distant buoy were audible. Tang glanced out at the moon-bathed waters of the inlet and realized that the time had come. He pulled himself up over the edge and began walking toward Han Ki Po.

Despite his youth, Tang was already a master at reading the eyes of his victims. In the eyes of Han Ki Po there was at first annoyance, and then terror. Quan was right; his reputation did precede him.

"Good evening, Comrade Chairman," Tang whispered. There was an ingratiating, almost condescending tone in his voice. Tang had been warned about the small electronic alarm on Han's chair, so when the old man's hand fumbled for the device, Tang stepped forward and disarmed it.

At eighty-two, Han Ki Po, incapacitated by a series of strokes, could not scream out and his struggle was brief. Tang stepped behind the wheelchair and began pushing it toward the rim of the overlook. Poised at the edge of the forty-foot drop, he reached down and partially disconnected the brake cable. He picked up Han's frail right hand and forced the brittle fingers around the brake handle. When he was satisfied with his staging, he pushed the chair over the edge.

There was the brief clattering sound of a

wheelchair ricocheting against the rocks as it plummeted forty feet into the boulders at water's edge. Then there was the even briefer sound of something crashing and being torn apart. Then there was silence, broken only by the sounds of the surf.

It was done. Colonel Quan would applaud him.

Datum: Thursday—2222L, October 9

Colonel Quan stared back at the defiant Russian and ordered the guard to take away his tray.

"My patience grows thin, Comrade Schubatis. Your continuing antagonism will no longer be tolerated. Perhaps we need to take stronger measures."

Schubatis did not reply. Nor did he look at Quan. Instead he continued to stare at the floor of his cell. Visibly annoyed, Quan paced back and forth in front of the cell, pausing just long enough to insert a cigarette in his ebony cigarette holder, light it, and exhale. A thin wafer of blue-gray, pungent smoke curled into the Russian's cell.

Still Schubatis did not respond.

"Very well, you will be denied all further privileges until you cooperate." Quan wheeled and looked at Lieutenant Yew. "Our reticent colleague will remain in his cell. He is to receive no further rations."

Yew acknowledged the order. "As you wish, Colonel Quan," he said. Then he hesitated. "The Colonel should know, however, that he continues to refuse to eat even when rations are provided. As you can see, he is already quite weak."

"That is his choice," Quan growled. "Let us see how recalcitrant he is if he has no choice in the matter. It is difficult to protest when one has no visible means of protest."

Quan was irritated. Schubatis's continued defiance was delaying the implementation of his plan. He turned abruptly and stalked out of the cell block. Outside, in the cool late-night breeze, he glanced at the shimmering moonlight on the reservoir and continued to his office. Inside the headquarters building, he was informed that he had a phone call.

Dung Lei Hong's voice on the other end of the line was barely audible. The senior Party committee member was obviously shaken. "Colonel Quan?"

"Yes, Comrade," Quan replied. He began to smile in anticipation. There would be only one reason for Dung's call at this hour of the night. Still, he knew he had to be careful. Dung was old and crafty, and Quan knew that if his response was not entirely appropriate, the elder would detect it.

"Chairman Han Ki Po is dead," Dung said. His voice was heavy with grief.

Quan's smile broadened; Tang had completed his mission. Finally he said, "When? How?" He was expecting Dung Lei Hong to describe how the Chairman had succumbed to another in a long series of strokes . . . or perhaps a heart attack. These were the ways in which Tang Ro Ji was both clever and skilled.

"He was murdered," Dung said flatly.

"Murdered?" Quan repeated. He had to be careful his voice did not betray him. "Are you certain?" He had no more than uttered the words when he realized he had deviated from his carefully rehearsed responses.

Dung's voice was suddenly stronger. "Earlier this evening, General Han Xihui, Chairman Han's son and commander of the garrison, went to see his father. He was just arriving at the gate to the gardens when he saw a man flee. The man escaped by rappelling down the wall into the rocks of the inlet. General Han managed to fire several shots at the man. He believes that at least one of the rounds found its mark. . . ."

Quan hesitated. He had to wait until he was certain of his composure. "What about the Chairman?" Dung would expect such a question.

"We found the Chairman's body in the rocks at the foot of the cliff. It is quite obvious that the assassin pushed him over the edge in his wheelchair."

Quan's mouth twitched. Tang Ro Ji had botched the job. His mind began to race. What if Tang was caught? What if Tang revealed their plot? He had to chance the question that was foremost in his mind. "What makes General Han think he hit the assassin?"

"General Han found bloodstains at the base of the cliff. If the assassin was not hit, he was injured in the fall."

Quan's mind was racing. "Is there any hope of capturing the assassin?"

"He escaped in a small fishing boat. General Han is rounding up the fishermen in the area for interrogation. He is confident we will have the identity of the assailant within a matter of hours."

Quan was silent. In all of the many scenarios he had played out in his mind, the discovery of his carefully designed plot to take over the leadership of the Fifth Academy and openly oppose the Kong Ho regime was not one of them. Finally he asked Dung Lei Hong, "How can I be of assistance, Comrade?"

For some reason, Dung Lei Hong's voice seemed to grow stronger. "Until there is a meeting of the Party committee and new leadership can be elected, I will assume authority. You will report to me."

Again Quan was silent. He stifled the inclination to rebel.

"At this time we do not know what we are facing," Dung Lei Hong clarified. "We must determine if this is the act of a single dissident, or if we are confronted with an insurrection. We will not have the answers to this question until we capture the assassin. In the meantime, you are ordered to take all necessary precautions. Double security. Allow no one without proper identification onto the Danjia compound, and arrange to have interrogation teams investigate coastal villages in your immediate area. If the assassin does escape, he can be expected to seek refuge any place on the island."

"As you wish, Comrade Dung," Quan said. "You will keep me advised?"

"Most assuredly, Comrade Quan, I will contact you as soon as we have any new developments."

"How do you want me to handle the news of the Chairman's death?"

Dung Lei Hong hesitated. "For the time being," he said, "no one must know. It will not be safe to reveal it until we are certain we are no longer vulnerable to outside forces."

Datum: Thursday—2357L, October 9

Tang Ro Ji's left arm was broken. The second of the three shots had splintered his arm just below the elbow, and he had difficulty swimming the three hundred yards to the spot where he had instructed the fisherman to wait. By the time he swam back to the boat, he knew the old man would have figured out that something was wrong even if he hadn't heard the sound of gunshots.

"Pull me aboard, old man," Tang sputtered. "I am hurt."

"I heard—heard gunshots." The man's voice quavered.

"They thought I was a poacher. There are deer in the compound."

Straining, the old man pulled Tang aboard and down into the bow of the boat. When he saw the nature of Tang's injury, he recoiled. A small bone protruded through the skin and he was bleeding profusely.

As the moon disappeared behind the clouds, Tang reached into the oilskin bag containing his dry clothes and pulled out a snub-nosed .22 Barkai. "Keep close to the shore," he ordered, "and don't use that motor. Just keep rowing until I tell you to stop. Understand?"

"You—you need a—a doctor," the man stammered.

"I need to get out of here. Now—old man—start rowing."

Tang had lost a great deal of blood. From time to time he nearly lost consciousness, but each time he managed to shake himself back. In the distance he could hear the police boats out of Huangliu. So far they were focusing their search south of the inlet where a fleet of fishermen were working through the night. Even though he had not anticipated trouble, the decision to use one of the smaller dorylike fishing boats had been a wise one; it enabled him to stay close to shore and utilize the shallows where the bigger boats refused to venture.

Now, despite his pain, he managed a small smile at the thought of the harbor police searching each of the fishing boats, looking for the man who had killed Han Ki Po.

Some two hundred yards offshore from the small village of Mianyang, Tang instructed the old man to move in closer to the beach. Moments later, in water no more than four feet deep, Tang struggled overboard. As he did, he grabbed the oilskin bag and wrapped a rag around the Barkai. The two shots he fired were point-blank—both to the head. The old man's body recoiled and toppled back against the gunwale.

Then Tang, with the small automatic tucked under his wounded left arm, pulled the fisherman's body overboard. With what little strength he had left, he managed to tip the shallow-keeled craft until the water began rushing in over the side. Within a matter of minutes, the boat that had carried him to safety slipped beneath the surface.

Tang Ro Ji knew that eventually it would be found, as would the body of the old fisherman—but by that time Tang Ro Ji would be a long, long way from Mianyang.

# Chapter Nine

Datum: Friday—0259L, October 10

There was a single incandescent light in the tiny room, and the windows, although small and usually left open on warm October nights, were shuttered and further darkened by layers of black tar paper.

After two hours of planning, it was obvious Le Win Fo was willing to leave nothing to chance. By Bogner's standards, he was exercising near-military precaution every step of the way.

"Quan's men," he explained, "frequently patrol the roads outside the perimeter of Danjia at night looking for poachers and thieves. They are not oblivious to the fact that their compound is an inviting target."

"As well as they've got the damn thing guarded," Driver said, "it's a wonder anything gets in or out of there."

Le Win Fo laughed. "When you possess a patrolled security fence and a mined area inside of the perimeter road, there is a tendency to be somewhat complacent, Colonel."

Bogner shook his head. "The way I see it, we've got two problems just getting to Schubatis. One, we've got to get past the security barrier, and two, we've got to find a way for Harry to clear that area between the cell block and the hangar."

"You are right—your friend must cover at least five hundred yards of very open space," Le confirmed. "But there is a way."

Both Driver and Bogner studied the layout of the buildings. "All right," Driver said, "let's go over it one more time."

"Originally," Le began, "I believed the best way to enter the compound was to swim ashore from one of the fishing boats, but that would not seem so now." He stepped past the two Americans and opened a door at the far end of the room. He pushed a small panel aside and revealed a door to what at first appeared to be a small storage area. The room was full of radio gear.

"At times," Le Win Fo continued, "we have learned a great deal by simply monitoring activity in the compound."

Driver stepped past Le Win Fo into a room where one of Hua's charges, a mere youth with a headset, sat monitoring a receiver.

"Then you do know what the hell is going on."

"Precisely," Le Win Fo admitted, "and earlier this evening, something very strange happened. Our friend Colonel Quan gave orders to activate several squads of his security detail. I learned of this when I returned from our earlier meeting in Haikou."

Bogner frowned. "What's going on?"

"Only that they are looking for a man named Tang Ro Ji. Quan has dispatched patrols to villages down the coast south of the Danjia installation."

"Tang Ro Ji," Driver muttered, looking at Le Win Fo. "The name mean anything to you?"

"I have to think it's something big if it's Tang Ro Ji," Bogner said. "He's the mouthpiece for the Fifth Academy. Tang is the one who called in after the explosion at Tuxpano in Mexico and after the bomb went off at the Royal Opera House."

"The name is familiar," Le said. "Here on the island we know little about the man—except that he is reputed to be one of Quan's agents."

Bogner looked at Le. "You said we were changing our plans. If Quan has put his people on alert, how can—"

Le held up his hand. "There has been a great deal of activity in the last few hours. There were, at last count, six J1H Komisko helicopters on Danjia. Quan obtained them from the North Vietnamese. He uses them primarily for patrols and reconnaissance. In the last two hours, all of them have been dispatched. They have been coming and going since then."

"I get it. Nobody even bothers to look up when a chopper goes over," Driver observed. He was smiling.

"So we slip in the back door," Bogner said with a grin, "and no one pays any attention. Is that it?"

"It is a long shot." Le sighed. "But as my people have long believed, in chaos there is order."

"Let's hear it," Driver said.

Le unfolded the map of the Danjia installation. "We have been monitoring the flights of the patrol. One group of the Komiskos appears to be concentrating their search in the hill country south of the installation. The other group is working the coastline. We must assume they are looking for this man Tang Ro Ji. We must also assume that they have not yet located him. Each group has returned to base once. They were refueled immediately and rejoined the search. We have been able to monitor some of the transmissions between patrol units. As recently as one hour ago, Quan dispatched additional ground patrols to the search area south of Danjia."

"What you're saying is there aren't as many

troops on Danjia now that Quan has them all out beating the bushes for this Tang," Driver said.

"If the Komiskos repeat the earlier refueling pattern, they should return sometime in the next hour," Le speculated. Then he glanced at his watch. "That gives us just enough time to prepare. I have already asked my young colleagues to move the Defender into the clearing. When the Komiskos are refueled and return to the search, we will go in. I can put you down on the roof of the cell block."

Le Win Fo paused.

"You will have a short amount of time to get Dr. Schubatis to a rendezvous point."

"Where do we take him?" Bogner asked.

"It will be too risky to chance more than one landing. I am afraid that once I put you down at Danjia, there will be no turning back. The entire plan is predicated on the word *if*. *If* Bogner is able to get Schubatis out of the cell block. *If* Driver can get to the airplane. *If* you can escape with the airplane . . ."

"Let's go over it one more time," Driver said.

"The hangar is located here," Le said, pointing to the map. Bogner watched while Driver circled the location of the largest hangar and traced his way to the runways.

"Wish me luck," Driver said.

"I have sufficient gear for both of you," Le

said. "Danjia equipment and supplies are readily available for the right price. The barter is often a trip for the seller to the Anxi atolls."

Driver measured the distance from the cell block to the hangar housing the Su-39 and frowned. "How the hell do I get from there to there? I may need a diversion of some kind."

Le looked at the two men. "It is too risky to attempt more than one touchdown."

"And if I don't make it back to that hangar before Driver flies that thing out of there?"

Le shook his head. "Then you're on your own, Captain."

Bogner leaned back in his chair and Driver hunched forward. "Okay," he said, "let's talk about that Su-39."

"Your task, Colonel Driver, is somewhat more daunting," Le said. "However, there is one thing in your favor. The Russian pilot, Borisov, I am told, is being quartered in that hangar in accommodations just above the ready room, which is here at the south end of the hangar. My source tells me that the schedule calls for the Russian to meet his Chinese pilot there to go over the training plan for the flight before proceeding to that part of the hangar housing the Su-39. At this point there appear to be two possible scenarios. Either you find a way to intercept and replace the trainee—or you replace

Borisov. That part, as you Americans like to say, is up to you."

"What do you think the odds are of you being able to fly that crate out of there?" Bogner asked.

"I think I've got better odds with a scenario where I get a chance to look at the controls of that thing before I have to start hitting switches. There may be a few bells and whistles on that crate I'm not familiar with."

Le waited a moment, then stood up. "Any further questions?" he asked.

"Yeah," Driver said. His voice was brittle. "You keep referring to 'your source.' How do we know we can trust him?"

Le smiled. "All fathers trust their sons, Captain."

"But I thought you were a priest."

"Let me paraphrase another old Chinese saying, Colonel Driver: 'Appearances can be and often are deceiving.' You see, I am not really a priest. As your friend Bogner already knows, the cassock is merely a convenient disguise. Under the circumstances, it serves me well."

Bogner looked at his watch. "We better get going."

Le walked across the room and opened a cabinet to reveal an odd assortment of weapons. "The selection is hardly extensive," Le apologized, "but they are all quite serviceable. Unfortunately, we must take what we can get."

Driver let out a whistle. "An M-16 with a grenade launcher, two M-4 SMGs, and an old Bullpup." He looked at Bogner, then at Le. "Take the nine-millimeter Spectre. If we need more than fifty rounds, we're both chin deep in a rice paddy."

Le handed them the clips, closed the cabinet, folded the charts, and turned off the light. "When we see the Komiskos return to patrol, we must be ready."

Datum: Friday—0817L, October 10

Gurin Posmanovich was being cautious. He checked in both directions and waited until the train had cleared the metro station before picking up the telephone and dialing the number. After three rings there was an answer.

"*Da,*" the voice said. It was dry and unfriendly.

"This is Gurin."

"One moment," the voice said, switching to English.

A second voice was silky smooth and feminine. "How nice of you to call, Gurin."

Gurin Posmanovich was suddenly uncomfortable with his arrangement, and he was tempted to hang up—but the thought of Savina was too much. "They have located Schubatis," he blurted.

"*Who* has located him?"

"The Americans. Ambassador Wilson received a communiqué early this morning. Schubatis is being detained at the Danjia compound. The Americans are planning to abduct him."

"When?"

"I don't know."

"How do you know this?" the voice pressed.

"I decoded the message myself before I gave it to Ambassador Wilson."

There was a pause before the voice thanked him. "You have done well, Gurin. We are pleased. I feel certain Savina will adequately express our gratitude."

Gurin Posmanovich was disappointed when he heard the metallic click on the other end of the line. He wanted to ask where and when the woman would call him. Finally, he hung up the receiver, stepped from the phone booth, and, as usual, felt pangs of regret over his actions. But he also knew that by the time he reached the street level and stepped out into the bustle of traffic on Zhdanov Street, the feeling of remorse would pass.

He buttoned his collar against the cold rain and headed back to the library. He knew it would be wise to hurry. The Ambassador would not expect him to be gone long. Besides, he wanted to be there when Savina called.

Datum: Friday—0037L, October 10

Tang Ro Ji stood in the middle of the tiny one-room hut, struggling to overcome the pain. Time had become his enemy. He had lost a great deal of blood and could feel himself growing weaker. "Over there," he ordered. He gestured with the Barkai automatic to put more authority in his command.

Thus far, the only one who had summoned up enough courage to talk to him was the old man. The woman and the three children, despite their anxiety, had remained stolid throughout. When they were finally clustered together, Tang ordered the oldest of the children, a boy Tang would have guessed to be no more than twelve or thirteen, to tie up the others. Then he turned to the boy's father.

"Now, old man, you're going to take me to Hai.kou."

"But I have only a horse and a cart," the man said. There was no defiance in his voice.

At last the woman spoke. "There is a bus," she hesitated, "that picks up the workers from the commune in Mianyang and takes them to Haikou for shopping."

"Mianyang is but five kilometers," the old man said. "And for your arm, there is a doctor in Mianyang."

Tang thought for a moment. "I will need something to wear," he said, "clothing that will not draw attention. Find me some."

The woman instructed the boy to gather up some of his father's clothing.

Tang struggled out of his wet clothes and into dry ones. When he removed his shirt he saw the shattered bone protruding just below the elbow. He wrapped a rag around it to stem the flow of blood.

"Now, old woman, just in case you are entertaining thoughts about telling someone what happened here tonight, think twice. As a precaution I am taking your son with me—a kind of insurance policy." Then he looked at the old man. "All you and the boy have to do is get me safely to Mianyang and that bus. If you do, you may live to tell about it. The boy is a different story; he stays with me right up to the time that I get on that plane in Haikou."

Tang prodded the old man across the room as the boy began to sob and ran back to embrace his mother.

Tang Ro Ji grabbed the boy, spun him around, and shoved him toward the door. Then he turned to the woman again. "Remember what I said, old woman."

Datum: Friday—0346L, October 10

Bogner crouched in the tall splay grass and waited for the thumping sound of the third of the three Komisko Russian-built helicopters to fade into the night. He checked his watch; it had taken the flight less than twenty minutes to refuel. While he waited, he methodically checked the contents of his aux belt. Le Win Fo had supplied each of them with a combat knife, two four-ounce cartridges of A7a plastic explosive, two spare fifty-round 9mm ammo clips for the SMGs, a pair of wire cutters, a flashlight, and a twelve-foot coil of .22-gauge stainless-steel wire. For a would-be priest, Hua's nephew exhibited all the savvy of a well-indoctrinated terrorist.

Bogner was dealing with factors other than the Komiskos. In the last thirty minutes, the sky had darkened and the breeze freshened as a deck of low-hanging clouds moved in from the Gulf. It had all the signs of an impending storm. Bogner began to feel occasional drops of rain, and in the distance he saw repeated flashes of lightning.

He heard Driver and Le moving through the grass toward him.

"We are in luck," Le said. "The weather will afford us even more distraction and cover. Those who remain on the installation will be driven inside. They will be less vigilant."

Driver scanned the low-hanging cloud deck and finally stood up. "Can't hear 'em. It sounds like they've cleared. Let's go for it. Let's get that Defender cranked up."

"One moment," Le cautioned. "There is still the small matter of disabling the observation post at the 2.5-kilometer marker. Colonel Quan located it there to observe activities at Zebo."

"Why in the hell didn't we take it out while we were waiting for the Komiskos to refuel?" Driver demanded.

"If they had not reported the arrival and departure of the search flight, Quan would have been alerted," Le said.

"How far is it?" Bogner asked.

"Less than five hundred meters. See that light just over the hill? It will be necessary to cut through the fence. But we are in luck. The rain will force them inside the shelter. They will be less alert."

It took less than fifteen minutes to get to their objective. The obs shack, located atop a twenty-foot security tower, was visible from the top of the hill. Bogner worked his way to the base, along the fence, used his wire cutters to cut a hole, and crawled through. Then he motioned for Driver and Le to stay back. "I think one of us has a better chance than if all three of us try to go in. Let me take it from here," he whispered.

Le Win Fo waited, Driver serving as a backup, and the rain had already started by the time Bogner circled the base of the wooden tower and started to climb the ladder. Le had guessed right. Quan's soldiers had forfeited security measures for sanctuary from the rain. The doors of the obs shack had been left open, and the two uniformed observers occupied themselves listening to music blaring from a small transistor radio.

Bogner inched his way onto the narrow observation platform outside of the shed and crawled along the deck until he was on the far side, away from the floodlights aimed at Zebo. In a narrow area where there were no windows he stood up. Both men had their backs to him. He removed the coiled choke wire from the spring clip on his aux belt and wedged one round from his spare ammo clip. Then he dropped the brass-jacketed shell onto the deck. It rolled off and clattered down into the gravel pad below the tower.

For Bogner it was all textbook and instinct after that. Everything happened fast.

The two observers looked up, there was a brief exchange of uneasy chatter, and the taller of the two picked up his rifle and stepped out on the obs deck to check out the noise. He had barely cleared the door when Bogner moved out of the shadows and slammed the butt of his SMG down into the back of the man's neck just below the skull. He heard the guard let out a semimuffled grunt, saw him go weak in the legs and topple over the guardrail. There was an ominous thudding sound when the man's body hit the ground.

Then he wheeled to confront the second man. When the young soldier saw Bogner he froze momentarily—then went for his revolver. The second one was even less of a challenge than the first. Bogner reached for his knife and threw, all in one motion.

For one split second between Bogner's throw and the eight-inch blade gouging its way into the young man's chest, their eyes locked. In that moment Bogner saw anger, hate, and finally terror. Then the guard lurched forward and fell to the floor. It was all over. There hadn't even been time to register a protest over dying. Right then and there Bogner asked himself whether or not Schubatis was worth the lives of two young men.

He rolled the soldier over, checked his pulse, found none, retrieved his knife, and smashed the radio gear. Then he scurried down the ladder, checked the man on the ground, crawled back through the fence, and raced for the place where Le Win Fo and Driver waited. As he did, there was a loud peal of thunder and a bolt of lightning razored its way through the Hainan sky.

Datum: Friday—0424L, October 10

An agitated Quan Cho snuffed out one cigarette and lit another. He glanced at the brace of telephones on his desk, stood up, and moved to the nearest window to watch the rain. Through it all, Lieutenant Yew had remained standing.

"How many men have you dispatched?" Quan demanded, still appraising the storm.

"All that are available, Colonel," Yew assured him.

Quan wheeled and glowered at the young officer. "And just exactly what do you mean by 'all that are available,' Lieutenant?"

Yew shifted his stance. When Quan was angry, he was often irrational. Yew measured his answer. "All personnel that are not on duty in the cell block or manning the security posts," he clarified. "I have also alerted the men who have just come off duty. They have been dispatched under Lieutenant Jing as part of the search party for Tang Ro Ji."

Quan's hollowed face formed a deep frown. Yew knew that look. The Colonel turned back to the window and watched the rain form a tiny river cascading down the stone walkway to the garrison ground in front of the headquarters building. From where he stood, the downpour all but obliterated the lights of the main hangar where the Su-39 was housed.

Further vexing Quan was the fact that there had already been two follow-up calls from the Huangliu compound where Han Ki Po's body had been found. The most recent call had been from General Han Xihui, the chairman's son.

Han did not try to hide his anger. Quan could tell from the sound of his voice that he had already begun to suspect a conspiracy. Furthermore, Quan realized that if Han located Tang before his patrols did, the General was skilled in ways that could make even a man like Tang Ro Ji talk.

Yew weighed his words before he spoke. "With the Colonel's permission, I will return to my post at the cell block to await orders."

Without looking back at the young officer, Quan nodded. "Send Major Zi Yu in."

"Major Zi Yu is with the patrols covering the coastal villages," Yew informed him.

Quan was still fuming when Yew left the

room. In the narrow corridor outside the Colonel's office, he put on the olive-green rain poncho, buttoned it tight against his throat, pulled up the hood, and stepped out into the rain. As he trudged across the garrison ground between Quan's office and the cell block, he heard the sound of a helicopter rotor. The Komiskos were coming and going with such frequency since the alert that he did not even bother to look up. He did not bother even though it occurred to him that flying one of the aging helicopters in weather such as they were experiencing would indeed be a sobering experience.

Almost as an afterthought, he stopped at a bank of vending machines between two barracks and rummaged through his pockets until he found enough money to buy a pack of cigarettes. It had already been a long night for Yew, and the prospects were for an even longer one before he was off duty.

In the intensity of the storm, the young security officer failed to notice Le Win Fo's small Defender helicopter settling onto the roof of Danjia's east cell block.

Datum: Friday—0439L, October 10

Bogner held his breath as a strong gust of wind yawed the tiny chopper into a sideways drift just a few feet above the roof of the cell block. He heard Driver suck in his breath and felt the Air Force veteran stiffen.

Le Win Fo fought the controls, leveled the craft, and began motioning. "Thirty minutes, that's all you've got," he shouted, "before the Komiskos will be coming back for more fuel."

Bogner, with the SMG slung over his back, threw his shoulder against the access door and jumped. He lit hard, fell forward, felt the tar and gravel roof abrade away a thin layer of skin on his hands. Then he rolled over, squinted his eyes against the rain, and scrambled to clear the force of the downdraft of the Defender's rotor. In the darkness he heard Driver land a few feet away from him.

Driver got to his feet, darted for the edge of the roof, anchored one end of his rappelling rope to an antenna base, threw the rest over the side, and shimmied over the edge. There was another loud peal of thunder and a flash of lightning. It hit close and the building shuddered. Bogner saw Driver hit the ground, grab the rope, and steady it. Then, just as Bogner wormed his way over the edge of the roof and started down, he heard the sound of another rotor, this one louder and more powerful than the Allison power plant on the Defender.

Suddenly a wide, sweeping beam from a searchlight on a twin-rotored Komisko penetrated the blackness. The shaft of light arced back and forth 180 degrees until it picked up Driver.

Driver dropped to his knees and opened fire. There were two quick spurts from the SMG and the hovering Komisko erupted in a ball of flame. Bogner dropped to the ground and for one split second the chopper appeared to defy gravity while it protested its fate. Then there was a second explosion, triggered by the ammo aboard the Komisko, and it plummeted to the ground, exploded again, and lay burning in the middle of the Danjia garrison grounds.

There were screams and the sounds men make when they are dying—and for Bogner there was once again that awful nightmare sensation of helplessness. There was the feeling of being consumed, of being torn apart and betrayed by his fears. He crouched in the shadows of the two-story cell block with the rain pelting down on him, knowing he was a pawn and hating it.

The Komisko had become a twisted mass of torched metal. Finally there was the inevitable mind-numbing moment when both men thought they saw the struggling figure of a man trying frantically to claw his way out of the flames.

But even before that searing image could etch itself on Bogner's cartwheeling brain, the figure was swallowed up by the flames and Bogner looked away. He felt his eyes burn and his throat constrict. It was happening all over again: that dizzying, bottomless black hole in time. The momentary image had triggered a flashback—to the burning, death-drenched, napalm-soaked rice fields, and the stench of cooking flesh. There was the nerve-screeching, ear-piercing cries of women and children. There were chain explosions played against a backdrop of sporadic gunfire. It was just one more burning Vietnamese village and again that aching realization that there was nothing he could do about it. He felt his throat go dry and his heart hammer. There was that same devastating sense of revulsion and the even more inevitable catapult back into a world of sweaty nightmares. His head was spinning, his senses reeling; then he felt Driver's hand on his shoulder, trying to extricate him from his dance with fevered demons and drag him back into the awfulness of Danjia. He wanted no part of it. But he knew he had no choice.

"Keep your head down," Driver whispered. "While they're occupied, let's get the hell out of here."

In the surrealism of the moment, black oily smoke, thick and wind-whipped, clawed its way up into the darkness. Bogner could hear sirens.

"What the hell's wrong with you? It's now or

never," Driver insisted. "They still haven't figured out what the hell's happening. If they had, one of their officers would have had the men fan out and start looking for us. They probably think that Komisko got hit by lightning."

Bogner pulled himself together, burrowed up against the wall of the cell block into the deeper shadows, pulled the SMG around, checked the clip, and tested the release. Everything had to be reoriented, reshaped, reconfigured. He bit down hard and pulled his poncho up close around his throat.

"Nothing's changed," Driver said. "We've still got to get Schubatis out of here and we've still got to get to that damned plane. We're on our own now."

Bogner pulled himself together. The nightmare was gone. The flashback, the excursion into his own private hell, had played itself out, and he was beginning to sift through the chaos of his thoughts, looking for answers.

"Still think you can fly that thing out of here without Borisov?"

Driver nodded. "Why? What's changed?"

Bogner's eyes darted to the burning Komisko and back again. "Because by the time we stuff Schubatis in there with you and me, there won't be any room for Borisov."

Driver looked at him. "No guarantees, swabbie. You know the risks."

Bogner had come all the way back. It was forced, but he even managed to sound as if he believed it. "All right—let's hit the bricks."

Datum: Friday—0447L, October 10

While Quan barked out orders to the handful of men milling around the burning Komisko, Bogner and Driver quickly devised a new rendezvous time and location—the ready room in the hangar where the Su-39 was housed. They synchronized their watches. They had given themselves one hour—exactly sixty minutes. If contact wasn't possible, each was on his own.

Driver, with seven to eight hundred yards to negotiate, had to work his way toward the hangar through a series of outbuildings and check out the Su-39. Bogner was to meet him there, with Schubatis in tow.

"Here goes nothing," Driver said. He stood up and sprinted across the access road. With the rain still pelting down on them, he was out of sight within seconds.

Bogner stood up slowly, keeping his back pinned to the concrete wall of the cell block, and began inching his way toward the south entrance away from the garrison ground. During the briefing, Le had indicated it would be the easiest way to gain access to the cell block.

He had managed no more than twenty yards when a personnel carrier rounded the north end of the building on the access road heading for the garrison ground. He crouched and waited until the vehicle roared past. The driver was too busy trying to navigate his way through the rain to notice him.

Minutes later he was within sight of the guard shack near the door. He moved cautiously, stayed close to the building, and inched his way to a place where he could see the guard. The man had stepped out from under the overhang to watch the frenzy around the burning Komisko. Bogner crouched to within three feet behind the unsuspecting soldier, reached back, and brought the butt end of the SMG down against the back of the man's neck. The guard's head was whiplashed to one side with a snapping sound, and he crumpled. Quick and clean; no sound and no protest. Bogner bent over and peered down at the soldier. With the guard's neck broken, Bogner knew the terrified eyes looking up at him could do nothing about his situation. The spasmodic twitching of hands and legs was the only indication that a thin thread between spine and brain was still clinging desperately to life.

Bogner fumbled through the guard's pockets until he located the cell-block keys; then he dragged the body behind the guard shack and slipped into the darkened entrance. Just inside the guard station was a small holding area containing a chair, a scarred table, and a stack of dog-eared magazines. At the far end was a heavy door with steel bars. Bogner peered in and saw a long corridor no more than four feet in width. The flagstone floor was flanked on each side by a series of timbered cell doors. A string of low-watt, incandescent lamps hung from the ceiling in twenty-foot intervals. Several of the bulbs were either burned out or missing.

Hurrying, Bogner found the key that opened the access door and slipped in. If the first part was risky, this was even more so. From this point on, he was vulnerable. Too vulnerable. If there was a guard at the other end of the cell block, or if one should happen to come in behind him, there was no place to hide.

Le Win Fo had said Schubatis was in the south wing of cell block 3, but as far as Bogner could tell, none of the cells was marked. He would have to check each one.

As he worked his way down the corridor, he reached up and unscrewed the lightbulbs. He needed every advantage he could get.

He was in luck; the doors to the first six cells were open. The floors were covered with a scattered layer of dirty straw and there was the pungent odor of urine and human waste.

The seventh cell was occupied. There was a small barred opening in the door, and Bogner stabbed the thin beam of his E-light into the recesses. He trailed the light over it twice before he saw the gaunt, hollow-faced shell of an old man staring back at him from a corner with eyes that betrayed his hopelessness. The man was dirty and naked and shivered in the chilled dampness. Bogner knew that even if he unlocked the cell, the old man did not have the strength to escape. He was too weak, and too far gone to cope with the world that lay beyond the barred doors.

The search slowed when he found six of the next seven cells occupied—one by an old woman, and two with men that Bogner was convinced had already gone to meet their creator. There was the undeniable smell of death.

He had reached the midpoint in the corridor when he noticed the crude chalk markings indicating cell numbers. On the right side, the third door carried the marking 3-8. He shoved the beam of his E-light through the bars and saw the distressed, unkempt figure of the man whose presence had triggered the Saint Martin's massacre.

"Schubatis?" he whispered.

For a moment there was no response. Bogner repeated the Russian's name and the man slowly lifted his head, squinting into the pinpoint of light.

"I'm here to help you."

The man tried to get up, stumbled, and fell back to his knees.

"Can you walk?"

Blinking, unsteady, and uncertain, the humorless Russian Bogner had met the previous Sunday had aged a lifetime since then. He struggled to his feet again and limped to the cell door.

"Dr. Schubatis, my name is Bogner. I was with you when you were attacked in Washington. Do you remember?"

The Russian's eyes searched Bogner's face. The thick glasses were gone, and he grappled with the fragmented pieces of recollection to make the connection.

Bogner glanced up and down the corridor and began sorting through the unmarked keys.

"You—you're—you're the American," Schubatis finally managed. His voice cracked with emotion. "You're with them. You're one of them. . . ."

"Keep your voice down, dammit," Bogner said.

"What . . . what are you doing?" Schubatis muttered. He looked at Bogner and backed across the cell toward the corner. "Stay away from me. Leave me alone."

"Look—we're here to get you out. Understand? You're going to come with me."

Schubatis was still shaking his head. "Leave . . . leave me alone. I have . . . have already told you, I will not . . . not assist you. Leave me alone."

The Russian's hands were crusted with blood and he was trembling. He was even weaker and more disoriented than Bogner had expected, and because of his leg, he was having difficulty moving. Just getting Schubatis to the hangar where the Covert was housed was going to be a great deal harder than either he or Driver had imagined.

"Stay away from me," Schubatis pleaded. His voice quaked. Then, from under his torn shirt, he produced a spoon that had been honed into a weapon on the stone wall of his cell. He thrust it at Bogner. His hand was shaking. "No, stay away."

Bogner grabbed the man's hand and twisted the makeshift knife away from him. "Dammit, I don't have time to explain. You're coming with me."

Schubatis recoiled again, but this time he was pinned in the corner. His eyes betrayed his confusion and anger. He started to cry out, but Bogner clamped his hand over the Russian's mouth before the sound could escape.

"Sorry about this," Bogner muttered as he

caught the Russian's jaw with a quick jab that dislodged the lower half of the man's false teeth. The stunned Schubatis sagged back against the wall and Bogner caught him before he hit the floor. He plied the dislodged plate from between the Russian's lips, threw it aside, tore off a piece of the man's soiled shirt, wadded it up, and stuffed it into the Russian's mouth. Then he picked Schubatis up like a rag doll and threw him over his shoulder.

At the door of the cell, Bogner checked in both directions before he started down the stone corridor. As he left the building, he checked his watch. He had already burned twenty-three minutes. He had exactly thirty-seven minutes to find Driver.

Datum: Friday—0510L, October 10: Hangar 3, Danjia

Driver was less than a hundred yards from the main hangar when the fuel truck pulled out of the fuel storage area and a returning Komisko settled onto the wet tarmac in front of Hangar 3 for refueling. The area was illuminated by three large banks of mercury-vapor floodlights along the front of the hangar.

Driver stopped just long enough to get himself oriented. He was on the north side of the building. According to Le Win Fo, his access was to the west—on the second level.

There were two light reconnaissance planes parked in an area immediately to his left. Beyond them was a maze of fuel storage tanks and maintenance sheds. He counted three armored vehicles, and noted there was no security fence around any of it. Le Win Fo knew what he was talking about; Quan's security had major holes in it.

Several hundred yards behind him he could still see the muted glow in the sky where the Komisko had crashed, and he could still hear the sounds of sirens and men shouting. Along the way he had counted three vehicles racing to the scene of the downed helicopter. Driver smiled to himself; the old joke about Chinese fire drills had some truth to it.

He waited while they finished refueling the Komisko, then worked his way to the fire escape at the side of the building, scaled it, and went in through the steel fire door on the second level. He was in luck. Just as Le Win Fo had sketched it for them, the big doors to the hangar were open, and the main floor was dark. Only two areas were lighted, at opposite ends of the hangar. One appeared to be a maintenance area and the second looked to be some sort of personnel dayroom. The door was open, the light was on, but there was no activity.

In the maintenance area at the south end of the building, two men were working on a truck. The hood of the vehicle was up and the men were talking. While Driver watched, the phone rang, one of the men answered it, talked briefly, nodded to his companion, and both men left.

He began working his way cautiously toward the north end of the hangar where Le had placed the quarters for flight personnel. From his vantage point on the catwalk, he could see the entire hangar. There were the two Su-27 Flankers armed with AAMs that Le had described when he reported seeing them fly over Hua's orphanage. Both of the Flankers appeared to be alert ready. The cockpit canopies were open, the roll-away mounts were in place, and the bank of red ready lights in each cockpit created a surreal glow in the semidarkness.

In the middle of the hangar was what they had come for. From where Driver was standing, the Russian Covert appeared to be slightly longer than the sixty-six-foot-long F-117X he had been testing at the site of the former Sandia Labs nuclear weapons facility southeast of Tonopah. It had a wider wingspan, a similar humpback design—and like the F-117, it was thick in the places where most aircraft are designed to be sleek.

It did not surprise him that it was faceted,

painted a flat black, and appeared to have a RAM coating. What did surprise him was the side-by-side cockpit layout. The Americans, for whatever reason, had long ago scrapped their plans to build a two-seated version.

Driver reasoned that if they had been successful in copying that much of the F-117's technology, they had probably been equally successful in designing a similar weapons system. If that was the case, Schubatis's Covert could carry and fire a couple of 2,000-pound smart bombs just like its American counterpart.

The rest of the main floor contained a MiG-23U trainer, two salty-looking MiG-21Rs, one of which was still painted with the insignia of the Czechoslovakian air force, and a MiG-21MF with the enlarged dorsal spine. Considering the vintage and condition of the rest of Quan's purchases, Driver was convinced the Covert technology was a bit more sophisticated than the 5A leader was ready for. Of course, he had no way of knowing what the other two hangars housed, but if Hangar 3 was any indication, Quan had reason to want the Covert. Without it, the dissident faction of Han Ki Po's regime had little clout.

On his way to the ready room and crew quarters, Driver took time to look for the ferry fuel tanks. If Borisov had actually flown the Su-39 from deep inside Russian territory, he would have had to strip out the weight of the plane's conventional armament to compensate for the installation of auxiliary fuel tanks.

The question of fuel was what had bothered him most. From the beginning, their plan hinged on the assumption that the Su-39 would be flight ready—and since it was being used to train Quan's pilots, that was a given. But the underlying question was always: How much fuel would she be carrying? If Le was right and Schubatis's pride and joy had been flying nothing more than training missions since its arrival, it was SOP in most third world countries to keep training fuel loads at a minimum. It was risky enough jumping into a plane he had never actually flown before—but trying to fly it out of there in a middle of a thunderstorm without having a handle on the fuel situation was asking for trouble. If they tipped their hand prematurely, the Komiskos would be waiting. The whole operation bordered on sheer insanity.

Driver was still working his way toward the ready room when he heard a phone ring on the deck below him. A uniformed officer hurried from the lighted room at the far end of the hangar, picked up the phone, listened momentarily, turned, and began shouting. Within seconds he was joined by three others. Two of the men were wearing flight suits. The only word Driver understood in the animated conversation was

"Quan." The four men reappeared moments later wearing ponchos and left by a side door.

Driver breathed a sigh of relief.

At the far end of the catwalk was a series of doors and an open bay latrine. Beyond that was a canteen area and the hall leading to the pilots' quarters. And, if Le Win Fo's information was right, behind one of those doors was a Russian by the name of Borisov. If Driver's luck held, the Russian would still be sleeping. If he wasn't, the task was going to be more difficult.

Driver discarded his poncho, double-checked the clip in his SMG, shifted it to his left hand, released the safety, and coiled his finger through the trigger guard. Then he took out his knife, tucked it in his belt, and slowly turned the doorknob. The door opened.

The only light in the room emanated from a small seven-watt security light plugged into a wall socket on the far side of the room. Borisov was sitting on the edge of his bunk, pointing a .45-caliber Makarov at Driver.

"Come in, Colonel," the Russian said in English. "Does it surprise you that I have been expecting you?"

Driver moved across the room and stood facing the Russian. "Yes," he admitted, "it surprises me."

Borisov laughed. It was muffled, but under the circumstances, surprisingly sincere. "We are all victims of our training, Colonel. All of us, I fear, are little more than the predictable products of regimentation. When one of my students reported that a Komisko had suddenly blown up and crashed, I became suspicious. That is the way the GRU trained you, is it not?"

Driver remained silent.

Borisov leaned back against the wall beside his bunk. He kept the Makarov pointed at Driver.

"When I learned that the fool, Quan, had engineered the capture of Schubatis, I knew that you, Comrade, were the one person that Kusinien could call upon. After all, who knows more about the Su-39 program than you do? Are we not indebted to you for much of the information made available to Schubatis in the early stages of development?"

"Simply a matter of money," Driver replied with a grin. "Believe it or not, it has nothing to do with political philosophy. Back in the States we've got a saying; 'When it's all over, the one with the most toys wins.' Over the years I've developed a taste for the finer things in life. The finer things cost money—a helluva lot more money than they pay an Air Force colonel."

Borisov was silent. He kept the gun pointed at Driver.

"You know what the problem with you Russians is, Arege? You people think too much. Let me give you an example. You think too much about political philosophies. You align yourself with some clown like Isotov, and the next thing you know, you're in a heap of trouble. Isotov doesn't stand a chance. Aprihinen will bury your Colonel General before this thing is all over. Shipping you off to this godforsaken hell-hole with the Covert was sheer stupidity. It forces Aprihinen's hand. He can't afford to have some half-crazed, senile old fart like Han Ki Po forming an alliance with Isotov. And he sure as hell can't afford to leave the Covert in the hands of some crackpot like Quan. So what's he gonna do? He's gonna send someone after it."

"Suppose Aprihinen doesn't win," Borisov said.

"Who gives a shit? I have the money—what else counts?"

Borisov shifted the Makarov from one hand to the other. To Driver he was little more than a shadow—a thing that would eventually have to be dealt with.

Driver leaned back up against a small writing desk with his hands in his pockets. "Know something, Arege? There's only two things in this world worth having; one is power and the other is money. Power don't mean much to me; it's restrictive—it keeps you tied down and people expect you to fix things that don't work, like the government. Money is different; you go where you want to go and you do what you want to do. . . . And when you got money, no one gives a damn about your political philosophy."

"So you return the Covert to Russia," Borisov said. "What then?"

"On the contrary, I've been told to fly the Covert out of here and ditch it. Aprihinen doesn't need it. Now that the Americans know he has one, they'll just pump more money into something that flies a little faster and a little higher. And Aprihinen will be right back where he started—sucking hind tit. But look at the bright side of it: Without the Covert, Isotov isn't much of a threat either, and he sure as hell doesn't want some half-baked kook like Quan to have it."

"What about Schubatis?"

"What about him? As goes the Covert, so goes Schubatis. The only instruction I have concerning Schubatis is to make damn certain I don't leave him in the hands of the Chinese. Actually, the Americans and the Chinese are the only ones who think he's important: If he goes down with the Covert, the Americans are never quite sure how much we know about stealth technology. And the Chinese don't know shit. Simple, huh?"

Borisov pushed forward and started to get up. Driver moved with the quickness of a cat. His right hand went for the knife, and he threw in one fluid and death-dealing motion. The six-inch blade buried itself in Borisov's chest and the Russian slumped over on the floor.

In dying, Arege Borisov never uttered a sound.

# Chapter Ten

Datum: Friday—0521L, October 10

Tang Ro Ji was in a great deal of pain, and with each passing hour he was growing weaker. His arm was throbbing, and in the last hour he had nearly blacked out. Twice he had found it necessary to loosen the tourniquet applied by the old woman to relieve the pain, and now the makeshift bandage was again soaked with blood. On the few occasions he had tried to talk to the old man, his thoughts were jumbled and his speech fragmented and incoherent. Each time the plodding horse-drawn cart passed over a rut in the rock-strewn road, he cried out in pain.

At first Tang had insisted on riding up front with the old man. But as he grew weaker, he had been forced to lie down in the bed of the cart. The cart had no springs, and the rough-sawed board bed of the two-wheeled cart was hard and unyielding. Despite that, he continued to hold the small automatic to the boy's head, using a threadbare old blanket to fend off the rain. The blanket had long since soaked through, and Tang, in addition to his pain, suffered from the chills.

Tang had instructed the old man to stay on the back roads to avoid Quan's patrols. On at least two occasions they had been close enough for Tang to see the lights of the armored patrol carriers on the main road just over the hill on the coastal road. Three times low-flying Komiskos with their sweeping searchlights had flown low enough that he was certain they would be spotted. Yet somehow they had managed to avoided detection.

Tang knew the Danjia base commander all too well, and he was equally aware of Quan's dogged determination. The man would keep his patrols out as long as it took to find him.

Tang had confiscated the boy's ancient battery-operated, two-band, six-transistor radio when they left the house. With it he had been able to monitor the Danjia security-band transmissions. He knew they were looking for him, and as the night had progressed, he knew Quan was no longer focusing his efforts on the coastal villages south of Danjia. He had expanded the search both north and inland. Twice within the last few minutes he had heard the patrols report in from villages within ten miles from where he was in hiding.

Early on, Tang realized his plan to take the bus into Haikou had to be scrapped. Quan's patrols would be stopping and searching every car, every bus, and every truck.

Despite his pain, he pulled himself into a sitting position and crawled up to the old man so he could hear him.

"I have . . . have changed my mind. We are not going into the village. Quan's men will be there."

The old man reined up the plodding horse and stopped the cart. He looked at Tang and waited.

Tang started to give the peasant instructions, then stopped. He was rattled. He closed his eyes against the pain and tried to think. "Where . . . where are we?" he demanded.

The old man squinted into the rain. "The village of Qianling is not far, perhaps a kilometer."

"Qianling is on the coast road," Tang said, his head clearing. "They will be looking for me in Qianling." There was another pause before he asked, "How far . . . far from Qianling is Zebo? There is an orphanage in Zebo. Take me there."

After a long silence the man protested, "The horse is old and it is lame. It cannot make it that far."

Tang shoved the barrel of the small automatic into the small of the man's back and felt the rain pelt against his own face. "The horse will not only be lame, it will be dead if you do not take me to Zebo. I am out of patience, old man, and I am in a great deal of pain. I need a doctor. If you and your son want to get out of this alive, you'll get me to Zebo."

Datum: Friday—0537L, October 10

Le Win Fo, with the aid of the older children, had pulled the Defender through the mud and back into the shelter, then closed the doors. While one group busied themselves smoothing out the tracks of the craft's sled undercarriage, others hurried to camouflage the rusting Quonset hut with cut kimho and shaq saplings. The smaller children brought in bunches of broom brush and heeled them into the mud until it looked as though the building had not been used in ages. Le knew that with the camouflage, in the rain and darkness, the old building was barely visible from the top of the hill.

Satisfied, Le trudged up the hill to the main house, where he knew Father Hua would be waiting and monitoring the transmissions from the Danjia radio. When Le entered the room,

Hua looked up with an undeniable expression of relief in his near-sightless eyes; the son of his sister had returned home safe.

"What about the Americans?" Hua asked, anxiety in his rasping voice.

Le's brow furrowed. "I do not know, Father. Just as I let them down on the roof of the cell block, one of the Komiskos returned. It may have spotted me, but suddenly the Komisko exploded, crashed, and burned. In the confusion I managed to escape. I do not know what happened to the Americans. Have the broadcasts indicated anything?"

Hua turned to the youth who had been operating the radios. "Yun Qin would know."

"They report only that they have widened the search for the assassin," Yun Qin said. "Nothing else."

Hua closed his eyes and folded his arms across his frail chest. "It would seem that Quan has erred greatly," he said.

Le waited for the aging priest to elaborate.

"The web is intricate, but to those who would see, the plot is apparent. This man they are searching for is called Tang Ro Ji. We have heard his name many times. Is this not the same Tang Ro Ji who has long been a confidant of Colonel Quan? Is this not the same Tang Ro Ji who is but an extension of Quan's greed?"

"You think Quan engineered the attempted

assassination of Han Ki Po?" Le Win Fo asked.

"Chairman Han Ki Po is dead," Yun Qin said. "It was announced less than an hour ago."

"One can only surmise that Tang Ro Ji's identity was discovered," Hua speculated. "If that is the case, and he is captured, it will not take long for them to uncover the plot. That is why Quan has thrown caution aside to capture Tang Ro Ji before Dung Lei Hong and Major Han's forces locate him. We must be mindful that Quan is not the only one with ambitions to take over the Fifth Academy. Capturing Tang would enable Quan's enemies to eliminate him as well."

Le Win Fo was putting the pieces together as Hua revealed his suspicions. Finally he asked, "Have Quan's patrols been here yet?"

Hua shook his head. "They will come," he said. "It is inevitable."

Le stood up. He looked at the youthful Yun Qin and instructed him to continue to monitor the Danjia transmissions. Then he turned to Father Hua. "We must pray for two things, Father. We must pray that Quan finds the assassin, Tang. And we must pray that our American friends succeed."

Father Hua closed his eyes and bowed his ancient head. He was already deep in prayer.

Le stepped from the shelter of the main house and out onto the flagstone deck. He peered up into the rain and wondered about the safety of the Americans. Far to the south and west, he could see the faint lights on the guard tower at the Danjia security fence. He wondered how long it had taken Quan's men to repair them. From time to time he could hear the distant sound of the searching Komiskos. Like Hua, Le Win Fo began to pray. He feared for the Americans' safety.

Datum: Friday—0537, October 10

Bogner had almost made it. He was within sight of the large hangar, and while he caught his breath he had ducked under the roof of a small shed containing oil drums and refueling equipment. He had put Schubatis down, propped him up against the side of the shed, and momentarily removed the gag.

The Russian was slipping in and out of consciousness. Bogner tried to reason with him, explaining that he was there to help him escape, but the frail little man was disoriented and frightened. If he understood what Bogner was telling him, he gave no indication.

The heavy rains continued, and for the last several minutes the downpour had been accompanied by repeated peals of thunder and occasional lightning. A Komisko circled overhead, preparing to land, and the refueling trucks scurried around the tarmac all but obscured by the spray of water created by the rotors' downdraft.

While Bogner waited, he tried to bring Schubatis around again. He shook the Russian until the man's eyes fluttered open. "Schubatis," he whispered, "can you hear me?"

The Russian nodded only once before he slipped back into unconsciousness, wincing in pain, and groaning.

Bogner checked his watch. He was running out of time. As long as the refueling teams milled around the returning Komiskos it was too risky to try to negotiate the final one hundred yards or so to the hangar. He sagged back against the side of the refueling shed and tried to see into the darkness.

"Where . . . where am I?" Schubatis mumbled. He was trying to sit up.

Bogner bent over him. He kept his voice low. "My name is Bogner. I'm an American. We're trying to get you out of here. . . ."

For the first time the Russian seemed to grasp what he was being told. He closed his eyes, then opened them and stared back at the man hovering over him. "Where am I?" he repeated.

"You're still in the compound—less than a hundred yards from the Danjia hangar. There are two of us. With any luck at all, we're going to get you and your plane out of here."

As Bogner spoke, he glanced out at the refueling crew milling around the Komisko. The fuel hoses had been disconnected and the pilot of the squat Russian helicopter was again pouring the power to the twin Glushenkov engines. The helicopter took off, hovered momentarily, then disappeared in a cloak of swirling rain and darkness.

Bogner could still hear the thumping sound of the Komisko's twin rotors when he turned back to Schubatis again.

The Russian had lost consciousness.

Datum: Friday—0540L, October 10

For Harry Driver, Arege Borisov's unexpected size was a convenience. The two men were about the same size, and the Russian's height and bulk enabled Driver to don his flight suit with ease. He rummaged through his closet, found dry clothes, and pulled on his flight gear. Then he stepped into the small latrine area and emptied the contents of Borisov's electric shaver into the palms of his hands. He rubbed the contents over his face to darken his otherwise sparse beard, and buttoned his flight collar high around his neck to conceal as much of his face as possible.

Driver had fallen into the habit of repeatedly checking his watch. He looked at it again and wondered if he dared risk a quick glance at the charts in the flight center. Le had told them that the flight center contained a small weather-briefing area, a few surface maps, and upper-air charts faxed in by the weather-reporting stations in Guangzhou, formerly Canton, and the WMO weather-forecasting center in Vientiane in Laos.

Listening to the rain pounding on the corrugated roof of Borisov's quarters, Driver wasn't as concerned about getting the Su-39 off the ground as he was about what to expect en route. The winds over Tonkin were tricky, and Driver was eager to avoid flying a craft he was unfamiliar with through a series of heavy thunder cells—especially over open water. Ditching over open water was a risk he couldn't afford to take. His survival depended on making it to land—friendly land. The Hanoi government provided that sanctuary.

If the Su-39 had been fueled for a conventional training flight, he knew he would be likely to have enough fuel to get him across the Gulf of Tonkin to Haiphong. It was that "if" that haunted him.

The plan was simple: When he was over Haiphong harbor he would bring the Su-39 around and head it back toward the gulf. Then he would eject.

From the latrine, Driver went back into Borisov's room to get rid of the body. He had no way of knowing how the Russian prepared for the flight, and if he deviated, it might arouse suspicion. He opened the window, felt the rain swirl in, and looked down. No more than fifteen feet beneath him was the tin roof of a makeshift storage shed. He pulled Borisov's body to the window, hefted it over the ledge, shoved, and heard the body land. Unless someone looked out the window, his body would not be discovered until long after he had taken off with the Covert.

At that point, Harry Driver paused. He was well aware of the fact that he was about to pass the point of no turning back. He was about to turn his back on his career, his country, and everything he had known. And, if Bogner had succeeded in getting Schubatis out of his cell and eventually made it as far as the hangar—all, in Driver's estimation, long shots—Bogner had to be contended with as well.

Datum: Friday—0545L, October 10

Shu Li was awakened by the incessant ringing of the telephone, punctuated by a loud peal of thunder. She shuddered, forced her eyes open, and realized the hour. She groped in the darkness for the phone, found it, and tried to clear her head.

Thinking it would be the hotel operator, she muttered a barely audible "What is it?"

Zhun Be's voice surprised her. "I must talk to you," he said.

She looked at the clock. "Come on, Zhun, can't it wait?"

"It is urgent."

"Very well, room seven fourteen. But give me a few minutes to get presentable. Okay?"

"I'll be up in five minutes."

Shu Li hung up the phone, got out of bed, put on a robe, and went into the bathroom to straighten her hair. Still half asleep, she wondered what could be so urgent that Zhun Be would risk coming to the Haikou. Normally he was far too cautious to risk revealing his contacts. Before she had time to think it through, she heard his knock.

When she opened the door, she saw that his clothes were soaked and his face was flushed. "Where are the Canadians?" he blurted.

Shu Li knew they had returned to Zebo with Le Win Fo, but she hesitated. "I don't know," she lied.

"They did not return to the hotel tonight," Zhun Be said. "I called their rooms, there is no answer. They must be warned."

Shu Li sat down on the edge of her bed. "Warned about what?" She knew Zhun was upset; he was disheveled, and he hadn't even commented on the fact that she was wearing only a robe. That wasn't the Zhun Be she knew.

"You have not heard the news?"

Shu Li shook her head. "What news? What are you talking about?"

"Han Ki Po has been assassinated, and the killer has escaped."

Shu Li was stunned. "Assassinated?"

"They are looking for a man named Tang Ro Ji. Patrols are everywhere. The police have been instructed to round up all foreigners. They have already taken the Russian Provnosky into custody—and they are looking for the two Canadians from Jade."

Shu Li knew the name Tang Ro Ji. She had never met him, but she had heard Ti Minn talk about the man. Ti Minn had called him a beast.

Shu Li hesitated before she admitted, "I know where the Canadians are." She was banking on the fact that Zhun Be wasn't playing both ends against the middle and trying to help the Haikou police. The Haikou police were known to be loyal to Quan.

To her surprise, Zhun Be did not ask where. He simply repeated, "They must be warned."

Shu Li stood up. "You are right. They are in Zebo."

"Zebo . . . the orphanage of Father Hua?" Suddenly Zhun's face broke into a small smile. "Of course," he said, "the orphanage. Then it is true: Hua is a contact. I have heard the rumors for years . . . and you, you are one of them."

Shu Li walked slowly to her dresser, opened the drawer, and brought out a small revolver. She turned and leveled it at Zhun. "I don't always trust you, Zhun. This could all be a trick. So now you have the opportunity to prove just which side you're on."

"I would not have come here—"

"You are coming with me to Zebo," she said as she grabbed some clothes from the dresser and stepped behind a small dressing screen.

"The police have set up roadblocks," Zhun protested. "They are checking everything coming into and going out of the city. We won't be allowed to leave."

"I know a back way," Shu Li said, "over the hill road through the old commune."

"That road will be treacherous; it has been raining for hours. I know that road, it is full of washouts."

Shu Li stepped out from behind the screen. She was wearing a dark turtleneck sweater, black slacks, and boots. Over her arm she carried a rain cape. "Do you know this man they call Tang Ro Ji?"

Her question surprised Zhun Be. "I have met him," he acknowledged. "He is dangerous. It is rumored that he works for Colonel Quan."

Shu Li started for the door. "We will use the back elevator. My car is parked out back of the hotel. We will take the side streets until we get to Hangko Park; then we will go by way of the old airport road."

Zhun Be swallowed hard. Warning the Canadians was one thing. Driving to Zebo by treacherous back roads in the middle of a prolonged storm was another.

Datum: Friday—0555L, October 10

Bogner, again carrying Schubatis, located an access door at the rear of the refueling depot. He unscrewed a small light over the door and entered a darkened area littered with spare aircraft parts and workbenches. Through the open door he could see into the main bay of the hangar. With the exception of a lighted area at the far end, it was dark. The only light came from a bank of floodlights on the roof overlooking the tarmac in front of the hangar.

Bogner waited and listened. When he was

convinced no one had heard him, he propped the unconscious Schubatis in an area between two benches, stuffed the gag back in the Russian's mouth, unshouldered the SMG, and stepped out into the hangar, staying close to the wall in the shadows.

A small utility vehicle pulled into the hangar through the main doors. A man got out and walked to a nearby bench, picked up some tools, got back in the truck, and drove away. Moments later, a man wearing a flight suit emerged from the shadows and walked toward the Covert. Bogner held his breath.

Driver circled the Covert, kicked the chocks away from the nose gear and load wheels, and began groping his way along the fuselage in the semidarkness. He was systematically familarizing himself with the plane's exterior features—many of which would let him know what to expect in the Covert's cockpit.

He knew the F-117 like the back of his hand. More than a year of testing the plane at Tonopah had ensured that. Thus far he hadn't detected anything that would make him think Schubatis and his engineers had deviated much from the original design. Schubatis was good—but he wasn't any smarter than the boatload of Lockheed engineers who had put the original *Have Blue* together. If Schubatis had made changes, they would be in the cockpit area where the Russians did their own thing—and they would be in the performance parameters. If the Russians held true to form, the Covert was bound to be heavier and its performance would be sluggish by comparison.

Driver's hands traced along the inboard edge flaps and the outboard elevons, around to the front of the wings and then on to the nose of the aircraft. The Covert had the same large suck-in doors on top of the air intakes that provided extra air to the F-117 during taxi and takeoff.

At the base of the boarding ladder, he tightened the laces of Borisov's G suit to compensate for their minimal difference in size, mounted, and lowered himself into the cockpit. His hunch about Schubatis tinkering with the cockpit layout had been right. Everything was there, but in a different configuration. There was the predictable HUD, head-up display, and the conventional FLIR CRT. The main control panel had three standard multifunctional display CRTs instead of two, as well as the large screen used to convey data during hostile engagement. The electro-optical unit was lower and not as conveniently positioned as the one in the F-117. Driver figured that was because the forward-looking infrared sensor turret was bulkier and diminished the pilot's field of vision.

In addition to the cockpit layout, Driver had confirmed one other thing: The red light he had spotted from the catwalk was in fact a warmer button. He was in luck: Borisov had spent too much time in alert hangars. The Russian's precautions would save him precious minutes when he fired the Covert's engines. He checked his harness and the position of the throttles. Unlike the F-117, the Covert had two, one on each side of the twin-seated cockpit. He released the engage pin, shoved it into a lock down position, and locked out the right-seat controls.

It occurred to Driver that he could get the Covert out of there—now. All he had to do was wait until the engine temperatures came up, confirm fuel load and full fuel flow, achieve RPM, and hit the throttle with the butt of his right hand. No complications. No waiting for Bogner or Schubatis. Instead he terminated the sequence, positioned it in the SR, stand by/-ready mode, and elevated the temp in the prewarming unit. Already the sensor was giving him an intermittent ready reading. When it gave him a consistent red glow, the Covert was ready.

A small smile played with the corners of Driver's mouth. The only thing that would be missing was a way of seeing the look on Quan's face when he realized some son of a bitch was high-tailing it out of Danjia with his Covert, stolen from right under his nose.

He had carried it as far as he could. The Covert was ready. He crawled out of the cockpit and examined the small area immediately behind the plane's flight station. He jerked out the wiring to the backup computer and the flight recorder; then he lifted the module out and sat it in the left seat. To make more room, he pulled out the firing mechanism for the left seat and inserted the hinged lock pin. If Bogner did make it and Schubatis had to be stuffed into the area behind the flight control center, the left seat wouldn't fire when Driver ejected.

This was the part of it Driver had though out very carefully. If by some miracle the Covert didn't disintegrate upon impact, and if the plane was recovered from the waters of the gulf, all they would find was the body of the missing Schubatis. Driver's smile intensified; let Colchin and his cronies try to explain that one to old Moshe.

He checked his watch and wondered if Bogner and Schubatis would make it. Time had run out; it was now or never. He picked up the computer module, climbed down, and headed for his rendezvous with Bogner at the north end of the hangar. If Bogner was there, so be it. It only ensured his being able to report that Schubatis was dead, somewhere in the depths of the Gulf of Tonkin. If Bogner didn't make it, the only difference was he wouldn't know how the two men had died.

Datum: Friday—0610L, October 10

Colonel Quan did not know the young officer by name, only that he had been recently transferred from the garrison at Huanglui. Thin and wet, still wearing a rain poncho, this officer was unlike the others. He did not cower. He stood erect and met Quan's eyes while he made his report.

"Are you certain?" Quan demanded.

"Yes, Colonel, one of the fire crew found the body of the guard after he helped extinguish the fire in the downed Komisko. He had been told to report for duty in the cell block. When he was unable to locate the guard, he thought he might be sleeping. He found the body behind the guard shack at the south entrance of the cell block. The guard's neck had been broken, and there is evidence to indicate that the man's body was dragged around behind the shelter to keep it from being discovered."

Quan reached for the telephone, but the officer held up his hand.

"I have already informed Lieutenant Yew. I

insisted that he take a small squad of men and search the area."

Quan frowned. The young officer's brazenness had taken him by surprise. "You insisted?" he repeated. "Need I remind you, Lieutenant, that I am in command here—that I am the one who countermands standing orders?"

The officer inclined his head forward in a mock bow. "Perhaps I should inform the Colonel that I was assigned here by order of General Han Xihui, the son of Chairman Han. I have been in contact with the General a number of times over the past few weeks, and as recently as one hour ago."

Quan rocked back in his chair. "Perhaps I should remind you that I am the commanding officer in Danjia," he said. "Your General Han has no authority here."

"I have orders direct from General Han. The General will soon assume leadership of the Fifth Academy."

"Han?" Quan laughed. "Your General Han is nothing more than a puppet. He holds his rank only because he is the son of Han Ki Po. Now, with the passing of Chairman Han, it is I, not your General, who will assume command of the Fifth Academy."

Instead of being intimidated, the officer leaned forward with his hands on Quan's desk and lowered his voice. "I was assigned here for a purpose, Colonel. We have known of your ambitions for some time now. We were aware that you had dispatched the man called Tang Ro Ji to assassinate Chairman Han."

"Lies," Quan said with a smirk. "If you knew, then why did you not stop him?"

"Because you were playing right into our hands, Colonel. General Han had it within his power to stop your man at any time."

The statement had caught Quan off guard.

"What you do not realize, Colonel, is that we have waited a long time for the passing of Chairman Han. We have watched the energy of our mission erode as the Chairman grew feeble and inept. Tonight, thanks to you, the Fifth Academy passed into the hands of an energetic new leadership, the command of General Han Xihui."

"Then you know that Tang Ro Ji—"

"General Han observed the assassin throughout. There was only one flaw: We did not capture the assassin before he escaped. Consequently, we were unable to force him to confess that you are the perpetrator of this insidious plot."

"Your allegations are groundless," Quan shouted. "You can prove nothing."

"On the contrary, Colonel, we have witnesses who will testify to what I have just said. Within the next few hours, General Han will board a flight to Danjia. His purpose will be to assume command of this installation. You see, Colonel, it is not a matter of *if,* it is merely a matter of *when.*"

For the first time, Quan was unnerved. He edged his chair toward his desk, put a cigarette in the ebony cigarette holder, and reached across the desk for his lighter. It was a gesture designed to distract the young officer. He did not see Quan open a desk drawer and reach for the revolver with his other hand.

Datum: Friday—0613L, October 10

Tang Ro Ji pulled the wet blanket tight around his head and shoulders and turned toward the dim and distant lights of Hua's orphanage. Even now, the lights were little more than a faint yellow glow in the distance.

Behind him, in a water-filled ditch, lay the bodies of the old man and the boy. Despite his shattered arm, he had managed to gather enough brush to hide the bodies. They would not be found for days. As a final precaution, he had led the horse, still hitched to the cart, down a steep incline into the water-filled wash beneath the bridge. He put the barrel of the Barkai tight up against the animal's forehead between the eyes, and pulled the trigger. There was a muted crack, a small explosion like the sound of a bullwhip, and the horse, still tethered between the traces, dropped and lay motionless.

Ro Ji squinted into the rain, looked off toward the lights, summoned what little strength he had left, and started up the hill. His pain had become intolerable, and he fell twice before he made it to the road. Each time he called on his inner resources, closed his eyes, and attempted to gain his equilibrium. He had come a long way from Huangliu. Zebo was now less than a kilometer away.

Datum: Friday—0615L, October 10

Bogner watched from the shadows as the figure in the G suit climbed down the cockpit of the Covert and crossed the floor of the hangar toward the maintenance area. He still couldn't be certain. He dropped to one knee, brought the SMG up to his shoulder, and held his breath. Then Driver passed momentarily through the faint illumination of a security light and Bogner recognized him.

"Harry, over here," Bogner whispered.

"You made it. Did you get Schubatis?"

Bogner nodded and motioned over his shoulder. "I've got him stowed away back there in one of the storage areas. He's a little the worse for wear, but at least he's alive."

Driver's eyes darted to the hangar doors and the first gray traces of daylight. Despite the rains and the low churning deck of clouds, in the last thirty minutes it had become perceptibly brighter. He pointed to the Covert and kept his voice at a near whisper. "There's our baby. I checked her out. She's had all the flight prep she's gonna get . . . and she's as close to ready as she's gonna get. That's assuming I've figured out what all those damn Russian words mean on the gauges."

Bogner stayed in the shadows. He checked his watch: 0617. Sunrise was only thirteen minutes away. They would lose what little edge they had with the coming of daylight.

Suddenly the access door at the end of the darkened corridor opened and three men entered. Bogner and Driver slipped back into the shadows. The men were wearing black rain slickers. Grim faced and weary, they were members of the refueling crew. They passed within ten feet of the two Americans and headed for the maintenance area containing Schubatis.

One of them flicked a switch and light spilled out into the hallway. When he heard their excited chatter, Bogner knew the refueling crew had discovered Schubatis. Bogner stood up, slipped the SMG off his shoulder, moved back down the hall, and stepped into the doorway.

With Driver right behind him, he leveled the SMG at the three men and shouted, "Freeze!" There was no way of knowing whether or not Quan's men understood English, but they understood the 9mm SMG.

Driver slipped around him, past the three men, and pulled Schubatis to his feet. The Russian, gagged and terrified, saw the Russian flight suit, took a step, and crumpled. Driver bent over and hefted the man over his shoulder. He circled past Bogner and headed back out into the hangar. "They're all yours, swabbie. Finish 'em off. We're runnin' out of time."

Bogner backed the three men through a door into the latrine and herded them into the emergency showers. Then he slammed the door and opened the valve on the water main. At the door of the latrine he pulled the latch, dropped the pin in place, and turned off the light. By the time anyone heard them, or they figured a way out, the Covert would be long gone.

As Bogner rounded the corner into the main hangar, he saw one of the Danjia security patrols pull up in front of the door. Two men crawled out; one headed for the north end of the hangar, the other stopped and lit a cigarette. When he saw Driver crawling out of the cockpit of the Covert, he shouted.

Bogner leaped out of the shadows, coiled his

arm around the man's neck, spun him around, and threw him to the floor. He had one hand cupped over the man's mouth and the other wedged under his chin. The maneuver was straight out of the pages of the survival manual. He shoved up and twisted, all in one motion. He heard the muffled scream, the stiffening in protest—and then the man went limp.

There was a marionettelike series of disjointed convulsions while the man's brain triggered commands to arms and legs no longer connected to a spinal cord—and then there was no movement at all.

As Bogner straightened up, he saw Driver running toward him. The first move brought the butt of the short-barreled SMG up into Bogner's stomach and crushed the wind out of him.

Dazed, Bogner doubled over, gasped for air, and pitched forward. He managed to get out the words "What the—" before Driver caught him with a second blow—this one to the side of the head.

He thought he heard the words "Sorry, swabbie" as he slumped to his knees. His brain was rattling around inside his head, and by the time he hit the floor there was the god-awful bitter taste of bile in his mouth and nowhere to go but down a long tunnel into his own private oblivion.

# Chapter Eleven

Datum: Friday, 0625L: October 10

Driver shimmied down into the cockpit of the Covert, pulled down his harness, buckled in, hit the switch to engage the canopy with one hand, and shoved forward on the throttle with the other. The hissing sound of the canopy sealing was drowned out by the deafening roar of the twin Tumanski R-34s blasting to life.

He counted as the EH needles began to climb: 5,000, 7,500, 10,000.

He scanned the indicators—oil pressure, hydraulics—and waggled the joystick. With no visual RrV, the pulsating green light indicated the reassuring movement in the V stabilizer and the telemetry displays sprang to life.

Mentally he was careening through a sequence that in the F-117 would have been second nature to him. He punched the sequencing switch and saw the fuel-flow pressure gauge level off at 5,000. He dropped his visor, bit down hard, and slammed the butt of his hand against the throttle. His head slammed back against the restraint and he felt the Covert rumble and surge forward. The G force was building.

As the Covert lurched from the hangar, it yawed and began to shudder. He eased back on the throttle and straightened the beast out as it catapulted out into the mercury-lamp-bathed wet tarmac. The taxi strip veered right and the 013 runway was straight ahead. The apron was wide, but the rain had intensified. The wash-back was blinding.

Out of the corner of his eye he saw one of Quan's armored personnel carriers hurtling toward him. He twisted the lumbering Covert violently to the right in an evasive maneuver just as the APC opened fire. The opening volley caught the canopy, splintering the Rmq, and the FLIR exploded in a barrage of fragmented acrylic and electronic components. He felt a hot, burning sensation in his shoulder, and through the tinted visor he saw a part of his G suit turn an ugly brown-black as the blood began seeping through. There was fire in his shoulder, and a bolt of pain raced down his arm, numbing the fingers of his left hand.

For Driver it was now or never. He began counting again. "Fifteen thousand, seventeen thousand." Pressure up. The indicator light was still red. "Dammit," he screamed, "Full up, you son of a bitch."

A second volley of shells slammed into the fuselage just as the green light began flickering in the fire stage. He slammed his hand against the throttle and plunged it to full stop. The Covert shuddered, lurched forward, and began to roll. The situation display on the CRT indicated alignment as the runway lights were absorbed in the swirling rain. He could feel his body being pinned deeper and deeper into the recesses of his seat as the G forces continued to build and the Covert began hurtling down the runway. Tiny pinpoints of light jetted by and he straightened the joy: flaps, lift, pull back, more throttle. No goddamn control tower on this one. His brain was processing the steady stream of information flashing across the GC-CRT. He was committed. All he needed now was for one of Quan's damned Komiskos to come limping into his flight path. Pull back, punch, lift. The Covert was rolling and vibrating. He could hear the plane shudder. Nose up. He stole glances at the ground-speed indicator and the altimeter. SLP, a steady .0047. Lift. Lift. The radio blared an incoherent stream of fragmented gibberish and static; voices betrayed confusion. The rain pounded against the broken canopy—there was no visual, only a pencil-thin streak of light on the horizon. H-DR indicator: red light blinking. Malfunction. Fuel pressure. Fuel pressure.

The Covert broke free and he was airborne—but the fuel-flow indicator was plunging. Harry Driver had no way of knowing that one of the shells from the APC had ruptured his fuel line.

Datum: Thursday—1731L: October 9

Robert Miller stood at the window watching the rush-hour traffic on Pennsylvania Avenue slow to a crawl. It was a gray, overcast day and the light rain on the city served only to slow traffic even further. Behind him, on his desk, was a stack of reports he had been meaning to tackle for several days, and the congestion was a further impetus to get a few of them out of the way before he left for the day.

He had just turned to face the task when the phone rang. He picked up the receiver, slumped down in his chair, half expecting it to be his wife, Betty, wondering what time he would be home for dinner.

"Miller here," he said.

"Agent Miller?"

"You got him."

"This is Major Fanning of base security at Nellis Air Force Base."

Miller straightened in his chair. "Yes, Major, what can I do for you?"

Fanning hesitated. "Lieutenant General Belding, the base commander here at Nellis, suggested that I contact you. But before I begin . . ." He paused. "Is this line secure?"

"Secure on this end," Miller laughed, "or at least it was the last time we ran a check. Why? What's up."

Fanning was the cautious type. He weighed his words carefully. "You have a Colonel Harry Driver currently assigned to you TDY from 4450th TG?"

"Affirmative," Miller said. "But I'm not at liberty to discuss—"

"Inside or outside the ZI?"

"Classified," Miller said. "What's this all about?"

Miller could hear a muffled exchange on the other end of the line before Fanning continued. This time his voice was only slightly less guarded. "What I'm about to tell you is extremely sensitive, Mr. Miller."

"I'm all ears," Miller said, sobering.

"Three days ago the body of a man was discovered some thirty miles from Nellis. The man had no affiliation with Nellis. The authorities believe the man died of a heart attack. During the routine investigation that followed, however, we uncovered certain documents that would lead us to believe the man was acting as an agent for foreign interests. . . ."

"Go on," Miller urged.

"We also found papers that would indicate there has been some sort of ongoing relationship between the dead man and Colonel Harry Driver."

"What kind of relationship?"

Fanning cleared his throat. "Nothing conclusive," he hedged, "but we have reason to believe that Colonel Driver may be acting in the capacity of a foreign agent—"

"For Christ's sake," Miller interrupted, "the man's a test pilot at Tonopah. He's been assigned to the F-117 program since the early nineties."

"The dead man was carrying top-secret file photos and classified information," Fanning said. "The file photos, all marked Top Secret, were signed out of FLT-OBS by Colonel Driver."

Miller let out a whistle. "Okay, I hear you, Major. But before I can release any information on Colonel Driver's whereabouts, I'll have to check signals with my superiors. As soon as I do, I'll get back to you."

Fanning hesitated again. Miller could hear him speaking to someone in the room with him. Then he came back on the line. He repeated two telephone numbers and gave Miller the name of the on-duty base security officer.

"Does it look incriminating?" Miller asked.

"Let me put it this way," Fanning said. "If we confirm our suspicions, this could make that CIA agent they caught last year in Washington look like kid's stuff." There was another pause before he said, "We'll wait for your call."

Miller hung up and dialed Packer.

The ISA bureau chief answered on the third ring.

"Sorry to bother you at home, Pack, but I thought I'd better get right on this. Just got a call from the security detail at Nellis. Driver is being investigated. . . ."

Packer laughed. "Harry always did have a way of irritating the head shed. What is it this time?"

"I think it may be a little more serious than pissing off the Chairman of the Armed Services Committee. According to the people at Nellis, it appears that our man Driver is suspected of consorting with some guy the folks at Nellis believe is a foreign agent."

"You're hedging, Bob."

"Nothing confirmed yet."

Packer was silent for a moment. "All the same, I think we better let Bogner know. Tell T. C. to keep an eye on him."

Datum: Friday—0637L: October 10

The first thing Bogner remembered was the unpleasant wailing of the alert siren. The discordant, undulating sound cycled over and over, and he finally managed to get a message past the throbbing sensation in his head to his eyes. Open, dammit. Open. What the hell is going on?

Beneath him he could feel the cold, damp concrete flooring of the hangar. He clawed at it, trying to crawl through the hole in his confusion and pain back into reality.

He could hear footsteps and men shouting. There was chaos and noise—and the frantic sounds men make when they hurry. Somewhere off in the distance there was a rumble and yet another uncataloged sound—like someone pounding a staccato beat on metal. It was the rain hammering on the metal roof of the hangar.

He tried to move his legs, and to his surprise they worked. Then he tried his arms and hands. More success. Finally, there was the matter of putting the two together, to move everything in unison—to make something happen, to feel in control. His head throbbed, and even though the parts were responding, the only thing he could manage was a crawling motion. Even that made him sick to his stomach. It was dark and cold and the world was a Rorschach, a blur on a blur.

He inched his way under a workbench—not because he was planning anything, but because it was a sanctuary. He saw the face of a man, a man with a serpent's tongue. Then there was a fire, out of control, and people screaming. His head hammered and he closed his eyes.

He heard the sound of engines, jet engines, turbos, the clanging of metal, more shouts—and the roar increased. He saw movement—great behemoths, spitting fire, angry and roaring—and put his hands over his ears to shut out the furor.

Finally there was nothing left but the shouts of the men. Eventually, even they died out—and he felt alone.

Slowly the face of Driver materialized and he saw the butt of the SMG arching down toward him. He winced and felt the blow to his mid-section for a second time. To stop it, he closed his eyes again, but the image stayed with him.

Finally the noise ceased, and the silence was frightening. He was alone—with no idea where he was.

Bogner pulled himself up on his hands and knees. He was shaky and weak, but the pieces were starting to come together. He saw a face. Driver. Driver had put him down. Why? He shook his head to clear the hurt and the cobwebs, but there was no relief. The only thing that was certain was that the hangar was dark and the Covert was gone—but so were the Flankers. More of the puzzle came together, merging, connecting, one piece at a time. The reasoning, like the images that played out in his head, followed a line of jumbled logic: Driver had escaped with Schubatis in the Covert and Quan had sent the Flankers after him. But why had Driver . . . ?

Bogner steadied himself just long enough to stumble toward the nearest door—the one with the red light over it. The rain . . . the rain would help. He needed to clear his head. He fumbled with the knob, managed to get the door open, and stumbled out into the rain. What the hell was Driver up to?

The rain pelted down on him. He shook his head again to clear his thought patterns, but the gesture only increased the throbbing. He leaned back against the side of the hangar to steady himself and closed his eyes. He knew he had to get his act together, to think straight, before he could calculate his next move. His only allies were the rain and semidarkness—and he was fast running out of the latter.

He had to try again. He looked around him.

In the cold gray light of the emerging dawn, he continued to put the pieces together again—to identify possibilities. He had stumbled into what appeared to be a motor-pool area. There were two trucks and a third vehicle that resembled a personnel carrier. The area was fenced, bordered on one side by the rear of the hangar, and on the far side by a shed with a low roof that provided an overhang no more than forty or fifty feet from where he was standing.

A plan was starting to formulate: By keeping his back to the wall until he could dodge between the parked trucks, he figured he could get across the opening to the shed door. But then what? Beyond that he had no plan—he didn't even know where he was. He knew he still wasn't thinking straight. The thought repeated itself: *Trust your instincts, Toby, trust your instincts.* They taught you that in psych warfare; work out the rest of your plan after you've conquered the first hurdle. The biggest mistake is to do nothing.

He managed the first part, getting to and hiding between the trucks. The next hurdle would be clearing the thirty, maybe forty feet to the overhang.

He was still crouched between the two trucks when he saw the door to the shed open and two men emerge. One was obviously one of Quan's men; he was wearing a uniform. The other appeared to be one of the villagers Le Win Fo had described; he was wearing a rain poncho with a hood. Just as they were closing the door behind them, Bogner heard a phone ring. There was a brief exchange of words, and the one in uniform went back in the building to answer it.

Suddenly Bogner saw his luck turning. The smaller of the two men, the one in the poncho, was headed straight for him.

Bogner dropped to the ground, shimmied under the truck, and waited. The man walked by him, and just as he started to crawl in the cab, Bogner reached out with one hand and took the man's legs out from under him. When he hit the ground, Bogner dragged him under the truck, rolled him over, and buried a left hook in the man's midsection. The little man was older than Bogner had anticipated, and one blow was all it took. There was no fight in him. The wind gushed out of him and he lay there, looking at Bogner, terrified and gasping for air.

"Sorry about that, old-timer," Bogner muttered, "but right now I need this truck a helluva lot worse than you do." He peeled the man out of his poncho, crawled out from under the truck, climbed into the cab, and waited.

Minutes later, the soldier came out of the building and darted through the rain for the truck. As he opened the driver's-side door and started to get in, Bogner reached out, grabbed him behind the head with one hand, and bolo-punched him with the other. By the time Quan's man knew what was happening, it was all over. Bogner jerked his head down, brought up his knee, felt the reassuring collision of knee against face, heard the man's semimuffled protest, and slammed his face against the steering wheel. Mouth bloodied, nose crushed to one side and pumping blood, the soldier fell back against the seat. Bogner pried the keys out of his hand, pushed the door open, and shoved him out. He jammed the key into the ignition, twisted, and heard the engine rumble to life.

Datum: Friday—0644L: October 10

Su-27 4107, the lead Flanker in the formation, was being flown by Flight Captain Feng. His wingman, Lieutenant Chang, in the Su-27 4211, managed to maintain his position some thirty yards off Feng's right wing despite the soup and chop at the 3,000-foot level.

"See anything?" Feng asked. He had dropped his mask-mike to scrutinize the electronic-warfare panel.

"Negative on EW," Chang answered, "but all the radar is degrading. If he's heading for Haiphong, as Colonel Quan thinks he is, I should be picking him up on acquisition."

Feng eased the throttle back and brought the nose of the Flanker down a full degree. The presence of repeated flashes of cloud-to-cloud, an intercloud lightning, was making their mission all the more difficult.

"Danjia five-four-oh, this is Songbird 4107."

Feng heard his voice filter through on feedback. The transmission was punctuated with static, and he wondered if Danjia TO was receiving his transmission.

"You're breaking up," Chang confirmed. "Garbled."

Feng continued. "We're easing down to twenty-five hundred to see if we can get under this mess. Experiencing severe turbulence."

There was no confirmation from Danjia TO, and in the heavy wash of rain slipstreaming over his canopy, Feng was beginning to have second thoughts about his decision to go lower. Despite that, he twisted the knob on the pressure altimeter to match the reading on the radar screen.

"Experiencing extreme turbulence," Chang reported. He was fighting the stick, working to keep the wings level and the steering centered.

"VDI active," Feng announced. "Watch your ordnance panel. Report target acquisition on count."

Chang, momentarily distracted by the lightning, sequenced all vector displays. "Oh-four, oh-two, oh-ten, oh-eight-sweep. I get negative. Chaos."

"Severe chop," Feng reported. "We're too low. I'm having trouble maintaining altitude—"

"Target acquisition," Chang cut in. "MN-55. Profile on log two." He flipped the switch and the scroll began, stopping with the NON-IDENT red light blinking on and off as the computer struggled to identify the target.

"That's good enough for me," Feng said. "Who else would be out here on a night like this?"

"Target maintaining two thousand," Chang confirmed. He punched the SLO—secure and lock-on—into the accretion file. "I'm getting some kind of ID chatter. Coming up on target fast."

"Give me a precise location," Feng said.

"Fifty nautical miles due east of the Anxi Islands. Read 21.2 and 57.7 and mark."

"He's losing altitude. Symbol deteriorating."

Chang changed the angle on the acquisition indicator. "I've lost him. He's flying too low. He's under the net." Suddenly the Flanker began to shake. Chang felt the stick begin to vibrate and his Su-27 yawed violently in the cloud base turbulence. "Losing altitude," he reported. "I'm breaking off."

Chang didn't wait for Feng's confirmation. He

peeled off in a thirty-five-degree right turn and began his climb, passing through the cone of vertical turbulence in the center of the cell.

Feng waited for his wingman to break out and report. "4211. Do you read? Report breakout." He waited several seconds and repeated his transmission. "Four-two-one-one, verify."

Feng changed frequencies and tried again. Then he put the signal on A-SCAN. He activated his recorder and turned the switch to Vo-Act. "I think I've got him on ACQ." He retarded the throttle to drop to 2,000. "Four-two-one-one, if you're reading this, report 4107 AAT-POS at 0649L."

Datum: Friday—0650L: October 10

Driver had been monitoring the transmissions between the two Flankers, but now his attention was focused on the FFI. It had dropped from 3,500 to 2,500hh in the last four minutes. A computer check on the flashing red indicator light on the CFMG, central fuel monitor gauge, verified the rapid fuel loss.

His fears were confirmed. The CFMG had indicated seven thousand pounds of fuel at takeoff. Either a fuel line had ruptured or one of the shells from the APC had severed it. Either way, he did not have enough fuel to make it to Haiphong.

The transmissions between the trailing Flankers had broken off. He rotated to the HSD, horizontal situation display, and scanned his flight path. Nothing but water. He activated the 360-degree scan on the center display. One blip, not two. One of the Flankers had either broken off or ditched. Regardless, one was still on his tail—and closing. If the Covert had been armed, and if he had fuel, he could circle back and engage—but he had neither. If the pilot of the Flanker knew what he was doing, Driver was a sitting duck. His only defense was the Covert's stealth profile. Between the rain and the RAM, he had to hope the jockey was still unable to get a fix. All bets were off if the Flanker pulled within the 25-n.m. range. The AA-9 missiles the Flanker was carrying could find Driver in a fog-shrouded swamp—there was no way to shut down the plume. That plume was like a whore in heat: find me—catch me—fuck me.

He throttled back again, inclined the nose three degrees, and wondered if the Covert would hold together on wave impact. The inflate ring would give him enough time to crawl out if she held together going in. If it didn't, the odds of buying the farm soared.

Torrents of rain swept back over the canopy and lightning flashed all around him. The SD was flat, feeding him a steady diet of blue-black ocean, and to top it off, the radar altimeter was flickering. He concentrated on the altitude indicator and only occasionally glanced at the FFI.

By now he knew the Flanker had him in target range. He dropped the nose and began an evasive descent.

There was another lightning flash just off his right wing, and the instruments flickered. He could tell by the popping sound that one of the circuit breakers had kicked out.

Suddenly, there it was on the screen, a chunk of rock right in the middle of the damn water. He located the SD reference switch and watched the coordinates scroll out in flashing green symbols. The words ANXI-1 and ANXI-2 appeared on the screen just as the gyro blipped. There was a snapping noise and the acrid smell of burning wires. Two tiny dots appeared on the HSD, minute phosphorous explosions—there one second, gone the next.

Le Win Fo had said something about two tiny islands, actually little more than rocks in the middle of the Gulf. What had he said about them—something about taking Quan's political refugees to a pickup point?

Another lightning flash—close. Then the distinct smell of something burning. One by one the displays begin to extinguish. The SD panel was out. He unfastened his oxygen mask and hung it on the umbilical hose to the air supply.

With his good arm he fumbled in the E-kit for an emergency flashlight. It was under the ANGMQ on the F-117. Not there. Where the hell was it?

The breakers clicked out.

The cockpit went dark.

He fumbled along the instrument panel for the emergency power switch. There had to be a backup—an E battery—but where the hell was it? Beads of sweat began to trace their way from under his helmet and down across his forehead. His palms were wet and the lightning razored through the blackness, giving him little more than transitory perceptions of a churning, storm-tossed hell only a few hundred feet below him.

Driver hammered forward on the throttle, pulled back on the stick, and dropped the flaps. He was going in . . . and there wasn't a damn thing he could do about it.

The tail dropped, the nose of the Covert pointed skyward, and Driver felt the impact before he heard it. The swell caught the Covert's stabilizer and jerked it down. There was a thunderous thumping sound and then a violent pitch forward. Harry Driver's body slammed forward against the restraint harness, and for a split second he felt as if the force of the collision would crush him. There was a stabbing pain in his chest and the wind rushed out of him. He was momentarily helpless, gasping for breath, and reaching for anything he could hold on to.

The Covert twisted violently, corkscrewing its fuselage into the chop and breaking off the left wing, then toppled over and slammed down on the surface of the water.

Driver heard hissing sounds and the canopy fogged over. A wave slammed into the broken carcass of Schubatis's brainchild and he knew he had only seconds before the aircraft started breaking up and was sucked down under the churning salt water—tons and tons of salt water.

He grabbed the ram handle on the canopy release, heard the seal disengage, and felt the rush of fresh air as the canopy lifted. At the same instant he was inundated by a wash of seawater. The survival sequence had been drilled into him, practiced hundreds, maybe a thousand times. He ripped off his helmet, released the seat harness, pulled himself up and out of the flight deck, and triggered the mechanism for the flotation device. Another wave of salt water pounded in on him, and for the first time he could see the extent of the damage. Schubatis's wet dream, crude and powerful, was deep-sixing. It was going under. It was only a question of how soon.

As the swirling sea poured into the cockpit of the Covert, Harry Driver, with one good arm, pulled the O ring trigger on the ASaR to release the raft. He gripped the crip handles on the wall of the cockpit, pushed up, cleared, and jumped. He lit in the water over the right wing and managed to flail his way to the raft just as he heard Milo Schubatis's scream for help. Driver caught himself thinking that it was a damned unfortunate time for the old bastard to regain consciousness. He dragged himself into the raft, lay there for what seemed like an eternity, and finally managed to pull himself into a sitting position to check his surroundings. To Driver's astonishment, he could see land. In the half-light of the storm-tossed water, he could see the faint outline of one of the two Anxi islands. He had come down less than a thousand yards from one of the rocky outcroppings.

With the rain still pelting down on him, he grabbed the raft's single oar, winced in pain, and began to row.

Flight Captain Feng brought the nose of his Flanker up and leveled off at 5,000 feet. The worst of the storm was behind him. He changed frequencies, fingered the transmit button, and prepared to repeat his transmission at the request of Danjia ops personnel in the tower.

Somewhere below him the Su-39 was awash

in six-foot swells, and in all probability, the man piloting it was either dead or dying. It was Feng's first combat mission, and in all probability, his first kill. He had achieved his objective by simply outflying the Russian—the Russian that Colonel Quan had brought in to teach them how to fly the strange-looking plane.

Feng had no way of knowing that the Russian, Borisov, had died long before the Covert ditched, or that in its final flight it had been piloted by an American. In fact, Chi Feng knew nothing of the details of the intricate drama in which he had played such a major role. He simply knew that his first real combat mission had been a success. There was a sense of elation—and a sense of sadness.

He pressed the switch and repeated his message. He gave the coordinates, the time, advised the tower of his location, and the confirmation "target acquired and destroyed."

# Chapter Twelve

Datum: Friday—0654L: October 10

Tang Ro Ji discarded the heavy wet blanket he had stolen from the old man's cart and dropped to his knees beside the road. The pain and the long night had taken their toll; he was near exhaustion.

With the first light of dawn, he had been able to find his way with less difficulty. Then the rain had slacked off to little more than a steady drizzle. But in the rice fields to the west, near the backwaters of the reservoir, a layer of thin, silver-gray fog had begun to form. At first it hugged the ground and only made the footing uncertain. Now the night-long cold rain and warm earth combined to paint a thick, concealing fog that made the job of the patrols even more difficult. But it was creeping up from the low land, filling in the swales and forming a bond with the low-hanging scud clouds—the aftermath of the storm.

For the last several minutes, his visibility had been restricted to no more than a hundred feet or so. Disoriented from the pain and confused by the fog, he had mistakenly traveled several hundred yards in the wrong direction—away from Hua's orphanage. When he discovered his error, he had to retrace his steps back to the hill overlooking the settlement. Even now he could not be certain. It would take what little strength he had left to descend the hill and reconnoiter the situation before entering the village.

Twice within the last hour Quan's patrols had passed within a few hundred feet of him as they scoured the countryside. Each time he had sought refuge in the tall grass that lined the road, and the patrol's probing and sweeping searchlights had passed over him.

He strained to see down in the shallow valley and held his head to one side, listening for any sound that might reveal his whereabouts. A wet hare came within a few feet of him, only to sense the danger and race away. In the distance, a dog barked a few times, but otherwise there was silence.

Tang waited for several more minutes before deciding he was ready. He ran his fingers over his blood-soaked arm and searched through his pockets until he could feel the reassuring bulk of the Barkai. He had not checked it since leaving the old man and his son, and he did not know how many shells he had left.

He had just struggled to one knee when he heard an approaching car. It was moving slowly over the muddy, rutted road, and he realized that the driver was probably having difficulty seeing as his headlights reached out only to be absorbed by the wall of fog. The car slowed and finally came to a stop no more than two hundred feet from where Tang Ro Ji was hiding.

He heard doors open and the sound of voices. One was that of a woman, the other a man's. Ro Ji inched forward in the grass and listened.

"Are you sure this is it?" the man asked.

"It has to be," the woman said. Her voice was confident.

"With all this fog, how can you tell?"

"Zebo should be just down that road a quarter of a mile or so. . . ."

Tang stood up, moved forward, and stopped when he could actually see the two figures standing beside the car.

"I have been here many times," the woman said. "See that old cemetery over there, and that rock road leading down the hill? This is it."

"If we go stumbling into one of Quan's outposts or one of his patrols, we'll have a lot of explaining to do," the man said. His voice was edgy and uncertain. "They may be the kind that shoot first and ask questions later."

The woman went back to get a flashlight from the car, walked several feet away, aimed the light down the hill, and repeated that she was sure they were in the right place.

A car was what Tang needed, but with his shattered arm he knew he couldn't drive. His fevered mind began formulating a plan. He could get rid of one of them and force the other to drive him to Haikou. In Haikou he knew a doctor who would ask no questions. Money did the talking in Haikou.

Still concealed by the fog, he fished out the Barkai, stepped out on the road, and approached the car. Shu Li saw him first, but Zhun Be was the one who recognized him. He blurted out Tang Ro Ji's name before he realized.

"Most unfortunate," Han Ki Po's assassin said ominously, "that you should recognize me. Such irony. Quan's troops have been searching for me throughout the night—and you are the ones who find me."

Shu Li's eyes were fixed on the Barkai. The man holding the small automatic was visibly weak and unsteady.

"The gods are with me, wouldn't you say?" Tang said softly. "I am in need of a car, and you have one."

"You can have the car," Shu Li said. "Just leave us alone."

Tang managed a crooked half-smile. "I'm afraid it isn't that simple. As you can see, I am somewhat incapacitated. Driving would be difficult . . ."

Shu Li looked at the bloodstained left arm hanging at Tang Ro Ji's side.

". . . I have lost a great deal of blood and . . ."

"Zebo is just down that hill," Shu Li said, pointing. "Father Hua can help you. He will know what to do."

Tang shook his head. "No, there are too many people down there. Have you not heard it said that one man cannot know the minds of many? While the good father is tending to my arm, others could go for help. If Hua was my only alternative, I would chance it. But your rather fortuitous arrival gives me a more desirable alternative. Instead, you will drive me to Haikou."

"You'll never make it that far," Shu Li said. "You've lost too much blood already."

"You underestimate me," Tang said. He had begun gesturing her back toward the Renault with the snub-nosed Barkai.

Shu Li looked at Zhun Be. "What about my friend?"

Tang was weary. "The Americans have a saying about being in the wrong place at the wrong time. I am afraid that is the situation your friend finds himself in. I cannot let him go, because he will inform Hua of what has happened. I cannot take him with us, because, under the circumstances, I cannot watch the both of you. He is, how do you say it, excess baggage . . . out of luck."

Zhun Be eyed the fog and wondered how far he would get if he started running. Tang was weak. Was he too weak, too unsteady to get off a good shot? It would be a calculated gamble.

Tang gestured Shu Li toward the car again and Zhun Be seized the opportunity. He bolted into the high grass and didn't look back. He heard Tang's shout and then a shot. There was a sudden, bone-jarring pain in his lower back and his legs went out from under him. He stumbled, pitched face first into a tangle of tall weeds, and rolled over, clutching his stomach. When he looked at his hands, they were covered with blood and there was a spreading red-black smear across the front of his tailored silk suit. Already his lungs had begun a frantic search for air. He began coughing up blood and a fire burned in his stomach—a pain unlike any he had ever experienced. He wanted to cry out. Instead, he rolled over on his back and stared up into the swirling fog. Any moment he expected Tang to stumble into the thicket after him. If he lay still enough, there was the slim hope that Han Ki Po's assassin would not find him. Zhun

Be held his breath and realized that he was praying.

An eternity passed before he heard the Renault engine sputter to life. There was the grinding of gears, and then the sounds of Shu Li's car splashing back down the road toward the old commune and Haikou.

Finally, when he thought it was safe, he tried to get up. He fell back and began coughing, choking on his own blood.

Datum: Friday—0731L, October 10

Quan frowned as the two Flanker pilots described their encounter with the Covert. At last he cut them off. "Did you establish visual contact?"

Both men shook their head.

"If there was no radar and no visual contact, how can you be certain?"

"Radar signature on such an aircraft is not possible," Feng reminded him. "However, both Lieutenant Chang and I were able to profile heat-sensor indications of the aircraft's engines."

Quan waited for his senior officer to continue.

"At the time of impact, our target was flying

at an altitude of less than two hundred feet."

"Why did you not fire your missiles?"

"It was not necessary," Feng said. "All heat-sensor significations terminated at 0651."

"Meaning?"

"The aircraft's flight had been abruptly terminated."

"And your position?"

"FLC 21.2 and 57.7, approximately fifty nautical miles due east of the Anxi atolls." Feng pointed to the charts. "The Covert's flight would have been terminated right here—just east of the first atoll."

Quan walked across the room to a map of the Gulf of Tonkin on the far wall of the ops center. He traced his finger from Danjia, across the tiny Anxi atolls, to the coast of Vietnam. He paid particular attention to the water depths around the atolls.

Feng cleared his throat. "Colonel Quan, sir, both Lieutenant Chang and I have wondered why the Russian would attempt such a flight."

Quan lit a cigarette and continued to study the map. Then he turned to his security officer. "Perhaps Lieutenant Yew would like to explain that. It seems our Danjia security is somewhat embarrassed by what has happened in the last few hours."

Yew looked at Quan before he began. His voice was strained. "Major Borisov was not flying the Covert aircraft. We discovered Major Borisov's body less than an hour ago."

Feng looked at Yew. "Then who was piloting—"

"Perhaps you should also ask Lieutenant Yew about our esteemed colleague Dr. Schubatis," Quan said.

"There has been a breach of security," Yew admitted. "One of the perimeter posts has been knocked out and Dr. Schubatis is missing."

"Missing? But how is that possible?" Feng asked.

Quan studied the faces of his young officers. "It is possible only because our security people have been derelict in their duty. We have determined that Major Borisov was murdered, thrown from his window to make it look like an accident. Within the last hour we learned that our perimeter had been violated at some point during the night. The security tower at E-7 was disabled and the fence cut. The security patrols discovered the intrusion. It is quite apparent that we have had visitors—unwelcome visitors—and it is equally apparent that they came to Danjia for the specific purpose of stealing the Su-39 and releasing Dr. Schubatis."

Feng looked around the room. "But it would take someone who was familiar with the aircraft to attempt such a flight."

"Precisely," Quan said.

"The Russians would have no reason," Chang speculated, "and if not the Russians, who?"

Quan was silent. Schubatis's escape and the theft of the Covert were indefensible; Han Xihui would be outraged. He turned back to the map. He was running out of time. His patrols had still not located Tang Ro Ji, and the young officer had indicated that General Han would soon be on his way to Danjia.

In the power struggle with Han Xihui, he had counted on his relationship with Isotov and possession of the Covert to influence the leaders of the Fifth Academy to rally behind him instead of the son of Han Ki Po. Now, because of Tang Ro Ji's blunder, he would have to find a way to assuage the General until he could regain his advantage. That meant he had to be able to turn over Tang and convince the other 5A leaders that the Covert had crashed during a test flight.

With heavy fog covering the entire island, Quan knew that Han's flight would have trouble getting off the ground at Huanglui. The fog would buy him time, but he still had to produce the body of Tang and convince Han that Tang was acting on his own.

Quan turned to his security officer. "Have the body of Major Borisov taken to the docks and have one of the patrol boats made ready. Inform the Captain we will be going to Anxi."

Yew saluted and left the room. When Feng and Chang looked at him, Quan smiled. "Does it not seem obvious that if Major Borisov was flying the Covert at the time it crashed—his body would be found at the crash site?"

Feng nodded.

"Then it is incumbent upon us to tend to the obvious."

Datum: Friday—0741L, October 10

Even though he had managed to tunnel his way under the perimeter fence through a drainage covert, Bogner had to work his way north and east in the general direction of Zebo by staying close to the fence. He knew it was sunrise, but the fog blotted out the sun and hung like a damp cloak around him. In the last thirty minutes it had seemed to grow thicker, limiting his visibility to no more than a few feet. As far as Bogner was concerned, the good news was that the rains had stopped and the winds had gone calm—and although he couldn't see Quan's patrols, he could hear them long before they got close to him.

To throw the patrols off, he had ditched the truck along one of the camp's side roads, headed it in the opposite direction, and lifted the hood to make it appear as though it had motor trouble.

For the last hour there had been increased patrol activity. It was obvious now that Quan's patrols knew the security systems weren't working and the tower at E-7 had been knocked out. As the fog had increased, the Komiskos had returned to base. In all, Bogner had counted five returning choppers. To the best of his knowledge, they had not gone out again. That was more good fortune; the fog had rendered that part of Quan's search effort useless. Bogner knew he had been places in the last hour where there would have been no place to hide from the Komiskos.

What he didn't know was whether or not they had located the man accused of assassinating Han Ki Po or why Driver had left him behind.

Bogner was still trying to put the pieces together, but there was every indication Driver had escaped. He hadn't heard the Covert take off, but Quan had scrambled his Flankers. Now they were back; Bogner had heard them return to base. None of it made sense.

Now it was a matter of survival, of avoiding Quan's patrols, and heading in the general direction of Zebo. He made his way through the undergrowth, keeping the fence in sight, always heading north.

He was approaching a small rise when he first

heard the voices. He stopped, crouched down, and listened. Then he saw it, a sweeping, a faint yellow glow in the fog, moving left to right. He waited, began to count, and saw it again. It repeated on the number seven. It was the searchlight on E-7. Quan's men had it operating again.

Bogner stayed low to the ground and worked his way to the top of the rise. Even in the dense fog he could make out the figures of three men. From the way they were dressed, two of them appeared to be villagers. The third was wearing a uniform and carrying a rifle. While the laborers shoveled dirt into the backfill against the base of the fence, the guard watched two men working on the light in the tower.

Bogner backed down the hill. The tower was the landmark he was looking for. Now he knew how far he had to go. Straight north and fifty yards or so beyond the security tower was the narrow footpath, all but concealed by rice grass, leading down to where they had seen the first of the Komiskos fly over earlier that night.

He backed down, circled around, and used the tower for reference until the voices of Quan's workers faded and the light was no longer visible. Then he worked his way back to the north again and found the trail. Bordered on both sides by terraced rice paddies, the trail would eventually lead him to the rutted road. At that point, he would be less than two miles from

Zebo. All that he needed now was for the fog to hold for another hour or so.

Datum: Friday—0832L, October 10

The raft undulated on the slow heave and swell of the waters lapping at the outcropping as Harry Driver opened his eyes to a half-world of uncertainty. It was a red sky, streaked with occasional slate-gray remnants of stratus clouds, diffused by the rays of the morning sun and dappled with patches of elevated fog. He was wet and chilled, and his body ached. His arm was no longer bleeding; the pain had subsided and the arm was numb. It took considerable effort to move it.

Shivering, he rolled over and peered over the edge of the raft. It had washed up against the rocks jutting out of the shallows of the atoll some two or three hundred feet from the shoreline.

The water, clear and briny, was no more than three or four feet deep, and the floor of the atoll was dotted with plant life and mollusks. The shoreline was laced with patches of shallow ground fog where the cold rains had collided with the warm earth, and although he could hear voices and see the tops of what he knew had to be stunted shiatzo trees, he could not be certain where he was. He knew it was one of the Anxi atolls, but which one? There were three in all, two of which were designated Anxi One and Anxi Two; the third did not have a number. All three were surrounded by a series of tiny, uninhabited, combination coral and rock satellites. Was he on one of the atolls or one of the satellites? At the moment there was no way to tell.

He rolled over and turned back to the east where he could still see the V stabilizer of the Covert jutting out of the water. It was difficult to judge the distance, but he estimated it to be several hundred yards.

From all appearances, he had crashed in water no more than thirty feet deep—deep enough to inundate the cockpit, but not deep enough to conceal the stabilizer. If Quan sent out his search planes or patrol boats, and Driver was sure he would, the black fuselage of the Covert would be highly visible against the crag-dotted shallows like some kind of sea monster.

The voices grew louder, and Driver turned his attention back to the shoreline. Gradually he realized they were the voices of children playing at the water's edge. Because of the patchy fog, they had obviously not spotted either his raft or the remains of the Covert.

While he waited, he rifled through the contents of the raft's survival kit. There were flares, a flare pistol, food rations, rain gear, some tools, including a shovel, a small battery-driven two-way radio along with a primitive hand-crank generator, and a booklet containing survival instructions. The instructions were printed in Russian. At the bottom of the pack was a 9mm Makarov. It was sealed in a watertight envelope along with a carton of cartridges. He slipped the Makarov inside the waistband of his flight suit, opened one of the cans of rations, and ran his finger through a brown paste that he supposed was intended to taste like a meat product. It was bland and unappetizing, but he was hungry, and in no time at all he had emptied the small tin.

Not long after that, the voices of the children faded, and Harry Driver slipped over the edge of the raft into water up to his thighs and waded to shore.

Onshore, Driver hid the raft in the rocks and worked his way inland. From the nearest rise, looking west he could see the north side of the horseshoe-shaped basin. The rocks ended abruptly in a drop-off. To the south, the landmass became a series of small rises dotted with boulders, tall grass, and small shiatzo trees. The water's edge traced its way inland, creating a series of tiny inlets before giving way to a cleared area with three ramshackle structures and a Quonset hut. Harry Driver was in luck; the raft had washed ashore on the Anxi atoll where Le Win Fo had indicated he flew the political refuges from Danjia. If this was the atoll where arrangements were made for the boats to pick up the refuges, he knew that eventually he would be able to find a way off the island.

He carefully hid the rest of his survival gear, slapped the clip into the Makarov, and headed for the cluster of buildings.

Datum: Friday—0913L, October 10

Shu Li had lost track of time. Tang had forced her to drive to the run-down Ghengdi section of Haikou. There, on the second level of tenements over a series of open-stalled market stands, he had prodded her down a darkened, narrow hallway to the cluttered back rooms of a doctor Tang referred to as "the Dutchman."

Hans Gosling was a dirty little man wearing a soiled linen suit. He had a broad piglike nose and a crooked smile, and despite the hour, he already smelled of whiskey. Gosling examined Tang's arm, rapped on the wall, and an old woman seemed to appear from nowhere. There was a brief exchange between the woman and Gosling before she took Shu Li by the arm and guided her into an adjacent room with only a bed and chair.

"Sit there," she ordered. Then she left and locked the door behind her.

Twice Shu Li heard Tang cry out in pain when Gosling set the shattered bone in his arm. Then there was a long period of silence. Finally the woman returned with a slender young man who would, she said, arrange for passports for Shu Li and her husband.

"He's not my husband," Shu Li protested.

The old woman paid no attention to her until Gosling came back into the room. "I trust my wife has made you comfortable during your wait," he said with a heavy Dutch accent. "The morphine will temporarily ease your husband's discomfort."

"Dammit," Shu Li said. "We're not married. Other than his name, I don't even know him. The man is holding me hostage."

Gosling ignored her, lit a cigarette, sat down, and turned his attention to the young man. "My client wishes for you to arrange tickets to Kowloon. He will need papers, a passport, and clearance documents for him and his wife." Then he looked at the clock. "An evening flight will be preferable. That will give me time to ensure there is no further bleeding."

The young man stood up, Gosling handed him an envelope, and he left. When the door closed, the Dutchman again turned his attention to Shu Li.

"And now, my child, something to help you relax . . ."

Shu Li looked at the old woman. She was holding a hypodermic needle.

"Without it," Gosling said, "it will be a long and difficult day."

Datum: Friday—0941L, October 10

Bogner continued sipping his tea while Le Win Fo, sitting across the table from him, updated him on the long night.

"Then, early this morning we received this communiqué from the American authorities . . ." He laid the piece of paper in front of Bogner. It was written in Chinese characters.

Bogner glanced at it and pushed it back across the table.

Le Win Fo understood. "Sorry," he said, "my young associate knows no English."

Bogner took another sip of tea. He was wearing dry clothes and the chill was fading.

"We received this at 0800 hours. It states quite clearly that we are to inform you that your associates have reason to suspect that your colleague, Colonel Driver, may be an agent for the Russian government."

Bogner shook his head. "If you had told me this yesterday, I wouldn't have believed you. He's a twenty-year man in the Air Force, not to mention the fact that he's been a test pilot on the F-117. He served with distinction in Vietnam and—"

Le Win Fo reached for his pipe. "We see only the veneer of a man. We do not know what is in his heart."

"It sure as hell would explain what happened last night," Bogner admitted. He watched Le light his pipe and waited for Hua's nephew to go on.

"Throughout the night we have monitored the transmissions from Danjia. At first there was atmospheric interference because of the storm. Much of our information about what happened during that first hour is fragmented. But we know that your friend Driver managed to take off about daybreak. Shortly after that, he was pursued by two of Colonel Quan's aircraft. What happened during that time is also obscure. However, we were able to monitor the transmissions between the returning aircraft and the Danjia tower."

Bogner leaned forward.

"One of Quan's pilots reported that the Russian plane crashed in the vicinity of one of the

Anxi Atolls. Which one, we do not know."

"Verified?" Bogner asked.

Le shook his head. "He reported that the Russian plane was flying very low because of the storm. He indicated he was within twenty-five nautical miles and trailing the aircraft when the heat and noise monitors shut down."

Bogner nodded. "It's possible. He could have had him on his E-system if he was flying right down his tailpipes. Otherwise his radar wouldn't have been picking him up."

"I must ask you," Le said, "what about the man, Schubatis?"

"We got him out, all right. The problem is, he was on board the Covert when Driver took off."

Le sighed. "What will you do now?"

"I wish to hell I knew. As far as I'm concerned, we don't know anything for certain. Quan's men aren't dead certain the Covert went down. Bottom line, we don't know if there still is a Covert, and we don't know whether Driver and Schubatis are alive."

"There is more," Le continued. "At approximately 0800 hours, Quan dispatched one of his gunboats to Anxi for verification of the pilot's report. If and when they report in, we will know."

Bogner stood up and walked to the room's only window. The sun was shining and the fog had completely dissipated. He turned back to

Le. "What did you tell me about Anxi? Isn't that where you said you fly political refuges and arrange to have them picked up by the Taiwanese government?"

Le Win Fo nodded. "It can be arranged only when there is a Nationalist freighter in the area."

"How do you do it?"

"We fly only at night."

"Then you can fly me there," Bogner concluded.

"It is very risky. The night skies are full of Komiskos and there will be Quan's gunboats. Until they find Han Ki Po's assassin, the patrol efforts will be doubled."

Bogner sat down again and poured himself another cup of tea. "Under the circumstances, I don't have a helluva lot of choice. I can't wrap this thing up until I know what happened to that plane and Schubatis."

Le Win Fo was distracted by a knock on the door. When he opened it he was confronted by two of the children from the orphanage.

"Father Le," the older one pleaded, "come quick. Little Yu claims he found a man's body."

"Where?" Le Win Fo asked.

"Hurry, Father, Yu says the man is still alive."

# Chapter Thirteen

Datum: Friday—1039L, October 10

From the wheelhouse of the Fange gunboat, Lieutenant Yew watched as Captain Shin slowed the craft to a near idle for the deployment of the trailing sonobuoys. One of Shin's men scurried topside near the radar, another took up position at the stern near the radar gear and winch, and a third scanned the area off the port side from the Fange's gun turret.

"You are certain this is the place?" Shin asked. He was a hollow-chested man with a hawk nose and sharp eyes. In the last two hours he had exhibited his mastery of several different dialects. So far, he had lived up to Quan's assessment that with seventeen years of service he was the most experienced of Danjia's patrol captains.

Yew unrolled the chart and pointed to the

spot where Feng indicated he had had the last indication of the Russian aircraft. "This is the area—if Captain Feng is correct, it should be somewhere just east of this atoll."

"The waters in this part of the Gulf are shallow," Shin confirmed, "but unless we have exact coordinates, it will be difficult to locate."

Yew rerolled his chart, climbed down from the wheelhouse, and worked his way toward the stern. Admittedly, he had no concept of the difficulty in locating something as small as the downed Covert in so large a body of water. If Captain Feng said it was offshore of one of the atolls, then that was where it should be. Instead Yew looked up at the clear blue Gulf of Tonkin sky and marveled that just a few hours after the fact there was no trace of the previous night's violent storm.

From where he stood on the stern, he could hear Shin order deployment of the trailing sonar and the confirmation by one of the crew that the task had been accomplished. In rapid succession he heard the man operating the apparatus read off a series of depth reports and relay them up to his captain.

In the distance Yew could see the horseshoe-shaped inlet of the atoll leading into what appeared to be little more than a rocky outcropping of boulders and a few sparse trees, with no sign of habitation. From the inland province of Hunan and the small village of Zunyi, Yew new nothing of the sea, only that Tonkin represented a very small part of it.

He walked forward again as Shin directed the Fange's helmsman to begin a crisscross pattern sweeping back and forth across the mouth of the inlet.

"These islands," Yew asked, "are inhabited?"

Shin continued to scan the horizon. He answered without looking away from the helm. "On occasion—but only by the Vietnamese. They have never been successful in their efforts to establish a permanent colony. The land is mostly rocks held together by a few grains of sand."

Yew scanned the atoll's interior with his binoculars. "I believe I see a structure of some sort."

Shin laughed. "You see what is left of the last settlement attempt—a few abandoned houses and a building that was used for stores during their war with the Americans thirty years ago. The atolls proved useless because of the shallow waters and the danger of the reefs."

Yew continued to scan the featureless landscape, intrigued by the emptiness and the land's lack of purpose. If the nature of their mission had not been so urgent, he would have urged Shin to allow them to explore the tiny island.

"I'm picking up something, Captain," the sonar man shouted.

Shin ordered the Fange to come about while the man verified his contact. At that point the Fange was heading due north. "There it is," the man reported, "in the shallows, 270.4 degrees—due west. I'm getting a steady reading."

"Distance?" Shin demanded.

"Two point four kilometers."

The Fange turned again to the west, sprinted a short distance, only to have Shin slow it to a near idle again. He instructed the young lieutenant to look in the water on the starboard side.

Yew peered down into the depths of the clear water and saw a series of what appeared to be metal canisters. They seemed to be floating, yet they were clearly connected by cables.

"As I suspected," Shin shouted. "Those, Lieutenant Yew, are percussion mines. The Americans laid them during the war to discourage the Vietnamese from enlarging their operations on these atolls."

Yew studied them and was about to express his disappointment when the spotter in the Fange's turret began gesturing, pointing off of the gunboat's port side. This time it was Shin who turned and scanned the area with his binoculars. To Yew's surprise, the man's craggy face betrayed a small smile. "I think we have located what you are looking for, Lieutenant."

Suddenly Yew could see it. Two vertical projections, no more than three or four feet above the surface—the twin black stabilizers of the Covert.

"Bring her around and launch the raft," Shin ordered.

Harry Driver lay in the tall sea grass at the water's edge and watched as the gunboat circled the area near the downed Covert. One thing the survival pack had not contained was a pair of binoculars. He could count five crew members in all. Three of the men were deploying a raft, and he wondered if they were coming ashore.

In the last few hours, Harry Driver had considered his options, playing out several different scenarios against a backdrop of "what if." The first, of course, had been what he would do if Quan's men came to search the island. Now that was a distinct possibility. Another had been how he would present himself if one of the Taiwanese freighters came to pick up refugees. A third had been to approach the children he had heard playing on the island earlier that morning. The last, however, proved not to be an option. A man had rowed ashore from a small fishing boat, called the children, and departed before Driver had worked out his plan. If it happened again, he vowed to be ready.

Driver checked the Makarov, inched forward, making certain the sea grass still concealed him, and watched the men in the raft struggle with a bulky sack of considerable size. They laid it in the bottom of the raft and began rowing toward the wreck of the Covert.

Win Yew was not prepared for what he saw when he looked down at the sunken Covert. The canopy was shattered and peeled back. Feng had instructed him as to what to look for. If the canopy was not missing entirely, then the pilot had not ejected.

In the cockpit, instead of the body of the pilot, Yew saw the Russian, Schubatis. The little man had a rag stuffed in his mouth and there was a curious look of terror on his face. His body was already slightly bloated, and discolored by what had no doubt been hemorrhaging. Even more disturbing was the fact that Schubatis's eyes were missing.

"The fish beat us here," one of the men commented.

While the third man in the raft donned scuba gear, Yew searched the waters around the Covert for the body of the pilot. A small school of yansi fish darted from under the broken left wing and a small lemon shark patroled just a few feet away.

The diver slipped into the water and began circling the craft. The water was so clear Yew believed he could reach out and touch him by merely putting his hand in the water. When he finally surfaced, the diver was shaking his head. "I find no trace of the other one," he reported.

Yew bent down and peered over the edge of the raft. "Could the body have washed ashore?"

The diver gestured, explaining how the tides and undercurrents worked in the basin of the atoll's inlet. "If the tide was strong enough to carry the body in this morning, the ebb tide would be equally strong—if the body did not get caught in the coral. The undercurrents in the claw of the inlet are three knots, perhaps stronger—in either case, sufficiently strong to take a man's body out to sea."

"Then the chances of finding the body are remote," Yew concluded.

A second diver joined the first and the search continued. It was Shin who finally called them off.

"You have found your Covert, Lieutenant Yew. What do you hope to prove by finding the pilot?"

"I had hoped to learn the identity of the man," Yew said.

"The sea knows the identity of the other man who died here—that is sufficient."

"You are right, Captain," Yew admitted. He

turned away and unzipped the body bag. Borisov was attired in his flight suit—complete to his flight boots and helmet. If the body of the Russian was eventually recovered, Quan was eager for it to appear that he was the one who had been piloting the ship at the time of the crash.

One of the divers pulled the raft into position over the Covert and Yew rolled the body overboard. The earthly remains of Arege Borisov undulated down in an eerie kind of death dance, caught briefly in the ebb and flow of the atoll's unseen currents. When he came to rest on the floor of the lagoon, with the acrylic mask of his flight helmet open, the Russian seemed to be staring up at Yew.

The gravity of the moment was lost on Shin. As soon as their grisly mission had been completed, he began barking out orders. The divers were brought in and the raft retrieved. The helmsman was given a heading of .090 and the Fange picked up speed.

Yew was, perhaps, the only one to reflect on what they had done. Down deep inside of him, in the pit of his stomach, perhaps in what his people called the "essence," he felt ashamed.

Datum: Friday—1059L, October 10

Colonel Quan stood at the window of his office waiting for the string of staff cars to roll through the security gate from the Danjia tarmac.

Han Xihui was the second son of Han Ki Po, the titular head of the Fifth Academy, and the man Quan knew he would someday have to overcome if he was to assume Han's place as head of the Academy. Quan was uncertain of his adversary's age, but estimated it to be mid-sixties.

Han was a portly man with a round, full face void of expression, excessive jowls, and an acknowledged penchant for cruelty. Quan had never seen the 5A general attired in any other fashion than in his full military uniform.

Han stepped from the black Mercedes, flanked by two of his staff officers. The second car disgorged three more members of his staff, all officers, all falling into step behind Han. Some of Han's retinue had been expected, but Quan was surprised at the size of this one in view of the death of the Chairman.

Quan moved behind his desk and waited. He knew Han well enough to know there would be little display of protocol. He expected Han to begin with an accusation.

The General conveyed arrogance as he entered the room. He ignored Quan's greeting and stepped up to the Colonel's desk. "You have located the assassin, Tang Ro Ji?"

"We have been searching since we first learned of this matter."

"You have not located him?" There was accusation in Han's question.

"We continue our search," Quan said flatly.

"I am told this man worked for you."

"I know him in the way that I know many men," Quan said. "No better than many and more than some. He is a man of few morals—at times a convenient man to know."

"And what about you, Colonel?"

Quan stiffened. "Is that an accusation, General? Are you accusing me of being part of a conspiracy?"

Han understood theater. This was theater handed down from dynasty to dynasty, from the intrigues of the Manchu rulers to the Kuomintang to the Chinese Communist Party, even to the Gang of Four. His own officers were dissidents within a dissident faction, many of whom had lived through the so-called rehabilitation of Deng Xiaoping—they had been witness to the ebbs and flows of power within the PRC. To accuse Quan of being the instigator of the assassination of his father and not be able to prove it was the action of a fool. His officers could, and would, switch their allegiance to Quan as easily as they could change their uniforms.

"It is not an accusation, Colonel. It is, however, well known that Han Ki Po's assassin, Tang Ro Ji, is a consort of yours."

"Tang Ro Ji is an animal," Quan replied, "a dangerous animal—an animal with ambitions of his own."

"Is not this Tang Ro Ji the same man who engineered the abduction of the Russian, Schubatis?"

"A scheme accomplished only with Han Ki Po's approval," Quan countered. "Arrangements were made between Chairman Han and the Russian, Isotov. Arrangements that as you well know were founded on like ideological beliefs."

Han continued to play his role cautiously. "Why has Tang been able to elude your efforts to find him?"

Quan knew that no excuse was acceptable. Nevertheless, he detailed the events of the long night—the storms, the crash of the Komisko, the theft of the Covert—weaving his way carefully through the events, making it sound more and more as though he was the one who had been betrayed.

"The Russian pilot," Han asked, "has defected?" There was incredulity in his voice.

Quan realized that his admission could be interpreted as dereliction. He hoped that Han would see it as one more intolerable distraction in the night-long search for Tang.

"How could this happen?" Han demanded.

"I suspect some sort of collusion between the Russians, Schubatis, and the pilot, Air Major Borisov," Quan said. "During his brief stay, Schubatis proved to be most uncooperative—and the pilot, Borisov, was not only slow, but actually hesitant to qualify our pilots to fly the Covert. I brought this to the attention of Chairman Han during his visit here yesterday."

"You have located this downed Russian aircraft?" Han pressed.

Quan seized the opportunity to demonstrate that he had regained control. "Within the past hour I have received verification that the downed aircraft has been located." Quan used his pencil to indicate the location of the Anxi atolls. "It is, according to Captain Shin, only partially submerged. His assessment is that a salvation operation is entirely feasible."

"What about the pilot and Schubatis?"

Quan was growing more confident by the minute. He was convinced that in the eyes of his fellow officers, Han's attempt to discredit him had been blunted. He did not answer the General directly. Instead he took time to tap out a cigarette. Han would recognize the gesture for what it was—posturing; a rebuke of both his position and authority—but he neither could nor would do nothing about it.

"Both bodies were located," Quan said.

"And recovered?"

Quan shook his head. "It would not be prudent, General Han, without the approval of the Vietnamese government. The Anxi Islands are a Vietnamese protectorate. However, if you wish me to make inquiries, I will contact—"

Han waved him off. He had been patient too long. He had allowed talk of the downed Russian aircraft to blur the charge that Quan was somehow involved with Tang Ro Ji in the plot to assassinate Chairman Han Ki Po.

"For the moment, the recovery of both the aircraft and its occupants is of secondary importance. For the time being, our efforts must be focused on the capture of Tang Ro Ji."

Quan inclined his head forward to acknowledge the senior officer's orders. But he, like the others in the room, knew Han had committed a major blunder. On the world stage, Han Ki Po was an obscure player. The Fifth Academy had not yet captured world attention except for a handful of terrorist acts. By most standards, the capture of Han Ki Po's assassin paled in comparison to the magnitude of the crash of the Covert.

Datum: Friday—1311L, October 10

It was early afternoon when Zhun Be first began to regain consciousness. He had lost a great deal of blood, and there was a period during which Le Win Fo had regarded his condition as critical. Soon after he was brought in, Le had sent for a young woman named Tia who had grown up in the orphanage and later studied to be a nurse. She had been able to stop the bleeding. Afterward, she explained to Le that one of the bullets had ruptured Zhun Be's spleen and damaged his left kidney. A second bullet had caused minor bleeding in his stomach.

"Wh-where . . . where am I?" Zhun muttered.

Le sat close and bent over to comfort him. "You are in Zebo."

"Ze . . . Zebo?" Still disoriented, he tried to look around the room. His eyes stopped when he came to Tia.

Win Fo smiled. "Not only is she pretty, Zhun, but I'd go so far as to say you owe her your life. Tia was the one who was able to get your bleeding stopped."

When Zhun saw Bogner he managed to get out the words "Cormea" and "Jade". Then he closed his eyes again.

For the next thirty minutes or so, Zhun Be drifted in and out of consciousness. Occasionally he would utter one word, depositing seemingly incoherent clues as to what had happened. Despite the obvious disorientation, Le was beginning to put the pieces together. Finally Le asked him, "Who shot you?"

Zhun Be closed his eyes and pursed his lips. It was a form of denial.

"Who shot you?" Le repeated. "We can't help you unless we know who shot you."

Zhun Be raised his head and tried to look around the room again. "You . . . you won't . . . won't tell anyone?"

Le Win Fo shook his head.

"He'll . . . he'll come . . . come after me. He . . . he said he would."

"It will be our secret," Le assured him. "Now, tell us who shot you?"

"Tang . . . Tang Ro Ji."

"Tang? Are you certain?"

Zhun Be closed his eyes and wetted his lips. "Yes."

"Where?"

Zhun opened his eyes and tried to focus on the face of Le Win Fo. "We . . . we were . . . almost to Zebo."

"We?"

"Shu Li Wan . . . me and Shu Li Wan. She was driving."

"Shu Li Wan was with you? Where is she now?"

Zhun Be looked confused.

"Damnit, Zhun, where is Shu Li?" Bogner demanded.

"She . . . she went with . . . Tang."

"Where?"

"To . . . to Haikou. Tang is hurt . . . needs a doctor . . ."

Bogner took Le by the arm and steered him out of the room. "Do you think Zhun Be knows what he's saying?"

"There's no reason to doubt him," Le said.

"You've been monitoring the Danjia radio. Is Quan still looking for Tang Ro Ji?"

"Less than an hour ago he ordered the Komiskos up again. He has ordered them to focus their search on the northwest quadrant of the island."

"What about Haikou?"

"Our friend Colonel Quan is far too arrogant. By now he's convinced himself that Tang won't be able to get past his roadblocks."

Bogner hesitated. "I've got an idea. Suppose we give Quan a little help."

"How and why?" Le Win Fo asked.

"What do you think Quan would do if he got a tip that someone had seen Tang Ro Ji in Haikou?"

Le began to smile. "That would be like looking for the proverbial needle in the haystack. We're talking about a couple of million people in the Haikou area. But one thing for sure, it would keep Quan occupied."

"Exactly what I was counting on," Bogner said with a grin. "It might make looking for that downed Covert tonight a little less risky for us."

Datum: Friday—1531L, October 10

By midafternoon, Harry Driver had surveyed most of the tiny island. To the east was the mouth of the atoll, shaped like a crab's claw. South and west the waters were shallow, as evidenced by the fact that the gulls were working the coral outcroppings just below the surface.

The north, Harry decided, was where the Taiwanese freighters could drop anchor closest to the atoll. There was a narrow strip of beach, no more than two or three hundred yards long, and even more revealing, evidence of footprints leading down to the sand from the small cluster of buildings.

It was apparent that Le Win Fo wasn't the only one who flew in to Anxi. In addition to the area where the helicopters landed, there was a pitted, and for the most part overgrown, place for a 1,300-foot runway—big enough to accommodate any number of small fixed-wing aircraft.

The old Quonset hut was no more than thirty feet long and eighteen feet across. Breaking in had been easy. It was empty except for five fifty-five-gallon drums of aviation fuel, some oil, a few empty crates, and an old rubber life raft similar to the one Driver had launched from the Covert.

The other three structures, all made of wood, had obviously been built with the intention of housing one or more families—shelter for the refuges waiting for pickup. Even by Chinese and Vietnamese standards, the shelters contained only minimum amenities.

In addition to having a roof over his head, Driver had also determined that if he was going to be there any length of time, his food supply was wholly inadequate. He had the provisions from the raft—namely, a few tins of something with labels printed in Russian and some tinned biscuits. But he knew it wasn't enough to sustain him more than a couple of days. Apparently the designers of the Covert hadn't conjured up a scenario where the plane went down very far from the proximity of immediate help.

With the exception of his wound, Driver was in good condition. He had probed the area where the bullet had entered his arm and the area where it had exited. The wound was clean, and the bleeding had stopped. The small first-aid kit in the raft had helped, but the gauze and tape were only partially adequate. There was enough to dress the wound a second time. After that he would be on his own.

On the plus side of the ledger, he had an island and a gun. If food got scarce, he could always jury-rig a fishing setup or shoot a gull. Bottom line: If Quan's gunboats came back, he would be ready. If one of those Taiwanese freighters came by, he would be equally ready with the Covert's flare gun.

He walked down to the water's edge and stared out at what was left of the Covert. Like the dorsal fins of two giant sharks, the vertical stabilizers were still visible.

Then, almost as an afterthought, he wondered what the two men on the Chinese gunboat had thrown in the water.

Datum: Friday—1645L, October 10

Chung Sho Hun had been prefect of police in the Ghengdi section of Haikou for seven years. A former member of the Central Commission for Disciplinary Inspection, he had been judged an infirm leader by the Special Party Conference, removed from office, and, because of his loyalty to the Party, assigned a token position as prefect.

Now, because of his inability to lower the crime rate and improve conditions in the infamous Ghengdi strip, Chung's once-bright future in the Party looked hopeless. He watched conditions in the overcrowded streets deteriorate with a steady influx of refugees and an increasing crime rate. A weary Chung Sho Hun had long since determined that there was little he could do about the problem.

But now he had information, information that could alter the course of his future. The call had come less than thirty minutes earlier. Tang Ro Ji, the caller had informed him, had somehow evaded Quan's dragnet and had made it to Haikou. Not only that, but to make it easier to find him, the caller had confirmed that Tang was in desperate need of medical aid.

Now Chung considered his options. He reasoned that Tang's plight limited the places he could go for help. None of the people's hospitals were located in Ghengdi, and if Tang sought help in any of the major medical centers, he would be recognized. The news of Han Ki Po's assassination and the search for Tang had been blaring over state radio since dawn, and his likeness was being broadcast on state-owned television every hour.

If Chung conducted his own search for Tang and was fortunate enough to locate him, the Party would be grateful. But if Tang escaped and it was later learned that Chung knew he was in Haikou and had not attempted to work with other prefect leaders, he would again be castigated by the Party. That fear motivated him to inform Quan. The call to Danjia was now being routed through to Quan.

"Yes." Quan's voice was brittle and impatient.

"Prefect Chung Sho Hun of Ghengdi-Haikou," Chung informed him. He did not wait for acknowledgment. "Less than thirty minutes ago we received an anonymous telephone call informing us that Tang Ro Ji was in Haikou—"

"Where?" Quan blurted.

"The caller would not reveal Tang's exact whereabouts. She simply indicated Tang was brought to Haikou to receive medical assistance."

"The caller's name?" Quan demanded.

"She refused to give it," Chung said.

On the other end of the line, Chung could hear Quan informing others. Then he was back. "We are responding," Quan said. "We will begin by cordoning off roads, closing the docks and the airport. Then we will begin a house-to-house search."

Chung prepared to offer assistance, but Quan had already hung up. It was then that he realized that he had again been rebuked by his superiors in the Party.

# Chapter Fourteen

Datum: Friday—2040L, October 10

A heavy cloud deck had moved in by the time Le Win Fo circled back for his second pass over the atoll. The Defender, an early model, was not equipped with some of the niceties Bogner would have preferred for a night mission. It did have an MMS, mast-mounted sight, for hull-down surveillance, IR suppression, and the standard navy package of haul-down ship gear and towed MAD, but the pop-out flotation bag capability had either been removed or never replaced. They would have to land on the atoll and row a raft to the crash site. In addition, there was no FLIR, no night-vision package, and no passive radar warning. The South Koreans had passed off a stripped-down version on Hua. As a result, there were times when Le Win Fo was all but flying blind.

"See anything?" Le asked.

Bogner peered down into the darkness. "We're over the atoll—but I don't see anything. Think it's down there?"

Le shook his head. "You heard the same reports I did."

"Picking up anything on the radio?"

Le nosed the Defender down until he had an altimeter reading of 200 MSL and activated the scanner. "Nothing," he said. "Haven't heard anything for the last thirty minutes—and that was one of the Komiskos working the mouth of the reservoir."

"What about surface transmissions?"

"Negative," Le assured him. "If one of Quan's gunboats was down there we'd be getting all kinds of chatter. It would seem"—he grinned—"that our little ploy worked. Ti Minn's call to that prefect in Haikou must have paid off."

"We're over water again," Bogner said, "shallows—looks like there's a strip of land just ahead."

Le checked the OR compass and glanced at the altimeter again. "We're on it."

Bogner activated the search beam and paraded the light back and forth across the beach. Then he dropped the MAD. Le brought the Defender around, circled back, and dropped to within thirty feet of the water.

"Down and in and trailing," Bogner confirmed. "Are you sure this thing works?"

"Don't know. Never used it before. The only thing I ever look for when I come out here is that chunk of rocks they call an atoll."

Bogner waved him off. "I'm getting something at 037—steady—steady—steady. There it is again."

Le Win Fo checked the OR. "Distance?"

"Three hundred yards."

"I'll take us out and over. Throw the light down there. See if you can pick anything up."

The Defender came around for the third time and Bogner saw it. "Bingo. I've got it. We're locked in."

"It should be there. When we picked up that gunboat's transmission earlier in the day, the captain was indicating it was in the mouth of the inlet in twenty to thirty feet of water. I'll put us down, we'll inflate the raft, and you can go have a look at it."

Harry Driver worked his way through the bunchgrass and rocks until he was no more than three hundred feet from the clearing. If the circling helicopter was one of Quan's Komiskos that had run low on fuel and was coming in for refueling, he would have to decide on his next move when he saw how many men were on board. If it wasn't—or if by chance it was a Vietnamese patrol—there was a good chance he had found a way out; a two-man crew he could handle.

He waited while the chopper swung out over the inlet to the atoll and danced its lights over the downed Covert. When it circled back a third time and came in at a lower altitude, he loaded the flare gun just in case it started to go away. Either way, he was ready.

The tiny Defender slipped in over the craggy shore of the island and Le put it down less than thirty feet from the water.

Bogner opened the access door and jumped out. Even before Le had brought the Allison engine to a waffling idle, he had jerked the RAM door open, grabbed the ReC gear, and begun inflating the raft.

Le opened the scanner switch for monitor, then jumped down out of the Defender. "The meter's running. You've got fifteen minutes at the most. Any longer than that and we're pressing our luck. No telling what's out there that we haven't picked up."

Bogner pushed the raft into the water, threw in the mask and scuba gear, and began rowing toward the Covert. By the time he reached it, he had stripped off his shirt and shoes and was donning the tanks. Thirty feet from the Covert, he dropped the small five-pound anchor and slipped overboard.

In the darkness he swam to the Covert, groped his way forward from the DLIR sensors along the top of the fuselage, and grabbed hold of the windscreen. At that point he estimated he was working approximately four feet below the surface. He turned on his halogen and worked the beam up and over the rim of the cockpit.

For Bogner, it was a scene straight out of a grade-B horror movie. Milo Schubatis's body had worked out of the area behind the commander's seat and was floating faceup in the cockpit. The gag was still in the little man's mouth, but the eyes were empty sockets and most of the fleshy part of the mouth had been eaten away. Bogner recoiled and swallowed hard. Colchin would have a hard time selling Aprihinen on the fact that his people had done a good job of taking care of his prized aircraft builder.

He spent the next few minutes looking for Driver's body. Either he had ejected or his body had been washed away by the tide. Finally, he swam back to the cockpit and looked for the flight recorder. There was evidence pointing to the possibility that there had been a flash electrical fire in the cockpit. The recorder housing was shattered and the B panel was lodged against it. It would take a Herculean effort to pry it out, and Bogner knew he was running short of time.

From the cockpit, he worked his way around the rest of the downed airplane, past the twin stabilizers, and around to the wing area, surveying the damage. All the while he was trying to make mental notes about the Covert's equipment.

Finally he came to the nose of the craft. The grid was smashed and the inlets had been ripped open. All things considered, Quan's prize had sustained no more than minimal damage. If Quan wanted to take the time and make the effort, it could be salvaged. That being the case, Bogner decided to go ahead with the second part of the plan. He swam back to the raft and slipped the small package of explosives out of the paraffin jacket, attached the primer and the timer, swam back to the Covert, and stuffed the charge in the suck-in doors on the fuselage above the inlet ducts. Then he set the timer.

Bogner had already started back to the raft when he saw the second body. The ebb and flow of the currents in the inlet had worked the body under the nose of the plane and wedged it into the rocks. There was no way of knowing what had motivated Driver, but Bogner had what they had come for: confirmation that both Schubatis and Driver had died in the crash. And in a few minutes, he would be able to assure the brass back in Washington that there was no way Quan could salvage the Covert.

He returned to the raft, crawled in, shed his scuba gear, and began rowing toward shore. He had burned twelve of his allotted fifteen minutes. If one of Quan's Komiskos or gunboats was in the area, Le had not given him the signal.

He pulled the raft up on the beach, ditched the scuba gear, ran across the clearing to the chopper, and opened the door.

Driver's foot caught him in the face. Bogner reeled backward and saw the figure leap from the plane. "I gotta hand it to you, swabbie. You got more goddamn lives than a cat," Driver snarled as he buried his shoulder into Bogner's midsection. Driver grabbed his head, jerked it forward and brought both knees up, and flipped Driver up and over his head. He heard him land on his back, roll over, and scramble to his feet.

Suddenly the effect of Driver's first blow took hold and Bogner's world went all fuzzy with pain.

Driver, shorter and heavier, and fighting with one arm, landed two more blows before Bogner managed to get his arm up to fend off the third. There was a burning behind his eyes and no way to breathe. He gasped for air and caught another blow in the pit of his stomach. When he managed to get his eyes open, Driver was standing over him with the flare gun pointed at him.

For Bogner it was a bewildering world of pieces and fragments. Driver was dead. He had seen him—out there at the Covert—floating facedown. Intermingled with the pain and jumble of sensations was an equation that defied logic.

"How'd you make it out of that hangar, swabbie. I left your sorry ass in that—" Driver's labored breathing caught up with him. The words broke off.

Bogner, still flat on his back, tried to push himself up on his elbows. He head was spinning and there was the feeling of drowning—of not being able to breathe, of looking up through a cloudy, undefined kind of liquid world. He tried to clear his head, but couldn't.

"I almost made it," Driver declared. "I almost got away with it."

"Why?" Bogner finally managed to spit out. It came out broken and funny sounding, but Driver understood him.

"You still don't get it, do you, swabbie?" Driver caught his breath and weighed his words. "While you were risking your life for fuckin' peanuts, I found a way to make a decent livin'. Those damn Russians poor-mouth it, but they had enough money to make me comfortable. All I had to do was slip them an occasional drawing and tell them what I was learnin' about that damned F-117."

Driver bent over with the muzzle of the flare gun six inches from Bogner's face. The hammer was cocked and his finger was coiled around the trigger. "I almost made it in that damn plane of theirs. If it hadn't been for Quan's goons runnin' my ass down, I'd have made it to Haiphong, turned over that weasel, Schubatis, and been a fuckin' hero—not to mention a whole lot richer."

Bogner shifted in the sand, and Driver pressed the barrel of the flare gun against his forehead.

"You got any idea what a gun like this does to a man, swabbie? Let me tell ya, it blows shit all over the place. I know, I seen it. Them fuckin' Vietnamese guards came into the POW compound one night and did it to my copilot. They beat the shit out of him and then they stuck a flare gun in his mouth. Did you ever see a man's head explode, swabbie? After six months of torture and some of the goddamndest things a man ever had to endure, I caved, swabbie—I sold out. I knew they was just lookin' for an excuse to give me one of their head jobs—they woulda done it to me, too, but I was smart enough to cut a deal. When they found out I had been a test pilot on those damned F-16s, I took on a whole lot of importance—they started treatin' me with some dignity. Hey, better that than gettin' my damn head blown off."

Driver paused to catch his breath before he continued.

"But you know when the deal really got sweet? It got really sweet when I was assigned to Tonopah and the *Have Blue* tests. That's when the Russians moved in."

Bogner tried to move, and Driver pressed harder.

"Now you know all this shit—it's too bad you ain't gonna live to tell about it. That's okay, it'll be our little secret what happened out here. . . ."

Bogner closed his eyes and the explosion rocked the island. The Covert was ripped apart in a rain of shrapnel. Driver looked away, and that was all Bogner needed. His leg came up, catching Driver in the crotch. The man's scream was lost in the roar of diffused air, and Bogner followed with his best one-two punch. Both of them were on target. Driver dropped the flare gun, staggered backward, regained his footing, and raced for the Quonset hut.

The rest of it was impulse. Bogner picked up Driver's gun, dropped to his knees, took aim, and fired. The flare and Driver arrived at the Quonset hut at the same time. The second explosion on Anxi One that night was almost as big as the first. The building erupted in a ball of flame when the fire got to the aviation fuel stored in the fifty-five-gallon drums.

Bogner did not hear a scream. He heard the

indescribable sounds of a building being consumed by fire, and for a few terrible moments it seemed as if the entire atoll was ablaze. The wooden huts went up quickly and the sky for a few reverential seconds turned a nightmarish red.

Bogner dropped the gun and waited for the nausea to pass. Only then did he begin to pick up the pieces. He got to his feet and staggered to the Defender. He found Le unconscious, slumped over the controls. Zebo's pseudo-priest sported a large swelling on his left temple, and a nasty gash that traced down from his ear where Driver had hit him with the barrel of the flare gun.

Like Bogner's, Le Win Fo's return from the world of darkness to awareness did not come easily. Twice he started to come out of it—and twice he slipped back. In a world dimly lighted now only by the array of instruments on the Defender's controls, the only sounds were those of the whirling main rotor and the occasional static crack picked up by the scanner.

Bogner lifted Le Win Fo out of his seat and strapped him into the observer's chair.

The voice transmission from a distant Komisko filtered through. "Shin Seven, this is Shin Two. We have a PiRep logged at 2100 hours. Pilot reports a bright flash of light in quadrant elevenB. Advise."

"This is Danjia control, Shin Seven. Better check it out. Anxi One and Two are in that quadrant. Verify fuel situation."

"Will verify," Shin 2 confirmed. "Fuel adequate."

"They're out there and they're heading this way," Bogner said. "We better get out of here."

"Think you can fly this thing?" Le muttered.

Bogner's blood-smeared face somehow managed a grin. "Now seems like a damn good time to learn."

Datum: Friday—2109L, October 10

Tang Ro Ji clawed his way out of his sedative-induced stupor to discover a stage on which he had become the principal player. He pushed himself into a sitting position on the examining table, winced with pain, and propped his back against the wall.

The Dutchman studied him for a moment, walked across the tiny room, and turned up the volume on the small radio. "It is most fortunate that you are awake. You should be aware that . . ."

Ro Ji could hear it. He recognized the tone and the manner of the newscaster as much as anything. The State Radio had a flat, unemotional way of reporting the news. It droned the carefully worded statements like a dung fly.

*". . . Haikou authorities continue their search for the man accused of assassinating beloved People's Party Chairman Han Ki Po.*

*"Tang Ro Ji, a nationalist, five feet eight inches tall, weighing 145 pounds, dark hair and eyes, is reported to be somewhere in the greater Haikou area.*

*"Tang, thirty-two, is reported to have been wounded by Han's guards last evening during the assault on Chairman Han and is believed to be in need of medical attention.*

*"As of four o'clock this afternoon, all roads in and out of Haikou were closed. Officials have closed the Haikou People's Airport and ordered the port authority to close the docks. A house-to-house search is being conducted by Haikou police.*

*"Once again, anyone having any information pertaining to the whereabouts of Tang Ro Ji is instructed to contact police or military officials."*

Tang shifted his weight, lit a cigarette, and looked at the Dutchman. "How do they know I am in Haikou, old man? Did you inform them?"

Gosling laughed. He was not easily intimidated. During the course of his sixty-seven years he had known more than one man like Tang. "I am curious," he said. "Are you the one?"

Tang refused to answer. He slipped down from the examining table, reached for his shirt, and started to put it on. The bulky splint made him clumsy. "Did you get the papers and the passports?"

Gosling nodded. "I have them. But under the circumstances they are no good to you. Your likeness is being continually broadcast by state television. . . ."

"Haikou police are fools. They will never find me."

Gosling pulled back the curtain and pointed to the street below. "Tell me, Tang Tang, does that look like the efforts of fools? Already they have centered their search in the Ghengdi."

Tang went to the window and looked out. Two of Quan's men, in uniform, stood on the opposite side of the street. Another was checking the papers of a shopkeeper. All were carrying firearms. Usually they carried only riot batons.

"How do I get out of here?" Tang demanded.

"There is still the matter of money," Gosling reminded him. "Money for, how shall I say it, 'services rendered'?"

Ro Ji reached for his coat and looked through the pockets for the Barkai.

"I took the liberty of removing your gun while

you were under sedation. You see, I have experience in matters of this nature."

Tang wheeled and caught the Dutchman with the back of his hand. Gosling staggered backward and Tang pinned him against the wall. "I don't have time for games, old man. You'll get your money—but right now you're going to tell me if there is another way out of here."

Gosling hesitated, and Tang shoved his arm up against the man's throat. "Now, how do I get out of here?"

"There . . . there is a door . . ." Gosling was gasping for air. ". . . at the end of the hall, one floor up. It is sheltered, concealed from the street."

"Where to then?"

Gosling's face was turning blue. "Go—go—go to number six, at the far end of the building. Ask for—for Rami—a black man—he'll . . ."

"How do I know I can trust you?"

With his free hand, Gosling reached inside his coat pocket and produced an envelope. When he handed it to Tang, he pushed the killer's one good hand away. Then he took a deep breath. "The simple truth, my friend, is that you don't know—either you do or don't—but then again, you don't have a lot of options, do you?"

"Now," Tang said, stuffing the envelope in his pocket, "what about the woman? Where is she?"

"She is in the next room. But I would advise

you to leave her. She will only slow you down."

Tang shoved Gosling to one side, stepped out into the dingy hallway, and opened the door to the room where Shu Li was being detained. The old woman stood up, and he pushed her back on the bed. Then he pointed at Shu Li. "Get her on her feet. We're getting out of here."

The old woman prodded the still-groggy Shu Li until she opened her eyes. Tang grabbed her hand, pulled to her feet, and shoved her toward the door.

Datum: Saturday—0037L, October 11

Bogner towered over the old priest and took his hand. "I am grateful to you and your nephew, Father," he said. "I'm afraid I got a little careless with some the equipment from your chopper out there. I'll see that it's replaced."

Hua bowed. "I am afraid that the passing of years has made it difficult to be of much service to our friends in America." His voice was barely audible.

Le Win Fo took his uncle by the arm and escorted him to his chair. Then he turned back to Bogner. "As they say in your country, what now?"

"I've got to get back to Haikou. There's a

bunch of people in Washington that by now are wondering if I've fallen off the ends of the earth. They sent me over to retrieve Schubatis and do what I could to get that Su-39 out of here. They won't be too happy when they learn I botched the assignment on both counts."

"Getting you back into Haikou will be difficult," Le reminded him. "You do not know Colonel Quan like I do. The man is the very personification of tenacity. He will maintain the roadblocks and keep Haikou captive until he finds this man Tang Ro Ji."

"Zhun indicated they got here by some back roads through an old commune. If they made it, why not me?"

Le Win Fo laughed. "I see you do not yet pay Quan his due homage. By now, Colonel Quan has seen to it that such oversights have been corrected."

"If I made it out of Danjia, I ought to be able to negotiate a couple of roadblocks."

Le frowned. "When I was first informed of you, I was told that you were a representative of a firm known as Jade, a Canadian arms dealer. Is that not true?"

"I'm not sure we fooled anyone."

"You still have your credentials?"

Bogner nodded. "Calling cards, identification, passports, papers, the whole nine yards. I've even got an inventory."

Hua's nephew smiled. He glanced across the room at the aging priest. "With Father's blessing, I might have a plan."

Bogner waited while Le consulted with the old man. Then he said to Bogner, "There is an element of risk in what I propose. You should know that we might be playing right into their hands."

"Let's hear it," Bogner pressed.

"How good of an actor are you, Captain Bogner?"

Bogner laughed. "Depends on the role. Like I said, let's hear it."

"How would you be at playing the role of a man at death's door?"

"With a busted nose and a mouth full of loose teeth, I feel like I already am."

"Very well, you will be a man who was in an automobile accident."

Bogner tried to grin, but the effort failed. "Grab a fistful of bandages and let's get going."

It was Le's turn to smile. "We will leave, Captain Bogner, when I am sufficiently convinced that you are hurt enough to merit being transported to a medical center in Haikou." Le turned away, then back again. "One more question, Captain. Is any part of your sense of urgency caused by your concern for the woman, Shu Li?"

Bogner hesitated. "It is," he admitted. "I know what Tang Ro Ji is capable of."

Datum: Saturday—0117L, October 11

"And you say the Dutchman sent you?" Rami asked. He stood in the shadows and became part of the room's darkness.

Tang sat at the small table in the middle of the room. He kept one eye on Shu Li and the other on the black man. Rami made him nervous. He was twice the size of Tang and carried a chromed automatic tucked in the belt of his pants. He wore an undershirt and was barefooted. He was playing classical music on a small transistor radio.

"Before we go too far, let's see the color of your money. Rami don't do shit for nobody until he sees the money."

Tang shook his head. "No money. But I've got something just as good."

"Ain't nothin' as good as money." Rami glowered. "I take it two ways: Singapore dollars or good old American greenbacks. No money—no deal."

Tang reached into his pocket, and Rami stiffened. "How about two passports and two sets of papers? You know what they're worth on the street."

Rami put his foot up on the room's only other chair. "You got any idea why I'm here?" he growled. "It sure as hell ain't because Haikou is my idea of paradise. It's because some white boy back in my Army days tried to sell me some bogus dream dust. That weed wasn't worth shit. It was talcum and cornstarch. Know what I did? I hunted that little fucker down and I cut him six ways from Sunday, long and deep. Shit, he probably ain't quit bleedin' yet."

Tang didn't flinch. "These papers are good. Gosling arranged for them. They're the best money can buy."

Rami started to laugh. "Now, what would I want with some bogus papers?"

Tang opened the envelope, unfolded the papers, and laid them on the table. "This could be your ticket out of Haikou."

# Chapter Fifteen

Datum: Saturday—0333L, October 11

At three-thirty in the morning, Le Win Fo had anticipated little in the way of traffic at the roadblock. His people tended to stay off the road when the military was active. He had guessed right; there were only two cars ahead of him at the Shinpo crossing—and three guards to conduct the searches. One of the guards had a clipboard and was asking questions; another poked his flashlight into the cars' interiors. The third appeared to have no particular responsibility; he stood beside the squad's PC and smoked a cigarette.

Le could read the fatigue on their faces. They were tired and disgruntled. It had been a long night, and so far, an unrewarding search for Han Ki Po's killer.

Le was driving the orphanage's ancient Volkswagen Microbus. Bogner was lying down, stretched out in the cargo area, covered by an old blanket. Bandages had been applied to his face.

"Get ready," Le Win Fo whispered. "We're next. Look like you're in a lot of pain, but don't overdo it."

Le rolled down the window.

"Name and papers," the guard said. He peered in while the second man danced the beam of his flashlight around the Microbus's interior.

Le Win Fo was again wearing the garb of a priest. He fumbled in the glove compartment for the documents. "I am Father Le Win Fo," he announced, "from Zebo, Father Hua's orphanage. I am taking this gentleman to the Guizhou Medical Center. He has been in an accident."

The beam of light fixed on Bogner, and the guard with the clipboard studied him.

"You have his papers?" the guard asked, gesturing at Bogner.

"His name is Cormea," Win Fo said. "You'll find his papers in the envelope. I believe you will also find they are in order."

"Your passenger is badly hurt?"

"We believe it is a broken nose and some broken ribs," Le said. "And he has been complaining of severe abdominal pain."

The beam of light shifted from Bogner to Le.

"How do you know this man?" the guard asked.

Win Fo braced himself. He was about to play his trump card. "Monsieur Cormea is with Jade Limited. He is in Haikou to do business with your superiors."

The guard, a corporal, still wasn't satisfied. "Identify this man you call my superior." There was arrogance both in his voice and the way he asked the question.

Bogner clutched at his stomach and moaned.

"I refer to Lieutenant Yew," Le Win Fo replied.

"And why would you be involved with Lieutenant Yew in these matters?"

"Because I agreed to act as Monsieur Cormea's interpreter. He is not fluent in Chinese."

To Le it was obvious the corporal was weighing his response. He turned to the guard with the flashlight and there was a brief exchange before he looked back at Le again. He opened the envelope and glanced at Bogner's papers. Le knew that the man couldn't read English, but the corporal was playing out his power game for the benefit of his fellow guards.

"Step out," the corporal said, "you are being detained."

Le shook his head. "This is most unfortunate. You realize, of course, that if this man has internal bleeding he could die."

For the first time, the guard hesitated.

"It is quite obvious," Le said, "that Monsieur Cormea is not the man you are seeking. We were led to believe that the man you are seeking is Chinese."

"How do we know your friend is not an accomplice?"

"Contact Lieutenant Yew," Le challenged. "Tell him you are detaining Monsieur Cormea and Father Le Win Fo. . . ."

The corporal hesitated. Then he stepped back and motioned for the Microbus to proceed.

Bogner felt the Microbus accelerate away from the roadblock and waited until Le gave him the all clear.

"We managed to clear that one, Captain Bogner, but that may not be the last one. I would advise you to maintain your vigil and be prepared to play your role again. Either that, my friend, or be prepared to pray for our safety."

Datum: Saturday—0410L, October 11

Tang heard the door open and a silver of light filtered in from the hall. Rami's footsteps were heavy as he approached the bed where Tang had been sleeping.

"Time to wake up," he growled.

Tang tested his arm. For a while it had

throbbed too much for him to go to sleep. Now it was numb in places, and where there was any feeling at all, it was a burning sensation. He sat on the edge of the bed trying to clear his head. From where he sat, he could see Shu Li, still asleep on a straw mat on the floor across the room. He had dreamed of what he would do with her had he not been encumbered by the pain in his arm.

"Come on, boy, chop chop. Get the lead out of yo' ass. The truck is waitin'. Rami here's got work to do."

Tang stood up. He was weak. The bandage was soaked through with blood again, and his vision was blurry.

Rami nudged Shu Li with his shoe. "On your feet, sugar. You and your boyfriend are hittin' the street."

"What about the patrols?" Tang managed to ask.

"I been doin' my route for the last two hours. Ain't seen 'em. While you been sleepin', I been doin' my homework."

Rami led them down a narrow hall, through a door, and out onto the roof of the adjacent building. There were few lights. The Ghengdi district was sleeping; the streets were deserted except for a handful of peasants with pushcarts scurrying up from the Haikou docks with fish and produce.

Shu Li began to shiver. Rami couldn't tell whether she was afraid or cold. He suspected both. "Where—where are you taking us?" she finally asked.

"Your boyfriend here wants me to take you and him to the Haikou Tower," Rami said with a grin. He had big, white, wide-spaced teeth, and a smile that revealed fleshy gums. "'Course, I expect he ain't thinkin' about yo' safety. He's probably already figured out what he gonna do with you when he gets you in that room."

Tang jerked Shu Li by the arm and she stumbled. When she fell, Tang ordered her to get up.

"But what about the tickets—the airport—leaving Haikou?" Shu Li asked.

Rami laughed. "While you was sleepin', sugar, your boyfriend here swapped your papers for gettin' your sweet ass to the Haikou. That's as far as you go."

Rami led them down two flights of stairs, down another hall, and out into a narrow alley where a delivery truck waited.

"Get in the back and keep your head down. When you hear me slap twice on the side of the truck, you'll be as close to the Tower as I think I can get you. From there you're on your own."

"What about the checkpoints?" Tang said.

"I've already checked it out. None of the checkpoints on our route are Quan's men. They're all locals. They know me. I've been runnin' this route for the last four years. They'll wave us through."

Tang crawled in, but Rami held Shu Li back. "What are you doing with her?" Tang protested.

"Pigeon here rides up front with me. Call it a little something extra for all the grief you put me through." Rami slammed the cargo door and shoved Shu Li toward the cab of the truck.

Tang felt the truck lurch and begin to move. In the darkness, he groped his way through a tangle of boxes and cartons to brace himself at the front of the truck. As Rami eased out of the alley onto the side street and gained speed, Tang shivered. The pain in his arm was mounting; Gosling's sedative had worn completely off.

Datum: Saturday—0440L, October 11

Tang felt the truck roll to another stop. But this one was different. Rami had not used his horn. He had slowed and obviously turned into another alley as he shifted down. The motor was still running, but Tang heard the cab door open and then slam shut again. He heard Shu Li's protest and then the signal, the distinct sound of Rami's huge hand pounding on the side panel of the truck. When the door opened Rami was glowering up at him.

"This is as far as we go. We got us a small change in plans, though. You ain't goin' back to the Tower; I got you as far as the Chanko district. I got friends in Chanko. Them friends and me, we made a little trade. In return for gettin' you on a freighter sailin' out of here for Singapore, they get the papers and I get sweet-ass. Your toy stays with me. I got use for her."

Tang was flustered. He blinked, trying to adjust to the light. Without the Barkai and with only one good arm, he was at Rami's mercy.

"As soon as I introduce you to my friends," Rami declared, "you're on your own."

Tang got out of the truck, and Rami pushed him ahead toward a truck and a man standing beside it.

Suddenly the doors of the truck swung open and three men armed with machine guns opened fire.

Shu Li screamed and turned away. When the shooting ceased, she looked back again. Tang Ro Ji's twisted body was lying in a pool of blood. A thin trickle of ugly crimson fluid was creeping toward the sewer hatch.

Rami tightened his grip on her arm as the man who had been standing beside the truck emerged from the alley's half-light.

He walked over to Tang Ro Ji and used his foot to roll the body over. Tang's eyes were still open, but there was no life in them. His mouth, likewise, was open, but there was no sound.

Quan turned toward Rami and lit a cigarette. When he exhaled, a thin veil of smoke momentarily obscured his face. By the time it cleared, Rami realized he was smiling.

"The people salute you, Comrade," Quan said. "You have rendered them a great service."

"Fuck the people," Rami growled. "A deal's a deal. This boy here was broke. You had the bread—he didn't. Rami always goes for the bread."

Quan stiffened. He stared back at the giant with the unpleasant smile, reached inside his tunic pocket, and handed him an envelope.

Rami snatched it out of his hand and backed away, still clutching Shu Li's arm. He opened the envelope and began to count.

"What about Mr. Tang's accomplice?" Quan asked. "Where are you taking her?"

"Does it matter?" Rami said.

"Perhaps an arrangement. We could return her to you after our interrogation."

"The way I figure it, by the time you got through with her, there wouldn't be a hell of a lot left for me. No, Colonel, you bought the boyfriend, you didn't buy her. She goes with me." Rami shoved his hand in his pocket and continued to back away. "Oh, and one more thing, Colonel, don't try to stop us. You're in Chanko now—not Danjia. These rotgut alleys are my territory. I've got friends—and believe me, Quan, they're all around you. If you or any of your men in that truck back there move before you hear my truck pull away, they'll cut your skinny ass to ribbons right where you stand."

Pushing Shu Li ahead of him, Rami backed into the shadows and disappeared.

Quan stood motionless until he heard Rami pull away. When Yew leaped from the bed of the truck, Quan held up his hand. "Wait, Lieutenant," he said. "We have what I want. Our friend Rami will only complicate matters."

The streets of Haikou were still dark, and Shu Li was frightened. Rami had been winding through the city's backstreets for what seemed like an eternity. In all of that time, he had not spoken. Finally, he pulled the delivery truck to a stop on a side street and looked at her.

"Where are we?" Shu Li asked. She was surprised at the strength in her voice.

Somehow Rami seemed different. Now there was no smile. In the shadows she could barely make out his features. He reached over and grabbed her wrist. There was great power in his massive hands, but when he spoke his voice seemed somehow less confident, less certain. "At this point, pigeon, you're what's known as excess baggage. This is where you get out."

Shu Li knew better than to hesitate. She

reached for the door, but his grip tightened.

"Somewhere back in the States, I got a daughter. I ain't seen her in years, but I figure she must be about your age now. I owe her, but there ain't no way I can pay her. I don't even know where she is." He hesitated, as if he wanted to say more. Then he said, "Forget what you saw tonight. I don't know how you got involved in all this—and I don't want to know. All I want is twenty-four hours. Then you can sing like a fuckin' bird to anyone who wants to listen. By that time, I'll be long gone. That's the deal. You buyin' it?"

Shu Li nodded. "Deal."

Rami loosened his grip; Shu Li opened the door and jumped out. She heard the truck pull away, but she didn't look back. She was already running.

Datum: Saturday—0713L, October 11

Shu Li Wan was exhausted. She turned off the water, stepped from her shower, and walked into her bedroom at the Haikou Tower. Without explaining, she had informed the hotel's manager that she would not be in her office until later.

She sat down on the edge of her bed and

turned on the television. She had already heard the announcement once, but this time she was hoping there would be more details. The images crystallized and she again heard the monotonous voice of the newscaster. Tang Ro Ji had been "apprehended." Apprehended, she decided, was a curious word for such a violent death. There was no way of knowing for certain, but she was convinced that Quan had been the one who released the information.

The newscaster finished reading the bulletin and immediately launched into a lengthy recitation of the details of Han Ki Po's state funeral. Shu Li turned it off.

What she didn't know was what had happened to Bogner and Driver. Twice she had tried to call Bogner's room, but there was no answer. Twice she had called the desk to see if there were any messages from the Canadians. Again, nothing. For the moment she was stymied. There was a telephone at the orphanage, but no one answered. On top of that, her car was tucked away on some unknown side street in the Ghengdi district. Even though she would report that it had been stolen, if the Haikou police worked the way they normally did, it would be days before they would locate it.

She was thinking about calling Bogner's room again when the phone rang. It was Bogner.

"Where are you?" she blurted.

"Never mind that, are you all right?"

"I'm fine. Well, maybe not fine—but at least I'm in one piece. Where are you?"

"At a place called the Guizhou Medical Center. Le figured this was the safest place to drop me off. It was the only place that wasn't crawling with Quan's men. Besides, I needed a little patch work."

There was a long pause before Shu Li's next question. "Do you know anything about Zhun Be?"

"Not so good," Bogner said. "He's in bad shape. The nurse at Zebo thinks the shot ruptured his spleen. He lost a lot of blood. Father Hua is doing what he can."

On Shu Li's end of the line there was silence. Finally she said, "How long will you have to stay there at Guizhou?"

"They just cut me loose. When he left, Le told me to stay put until he called. Apparently he talked to a Lieutenant Yew and then he called me back fifteen minutes ago. Yew told him they captured Tang and released his hostages. That's all I know. I have no idea what happened."

"It's a long story." She hesitated again. "Stay where you are. I'll send someone from the hotel over to get you. We can talk when you get here."

Shu Li hung up and called the desk. After she made arrangements to have Bogner picked up, she realized she hadn't asked about Driver. She lay back and fell into a deep sleep.

Datum: Monday—1330L, October 13

The winding road that would eventually lead him to the secluded dacha of Georgi Kusinien took Colonel General Viktor Isotov through the rolling Kovinsk foothills and past picturesque vistas where he could catch glimpses of the winding Moskva River.

Isotov, accompanied by an administrative assistant with the rank of major, and chauffeured by a young corporal from the Air Wing's support staff, sat in the rear seat of the black Moskovich staff car, ignoring the dispatches the AA had brought with him for Isotov's perusal.

"Did Secretary Kusinien discuss the agenda with the General?" Lvov inquired. Pyotr Lvov was a bookish-looking man who viewed his position as Isotov's AA as one of great importance.

*"Nyet,"* Isotov grumbled. He did not elaborate. Nor was he concerned. He no longer viewed the Party secretary as an equal. Moshe Aprihinen and Georgi Kusinien were two of a kind. They were lackeys, former comrades, men of compromise. The way Isotov viewed it, the moral fabric of the former Union was in shreds.

Ideologies had been mediated and re-dressed—negotiated until there was no longer strength in covenant.

"Perhaps in these communiqués there is some clue as to what is on the Secretary's mind. . . ." Lvov tried.

Isotov waved the man off as the staff car roared through the security gate and began the ascent to the main house. It was another mile before the driver brought it to a gentle stop behind a string of Volgas, Zaporozhets, and more Moskovichs.

When the two-man entourage from the Air Ministry stepped out into a fresh light snow, two guards standing at the door of the dacha's main entrance snapped to attention.

Inside, a member of Kusinien's staff escorted them through the Secretary's library to the Tartar Room. Kusinien's ancestors hailed from Suzdal, and with the ornate furnishings in the room, the Secretary paid homage to his Tartar heritage.

Isotov was surprised at the number of Aprihinen's staff members in attendance. He had expected a small, if not intimate, session with the Secretary.

Kusinien, with his parchment-thin skin and death-mask countenance, was already seated with his back to the roaring fireplace, a concession to his eighty-two years.

"Come in, Air Major," the Secretary said. "We were just about to get started."

Isotov and Lvov took their place at the end of the table as Kusinien nodded to Colonel General Suvorov to begin. Suvorov was the man said to be responsible for disassembling the convoluted intricacies of the GRU.

"Four weeks ago," Suvorov began, "you will recall, General Isotov reported the apparent loss of our second Su-39 Covert. This report was based on the fact that Air Major Borisov was not heard from again after checkpoint Tultue, fourteen September at 1142 local time. In a subsequent session of the staff, Isotov confirmed his earlier report."

Several members of the staff were reading the report along with Suvorov.

"Then how is it, Comrade General," Kusinien interrupted, "that we now have confirmed reports that the Covert which you reported lost somewhere in the foothills of the Uliastays recently crashed on a flight from Hainan Island?"

"I have heard no such report," Isotov blustered.

Kusinien nodded for Suvorov to continue.

"Hanoi Government Radio on October eleventh reported activity on Anxi atoll. The basis for these reports were two PIREPS, one from a Vietnamese military aircraft, the other from a British commercial airliner. Both reported a strange illumination in the sky ten October over the Gulf of Tonkin near the Anxi atoll cluster. Because the Anxis are a Vietnamese control point, a patrol was alerted. Debris from a downed aircraft was reported by two different pilots within twenty minutes of each other. Vietnamese patrol boats were requested; they investigated, and confirmed that the aircraft was one of ours."

Isotov rocked back in his chair with his arms folded. For the first time since he had taken his seat at the conference table, he realized the Gorgi Kusinien was watching him intently. "I do not see the—" Isotov began, but Kusinien cut him off.

"The report, Comrades," he said, "reveals that on ten October, twenty-six days after it was reported lost by General Isotov, the Su-39 crashed near Anxi Atoll One. It would seem, would it not, that Comrade General Isotov erred in his first report."

Isotov glowered. His eyes traveled from Lvov to Suvorov.

"Or was he premature . . . or careless . . . or even intentionally misleading in his preliminary report?" Kusinien continued.

Isotov leaned forward. "Your accusation is outrageous, Comrade Secretary," he snarled.

"And I contend that your report was meant to mislead us, Comrade Isotov," Kusinien challenged. He nodded at Suvorov and urged him to continue.

"We have since learned that the Su-39 took off from Danjia installation on the island of Hainan shortly before it crashed early the morning of ten October."

Drachev, the former GRU 3 Director, took up the report from there. "The Su-39 was destroyed, but our illegals managed to recover the bodies of two men. We have confirmed the identity of one, and are reasonably sure of the identity of the second. One was Air Major Arege Borisov. The second, we are almost certain, is Dr. Milo Schubatis."

Lvov could hear the stirrings around the table.

"Impossible!" Isotov shouted.

"Impossible? Not at all, Comrade General," Kusinien said calmly. "We have put together a rather cogent scenario of what really happened. Your antagonism toward the policies of President Aprihinen is well known. Your admiration for and your coalition with the Han Ki Po government is likewise well publicized. Therefore, we believe that when Air Major Borisov initiated his flight on fourteen September, he knew he was defecting. Let me state that more clearly: defecting under orders of Colonel General Viktor Isotov."

"Preposterous," Isotov said. He could feel

Lvov move away from him.

"Was this part of the plot to assassinate Han Ki Po?" Kusinien demanded. "Was this an arrangement between you and Colonel Quan Cho?"

Isotov stood up. "This is an outrage."

"Sit down, Comrade General," Kusinien said. "If there is an outrage in all of this, it is you who have committed it."

"I will hear no more of these ludicrous charges," Isotov said. He picked up his briefcase and started for the door. He was surprised when no one tried to stop him. He opened the door and started for the vestibule and his waiting staff car.

As the Moskovich pulled out on the drive toward the front gate, Gorgi Kusinien picked up the telephone.

"Colonel General Isotov's car is approaching the front gate. When it arrives, place the General under arrest."

Datum: Monday—1344L, October 13

It was unusual for Inspector Konstantin Nijinsky to work directly with foreign diplomats, especially Americans.

As he waited in the vestibule of the American

embassy, he was reminded of the more modest consulates of less-affluent countries, and at the same time he wondered how the Americans would respond to the news.

Nijinsky had seen the American Ambassador, Frank Wilson, on television many times. He knew what to expect. Still, it would be the first time for him to work outside the authority of his own homicide detail or not in conjunction with another government agency.

"Ambassador Wilson will see you now," the woman said, placing the telephone back in the cradle. She stood and escorted the inspector into Wilson's office. The Ambassador stood when they entered.

"Well, Inspector, what brings you out on a nasty day like this? Certainly not news of Gurin, I hope."

Nijinsky held on to his hat with both hands. It was still wet from the heavy snow. In addition to being uncomfortable about his appearance, Nijinsky knew his English was not as good as he would have liked it to be when he spoke to men like Wilson.

"We have indeed located Gurin Posmanovich," Nijinsky said. "Or perhaps I should say we have located his body."

"Body? What do you mean, 'body'?"

Nijinsky fished through his pockets and came up with a small brown imitation-leather notebook. Instead of handing it to Wilson, he began to thumb through it. He still hadn't clarified what he meant. "Have you seen this notebook before, Mr. Ambassador?"

Wilson glanced at the book and shook his head. "What did you mean when you said 'body,' Inspector?"

Konstantin Nijinsky squared his shoulders. "I'm afraid Gurin Posmanovich is dead."

"Dead?" Wilson repeated. "When? How? He said he was going to Zaporozhye to visit some of his friends for the weekend."

"He did not go to Zaporozhye for the weekend," Nijinsky said. He reached into his coat pocket and produced an unused airline ticket from Aeroflot. He laid it on Wilson's desk.

"Most curious," Wilson said. "Gurin had been planning that trip for a long time. Working here at the embassy as he does, he only gets one weekend a month off. He has always been very careful how he plans and spends his free weekends."

"I am curious," Nijinsky continued, still thumbing through the notebook. "Do these numbers mean anything to you?"

As Wilson looked at the numbers he made no effort to conceal his surprise. "They most certainly do, Inspector. Those are the sequences that open the codes on the embassy computer."

"Which does what?"

"Which enables someone to access and screen all coded messages coming into and going out of the embassy."

Nijinsky continued thumbing through the pages. "The book also contains *vestuka* numbers. Do you keep a record of telephone calls coming into and going out of the embassy as well?"

"Only official embassy business," Wilson admitted. "We do not log personal calls."

Nijinsky turned away from the desk and walked across the room. "What does the name Mikolai Korsun mean to you, Mr. Ambassador?"

The question caught Wilson off guard. On balance, Mikolai Korsun was not the kind of man someone in the position of Frank Wilson would be expected to include in his circle of friends. To admit that he knew Korsun was to forfeit some small part of his diplomatic immunity. "I don't think I know the man, Inspector," Wilson lied.

"Most curious," Nijinsky said. "According to Gurin Posmanovich's notebook here, you had an early-morning meeting with Korsun on Monday, six October, at the Vilnius on Butlerova Street. Or had you forgotten?"

Wilson knew Nijinsky had given him an out. But if he took it, he would forfeit his immunity. "I'd rather not answer that, Inspector."

"You knew, of course, that Korsun died shortly after that."

Wilson did not answer. He had not heard of Korsun's death.

Nijinsky looked over some of the items on the mantel of the Ambassador's fireplace. "I don't always believe that we are judged by the company we keep. Do you, Mr. Ambassador?"

Again Wilson thought it prudent not to answer.

Nijinsky picked up a statue of an elephant, examined it, and set it back down. "I have never seen a real elephant," he admitted. "I have seen them on television and in movies—but never in real life."

Wilson leaned back against his desk with his arms folded. "You still haven't told me how Korsun died, Inspector. Nor have you said how Gurin died."

"Both men were murdered." There was a matter-of-factness about the way Nijinsky said it that made Wilson think only a homicide officer could have phrased it that way.

Wilson had trouble with the word *murdered.* He repeated it twice.

Nijinsky folded his hands behind his back and stood with his back to the window. "I'm afraid it is a long and complicated story, Mr. Ambassador. But this same notebook, containing keys to your embassy computer access codes, also contains the *vestuka* numbers of people—people whose names our former KGB and GRU agents would find very interesting."

Wilson waited for Nijinsky to continue.

"This may surprise you, Mr. Ambassador, but Gurin Posmanovich was working closely with a GRU agent. After your meeting with Mikolai Korsun, Gurin simply informed his contacts what Korsun had told you. Someone determined that Mr. Korsun both knew and communicated too much . . . and the rest is history."

"But why was Gurin killed?"

"At this point it is only conjecture, mind you. We have not yet conducted an autopsy. Nevertheless, we are reasonably certain it happened shortly after he contacted his friends to inform them you had learned that both the Su-39 and Dr. Schubatis were located at the Danjia installation on Hainan Island. In return for that information, his contacts told him he would receive his 'usual reward.' "

"Which was?"

"An involvement with a young woman named Savina."

"I'm not sure I understand."

"Your young associate had a rather voracious appetite for women, Mr. Ambassador—so they arranged a liaison with the woman called Savina as his payoff. Apparently there was only one problem. Young Gurin believed he was in love with the woman . . . and when she wouldn't go away with him, he threatened to expose her friends for the political threat they were."

"And . . ."

"They killed him rather than have their position revealed. It seems these young people share the opinion that Mother Russia should return to the ways of Lenin."

Frank Wilson shook his head. He had spent eleven years in Russia and he still did not understand the workings of the Russian mind. Finally he asked, "Is there anything I can do, Inspector?"

"Actually there isn't," Nijinsky said. "When you contacted my department and expressed your concern about the missing young man this morning, we had already discovered the body."

"How did he die?"

Nijinsky could not suppress the smile small that played with the corners of his mouth. "He died in bed, Mr. Ambassador—making love." Then he sobered. "The signs are hard to ignore. At perhaps the critical moment in their love-making, his partner put the barrel of a gun to his temple and pulled the trigger."

Wilson closed his eyes against the image.

Nijinsky started for the door, then looked back. "My condolences, Mr. Ambassador. If you have any further questions, please call me."

# Chapter Sixteen

Datum: Wednesday—1658L, October 15

Robert Miller had made it a habit for the last five years. Every Wednesday, he left work a half hour early and dropped into the Riverside Club on Potomac. Luke Bailey of United Press and Reese Webster of First Bank made Wednesdays a habit along with Miller. The three had been friends since their graduate days at Capital.

Miller bought the first round of beers and lit one of his infrequent cigars. "So Reese, my man, tell me what the hell the Fed's gonna do about the interest rate. My investment club meets this Friday, and they think since I work for the government I've got inside information."

Webster started to laugh. "Tell them that if they wanna make more money they need to get a second job like Luke and me."

Luke Bailey raised his glass in a mock toast

and started to take a drink. At the same time, out of the corner of his eye, he was watching the television over the bar. The camera was panning across the scene of an airline crash. He nudged Miller. "Hey, look at that."

Robert Miller sobered and put down his glass. "Hey, Sam," he shouted at the Riverside's bartender, "will you turn it up?"

As the volume came up, Miller recognized Reed Barkley. The CNN anchor was to his generation what Walter Cronkite was to Miller's father's generation. Barkley's voice was somber as the scene again reverted to the crash site.

*"Once again, confirming our main story this hour: A Tupolev Tu-16 Badger was shot down by what has been described as "friendly fire" from an unidentified Russian aircraft over the Gulf of Tonkin earlier today.*

*"The incident occurred some fifty nautical miles due east of Haiphong.*

*"Observers on the scene report no known survivors."*

Barkley turned to his "on-camera" colleague.

"This is interesting, Blake. According to what we have been able to learn so far, the Tupolev's flight originated in Huangliu on the Chinese island of Hainan. . . ."

Blake Harold was nodding his head. "Indeed,

and it was just a few days ago that we received word that Han Ki Po, a man many believed would succeed Hong Ho, the current Chairman of the People's Republic, as the supreme Party leader in the PRC, had been assassinated as part of the ongoing political turmoil in that area."

Barkley was nodding. "The irony of this situation, Blake, is that the first reports received here at the CNN newsroom in Atlanta indicated that the Tupolev was said to be carrying a General Han, son of Han Ki Po, and the man some sources close to the situation believe was destined to take over the Fifth Academy faction of the Red Army."

"Has that been confirmed?" Blake Harold asked. Miller regarded him as a good journalist.

Barkley shook his head. "At this point we are unable to confirm the identity of anyone aboard the aircraft, nor, as a matter of record, have we even been informed of any fatalities. . . ."

Miller elbowed his way out of the booth and raced for the telephone. By the time he got through to his office, Packer was the only one still there.

"Pack," Miller huffed, "CNN is carrying a story about a plane crash in the Gulf of Tonkin. Apparently a Russian Tupolev was shot down . . . and they also have an unconfirmed report that Han Ki Po's son, General Han Xihui, was aboard that plane."

Packer was silent for a moment. Then he repeated what Miller had told him as though he was trying to get his hands around it. He concluded with a question. "Any idea when Bogner's coming in?"

"I think he's probably already in town," Miller said. "He indicated he was staying overnight in Washington, but he was very adamant that he wouldn't be in the office until tomorrow morning."

Datum: Thursday—0909L, October 16

Bogner had expected Miller and Packer to be there. He had not expected Lattimere Spitz.

Still sporting a brace of black eyes, a broken nose, and an assortment of cuts and bruises from his encounter with Driver on Anxi, he looked worse after this gambit than at any time either Miller or Packer could remember.

"How are you feeling, Toby?" Packer asked.

"Like I look." Bogner headed straight for the coffee and poured himself a cup. "I got the first good look at myself in a mirror last night, Pack. It occurs to me that I may be getting a little too old for this sort of thing."

Spitz sat down at the table and loosened his

tie. "Colchin wants a full report about what happened out there."

"I wish I knew," Bogner admitted. "I was there, and it's still all bits and pieces."

"Start with the Covert," Spitz said. "Colchin still has to button that up with President Aprihinen."

"I saw Driver fly it out of Danjia and twenty-four hours later I actually saw it buried in about twenty to thirty feet of water in an Anxi atoll . . ."

"And you're certain it was the same plane?" Spitz pressed.

"If you're asking me if I'm one hundred percent certain that the plane I saw Driver crawl into is the one I saw in that atoll, I'd have to say no. The only time I saw the Covert, it was sitting in a dark hanger with damn little in the way of lighting. The next time I saw it, it was mostly submerged in water and it was at night."

"Let me put it another way, T.C. Could Quan have switched planes on you?"

"What the hell is this, Lattimere? Are you trying to tell me you don't think that plane I saw was the Covert?"

"Take it easy, T.C., the boys over at Naval Intelligence have merely pointed out that it's a possibility. They point out that you weren't there when the plane went down. And they also point out that Quan would have had the opportunity to switch aircraft."

"What the hell kind of aircraft does NI think Quan dumped on Anxi?"

"Look, Toby, have you got any proof—solid proof?" Spitz demanded. "Something I can take to Colchin—something he can hang his hat on when he's talking to Aprihinen?"

"I saw Harry Driver cram Dr. Schubatis into the cockpit of that aircraft just moments before he took off. I saw what was left of Schubatis twenty-four hours later. He was dead and floating in the cockpit of the aircraft."

Spitz held up his hand. "Now don't blow a gasket, T.C., but I want to point out, finding Schubatis's body at the crash site doesn't prove anything."

Bogner looked at Packer. "What the hell is this, Pack? What's going on here?"

Packer got up, refilled his cup, and ignored Spitz. "Late last evening, CNN got a call. Want to guess who it was from?"

Bogner was tired of playing games. Parts of his body hurt—parts that he had other plans for—and he wanted to get a long way away from there so he could do a little healing. "All right, I'll play your game. Who made the call?"

"Quan."

Bogner's head snapped up. "Why?"

"He's taking credit for blowing that Tupolev out of the sky yesterday afternoon. And he assures us that General Han Xuhiu was aboard that Tupolev when it went down."

"More than that," Spitz continued, "according to Quan, the aircraft that knocked that Tupolev out of the sky yesterday was the Su-39. He said we could relay a message to some of his Russian friends for him: 'The armament package has been installed on the Covert and it's working just fine.' "

"He's bluffing," Bogner said.

"Is he?" Spitz asked.

Bogner lapsed into silence. He still hadn't responded when he heard the phone ring. Miller picked it up. He listened for a moment, then handed it to Bogner. "It's for you," he said.

"Heard you were back in town," Joy said. "In the mood to buy a gal dinner?"

Bogner managed a laugh. "Think we can find a dark café somewhere? Some place with low-level lighting—where black eyes and crooked noses aren't all that apparent?"

"I know just the place," she said. "I'll pick you up at six."

Bogner hung up and looked around the room.

"What do you want me to tell Colchin?" Spitz asked.

"Tell him I saw Schubatis's Covert lying at the bottom of one of the Anxi atolls. That it wasn't busted up enough to discourage a salvage effort and that I blew the damn thing to kingdom come. Tell him Schubatis is dead and Colonel Quan is dangerous.

"Tell him Harry Driver is dead. And tell him how I know: because I'm the one who fired the shot that killed him.

"Finally, tell him I have a date tonight and I don't want to be disturbed—not even by the President of the United States."

# R. KARL LARGENT

**The Techno-thriller Of The Year!**

# RED ICE

**"A writer to watch!" —*Publishers Weekly***

## RED MENANCE

After the USSR collapses, the United States and its powerful allies are content with the new world order. But Russian scientists are constructing a technological marvel that can bring their leaders the power they crave.

## RED SECRETS

Then Russian intelligence sends the Chinese spy who sabotages the project to the bottom of the Barents Sea—along with the last copy of the Lyoto-Straf's computer files. And whoever gets there first will control humanity's destiny.

## RED TERROR

Deep beneath the frigid waters lies the design for a doomsday device, and Commander T.C. Bogner is sent on a high-tech chase to retrieve it—at any cost.

_3774-2 $5.99 US/$6.99 CAN

**Dorchester Publishing Co., Inc.**
**65 Commerce Road**
**Stamford, CT 06902**

Please add $1.75 for shipping and handling for the first book and $.50 for each book thereafter. NY, NYC, PA and CT residents, please add appropriate sales tax. No cash, stamps, or C.O.D.s. All orders shipped within 6 weeks via postal service book rate. Canadian orders require $2.00 extra postage and must be paid in U.S. dollars through a U.S. banking facility.

Name_______________________________________

Address_____________________________________

City ____________________________ State______ Zip______

I have enclosed $______in payment for the checked book(s).

Payment must accompany all orders.☐ Please send a free catalog.

# LADY OF ICE AND FIRE
# COLIN ALEXANDER

**Colin Alexander writes "a lean and solid thriller!"**
***—Publishers Weekly***

With international detente fast becoming the status quo, a whole new field of spying opens up: industrial espionage. And even though tensions are easing between the East and the West, the same Cold war rules and stakes still apply: world domination at any cost, both in dollars and deaths. Well aware of the new predators, George Jeffers fears that his biotech studies may be sought after by foreign agents. Then his partner disappears with the results of their experiments, and the eminent scientist finds himself the target in a game of deadly intrigue. Jeffers then races against time to prevent the unleashing of a secret that could shake the world to its very foundations.

_4072-7 $5.50 US/$6.50 CAN

**Dorchester Publishing Co., Inc.**
**65 Commerce Road**
**Stamford, CT 06902**

Please add $1.75 for shipping and handling for the first book and $.50 for each book thereafter. NY, NYC, PA and CT residents, please add appropriate sales tax. No cash, stamps, or C.O.D.s. All orders shipped within 6 weeks via postal service book rate. Canadian orders require $2.00 extra postage and must be paid in U.S. dollars through a U.S. banking facility.

Name____________________________________________
Address__________________________________________
City ___________________________ State______Zip______
I have enclosed $______in payment for the checked book(s).
Payment must accompany all orders.☐ Please send a free catalog.

# WAR BREAKER

## JIM DEFELICE

**"A book that grabs you hard and won't let go!"**
**—Den Ing, Bestselling Author of**
***The Ransom of Black Stealth One***

Two nations always on the verge of deadly conflict, Pakistan and India are heading toward a bloody war. And when the fighting begins, Russia and China are certain to enter the battle on opposite sides.

The Pakistanis have a secret weapon courtesy of the CIA: upgraded and modified B-50s. Armed with nuclear warheads, the planes can be launched as war breakers to stem the tide of an otherwise unstoppable invasion.

The CIA has to get the B-50s back. But the only man who can pull off the mission is Michael O'Connell—an embittered operative who was kicked out of the agency for knowing too much about the unsanctioned delivery of the bombers. And if O'Connell fails, nobody can save the world from utter annihilation.

_4043-3 $6.99 US/$7.99 CAN

**Dorchester Publishing Co., Inc.**
**65 Commerce Road**
**Stamford, CT 06902**

Please add $1.75 for shipping and handling for the first book and $.50 for each book thereafter. NY, NYC, PA and CT residents, please add appropriate sales tax. No cash, stamps, or C.O.D.s. All orders shipped within 6 weeks via postal service book rate. Canadian orders require $2.00 extra postage and must be paid in U.S. dollars through a U.S. banking facility.

Name___________________________________________
Address_________________________________________
City ______________________________ State______ Zip______
I have enclosed $______in payment for the checked book(s).
Payment must accompany all orders.☐ Please send a free catalog.

# A KILLING PACE
# LES WHITTEN

**"Gritty, realistic, and tough!"**
***—Philadelphia Inquirer***

For George Fraser, dealing and double-dealing is a way of life. But with the body count around him rising higher, he decides he wants out of the espionage business. As a favor for an old friend, Fraser agrees to take on one last job: just running some automatic weapons—no big deal. Then the assignment falls apart, and Fraser is caught in the sights of terrorists determined to see him dead. Suddenly, Fraser is on a harrowing chase that takes him from the mean streets of Philadelphia to the treacherous canals of Venice. He is just one man against a vicious cartel—a man who can stop countless deaths and mass destruction if he can keep up a killing pace.

_4017-4 $4.99 US/$6.99 CAN

**Dorchester Publishing Co., Inc.**
**65 Commerce Road**
**Stamford, CT 06902**

Please add $1.75 for shipping and handling for the first book and $.50 for each book thereafter. NY, NYC, PA and CT residents, please add appropriate sales tax. No cash, stamps, or C.O.D.s. All orders shipped within 6 weeks via postal service book rate. Canadian orders require $2.00 extra postage and must be paid in U.S. dollars through a U.S. banking facility.

Name________________________________________
Address______________________________________
City ______________________ State______ Zip______
I have enclosed $______in payment for the checked book(s).
Payment must accompany all orders. ☐ Please send a free catalog.

# TIMOTHY RIZZI

**"Rizzi's credible scenario and action-filled pace once again carry the day!"** —***Publishers Weekly***

After Revolutionary Guard soldiers salvage a U.S. cruise missile that veered off course during the Gulf War, Iran's intelligence bureau assigns a team of experts to decipher the weapon's state-of-the-art computer chips. But fundamentalist leaders in Tehran plan to use the stolen technology to upgrade their defense systems. With improved military forces, they'll have the power to seize the Persian Gulf and cut off worldwide access to Middle-eastern oil fields.

Sent to stop the Iranians, General Duke James has at his command the best pilots in the world and the best aircraft in the skies: A-6 Intruders, F-16s, MH-53J Pave Lows, EF-111As. But he's up against the most advanced antiaircraft machinery known to man—machinery stamped MADE IN THE USA.

_3885-4 $6.99 US/$8.99 CAN

**Dorchester Publishing Co., Inc.**
**65 Commerce Road**
**Stamford, CT 06902**

Please add $1.75 for shipping and handling for the first book and $.50 for each book thereafter. NY, NYC, PA and CT residents, please add appropriate sales tax. No cash, stamps, or C.O.D.s. All orders shipped within 6 weeks via postal service book rate. Canadian orders require $2.00 extra postage and must be paid in U.S. dollars through a U.S. banking facility.

Name_______________________________________
Address_____________________________________
City ______________________ State______ Zip______
I have enclosed $______in payment for the checked book(s).
Payment must accompany all orders. ☐ Please send a free catalog

TIMOTHY RIZZI

**"Heart-in-mouth, max G-force, stunningly realistic air action!"**
***—Kirkus Reviews***

THE COBRA TEAM: F-117 Stealth Fighters, F-15E Strike Eagles, F-16C Wild Wealsels, A-10 Warthogs—all built from advanced technology; all capable of instant deployment; all prepared for spontaneous destruction.
THE SPACE SHUTTLE: *Atlantis*—carrying a Russian satellite equipped with nuclear warheads—makes an emergency landing right in the middle of a Palestinian terrorist compound. Soon everyone from the Israelis to the Libyans is after the downed ship.
THE STRIKE: The Cobra Team must mobilize every high-tech resource at its disposal before the *Atlantis* and its deadly cargo fall into enemy hands bent on global annihilation.
_3630-4 $5.99 US/$6.99 CAN

**Dorchester Publishing Co., Inc.**
**65 Commerce Road**
**Stamford, CT 06902**

Please add $1.75 for shipping and handling for the first book and $.50 for each book thereafter. NY, NYC, PA and CT residents, please add appropriate sales tax. No cash, stamps, or C.O.D.s. All orders shipped within 6 weeks via postal service book rate. Canadian orders require $2.00 extra postage and must be paid in U.S. dollars through a U.S. banking facility.

Name ____________________
Address ____________________
City ____________________ State ______ Zip ______
I have enclosed $______ in payment for the checked book(s).
Payment must accompany all orders. ☐ Please send a free catalog.

# KNIGHT'S CROSS

**E.M. NATHANSON, Bestselling Author Of *The Dirty Dozen* and AARON BANK, Founder Of The Green Berets.**

**"The ultimate secret mission—kidnapping Hitler!"**
**—Stephen Coonts**

THE TIME: The closing days of WWII, and the Germans are organizing their final plan to defeat the Allied powers. If successful, the Last Redoubt will extend the war and revitalize Nazi forces.
THE MAN: OSS Captain Dan Brooks—ambushes, raids, sabotage, subversion, and guerilla warfare are his specialties. He is the Allies' choice to damage the enemy war machine—and to take a dangerous assignment that no one else will dare.
THE MISSION: Get Hitler.
_3724-6 $5.99 US/$6.99 CAN

**Dorchester Publishing Co., Inc.**
**65 Commerce Road**
**Stamford, CT 06902**

Please add $1.75 for shipping and handling for the first book and $.50 for each book thereafter. NY, NYC, PA and CT residents, please add appropriate sales tax. No cash, stamps, or C.O.D.s. All orders shipped within 6 weeks via postal service book rate. Canadian orders require $2.00 extra postage and must be paid in U.S. dollars through a U.S. banking facility.

Name________________________________________
Address______________________________________
City ____________________________ State______Zip______
I have enclosed $______in payment for the checked book(s).
Payment must accompany all orders.☐ Please send a free catalog.

# ATTENTION PREFERRED CUSTOMERS!

## SPECIAL TOLL-FREE NUMBER

**1-800-481-9191**

***Call Monday through Friday***

**12 noon to 10 p.m.**

**Eastern Time**

*Get a free catalogue;*

*Order books using your Visa, MasterCard, or Discover®;*

*Join the book club!*

Leisure Books